this *is* love

a novel

Thanks for the support! Happy Reading

caroline nolan

This is a work of fiction. Names, characters, places, brands, media, and incidents are either the product of the author's imagination or are used fictitiously. The author acknowledges the trademarked status and trademark owners of various products referenced in this work of fiction, which have been used without permission. The publication/use of these trademarks is not authorized, associated with, or sponsored by the trademark owners.

Cover design by Okay Creations
Editing & proofreading by Indie Solutions by Murphy Rae
Interior design and formatting by JT Formatting

First Edition: October 2015
Library of Congress Cataloging-in-Publication Data
This is Love (a novel) – 1st ed
ISBN-13: 978-1518752469 | ISBN-10: 1518752462

For more information about Caroline Nolan and her books, visit:
www.facebook.com/authorcarolinenolan

prologue

SPREAD OUT IN front of me are an assortment of graphs, charts and floor plans, all of which are organized and color coded with Post-it notes. My living room looks like a rainbow, each color representing its own important purpose. *Head table, positioned. Chocolate fountain, rented. DJ booth, near dance floor but out of the way.* I look at it all, congratulating myself on a job well done. Not only had I successfully created an amazing floor plan, but I had finished it ahead of schedule.

Way to go, Rachel!

The wedding was only a few weeks away, but I was well on my way to becoming the most organized bride anyone has ever heard of. Dress bought, caterer booked, rings safely tucked away upstairs in our dresser and the groom—currently on his way home from the gym. Ben called from the parking lot while he let his car warm up.

"Goddamn, it's cold! I'll probably lose a finger from wiping all that snow off the car."

I could hear the heat vents on full blast in the background. I pictured him sitting in the driver's seat, knit cap covering his sandy blond hair, blowing hot breaths into his fisted hands.

"Well if you get home soon, I will make it my number one priority to warm you up," I say flirting, hinting, hoping it would get him home sooner.

It was only the beginning of December and already we had reached colder than usual temperatures with more snowfall than even we were used to seeing. Living near the lake, we are used to the cold and snow but this winter has already left a bitter mark for the beginning of the season.

"Just as soon as I stop seeing my breath," he answers between long exhales. "That gives you just enough time to think of at least three ways to raise my body temperature. All of them better include body heat."

I giggle. "Get here soon and I'll show you at least five."

I know Ben well enough to know he's already smirking.

"You're on. I just need to stop by the hardware store so I can fix that leaky pipe. I don't want it to freeze in this shit weather. After that, be ready, because I'm coming for you. In more ways than one."

It's nearly impossible to ignore the anticipation running through my body with such a promise. "See you soon."

I take a look at the seating plan I just finished after hanging up, relieved that the hardest task is now behind me. Luckily, our guest list is relatively small, but somehow it had still taken me two weeks to complete. It wasn't that we had clashes between our two families, or even within our own, but Ben and I came from two different backgrounds. His family came from a long line of police officers, almost like it was the family business. They all had very strong, very forward personalities. Fathers, brothers, and uncles, all extremely proud to wear a badge, and sometimes that pride caused friction between them. Each member of Ben's family had a strong temperament, and if you put them all together in one room, there was no telling what could happen.

A few weeks after Ben and I had started dating, he brought me to a family barbeque. Children were playing, their laughter and squeals heard from every corner of the yard, the smell of meat grilling filling the air, and just like any Irish family, a bottle of beer was never far from reach. The day seemed to be going perfectly until what started as an off-handed comment about the White Sox erupted into a full-out argument between two of his cousins. A picnic table toppled over, leftover food spilling all over the lawn. While the women shouted and the men laughed, the dogs scurried around to get all the food they could before it was cleaned up. One cousin ended up with a black eye, the other with a broken finger. Ben didn't seem too fazed by it all. He simply waved his hand in the air and told me not worry about it.

"Those two are always starting shit," he'd said passively. "It will all be forgotten soon enough."

He was right, because by the end of the day, both were drinking and laughing together like nothing happened. To them, there was nothing more sacred than family, even when they didn't agree. And soon, that would include me.

My family, on the other hand, was a little more conservative. They always kept in mind social cues and appearances. The most heated argument I'd ever witnessed between members of my family were slightly raised voices while discussing politics. We came from two completely different backgrounds but were lucky that both sides welcomed us easily.

When Ben asked me to marry him, I could not have said *yes* fast enough. I was always the girl who planned and imagined her wedding from a young age—the dress, the colors, the food. And now I had the groom. I couldn't wait to show him all I accomplished tonight, including the flowers I special ordered for the occasion. Being a florist with my own shop was definitely a perk when planning my own wedding.

I opened a bottle of wine, ready to finally relax with Ben as soon as he got home. Ben always has and always will be a beer drinker, but once in a while he'll humor me and have a glass of Pinot Noir. I'd watch him wince slightly with each sip, and with every swallow, I would love him more for it.

An hour passed since our phone call and my anticipation of his walking through the door now turned into slight annoyance. Having gone through half the bottle while waiting only fueled my agitation. A part of me wasn't surprised though, Ben could so easily become distracted. I'm sure his only intention was to run into the store and grab whatever tool he needed for our kitchen pipe, but it wouldn't take long for his eyes to start roaming the aisles and before he could help himself, he'd be discussing floor tiles with a sales associate.

I must have drifted off on the couch because the sound of the doorbell, followed by a soft knock, startled me awake. My eyes quickly glance to the small clock sitting on the mantle. More than three hours had passed since we spoke over the phone. Walking towards the door, I notice his house keys sitting in the bowl by the front entrance.

He forgot his house keys again.

I grab his keys out of the bowl, unlock and open the door.

"Forget someth…?" I begin to say but stop abruptly when I see Paul, his best friend and partner, standing in front of me. "Hi," the surprise of seeing him evident in my voice.

I open the door further, inviting him in. "Ben's not home yet."

Then, out from a few feet behind him, a uniformed officer whom I don't recognize comes up and stands next to him.

Paul takes two steps towards me, his face now completely lit up by the light from our front porch. I see red-rimmed eyes mixed with shock and devastation.

In the back of every police officer's wife's mind sits a dark fear that one day, there will be a knock on the door and someone will come to tell you that something terrible has happened. How they choose to live with this fear varies from woman to woman. Some choose to never think of it, refusing to acknowledge it every time their husbands leave for work, while others make sure to tell them every day how much they love them, surrendering to the possibility that it could be their last. I was never sure which category I fell into. Too afraid or not at all. It was something I put aside, always telling myself I would have plenty of time to it figure out later. Plenty of time to have my fears and get over them. Plenty of time to realize that what fate has in store for us does not change with the clothes one wears to work.

But right here, right now, my time had run out, and I wasn't ready.

My hand grips the door harder, needing the extra support for what I know I'm about to be told. Bile starts to make its way up from my stomach, to my throat and finally my mouth. It tastes awful and it stings, but I'm too frozen to do anything about it. Out of fear? Shock? Anger?

Paul's face flashes red and blue from the lights on top of the police cruiser parked in my driveway. There are no sirens, no loud ringing cautioning, preparing me that somewhere, there is a state of emergency. My face becomes hot, and I think I'm going to throw up. I fight for air even though the door is wide open and cold wind is hitting my face. I see Paul's lips moving, but only a few choice words are able to battle through the rapid beat of my heart pounding in my ears.

"*Black Ice*."

"*Tree.*"

"*They tried.*"

And finally…

"*I'm so sorry, Rachel.*"

After that, everything becomes dark.

chapter 1

One Year and a Half Later

AS I SIT in Dr. Embry's office, my eyes scan the room, examining all the details I'm sure were strategically placed in order to make people like me feel more welcome and open to sharing their feelings. A beautiful pine colored desk sits dominantly in the corner of the office with an unopened laptop perched on top. Just beside, a couple of frames displaying photos of her family. A husband, happy children. Today, like every other day I've come to this office, I park myself on a very comfortable cream colored leather sofa, which I know was chosen to encourage people to sit back and relax. The blue pillows next to me have me wondering if people have gone so far as to lay their heads down before divulging their thoughts like they do in the movies. Numerous degrees hang proudly on the robin's egg blue colored walls along with framed prints of waterfalls and clear blue skies. Working with color all day long, I've read that shades of blue can actually cause the body to produce calming chemicals, helping one to relax.

I wonder if that's true. I wonder if it's false. I wonder what it says about me that I feel nothing.

As always, Dr. Embry watches me from a modest looking chair, a small coffee table with art books displayed separating us. Just beyond her, I see an orchid plant on a bookcase filled with what looks like medical texts. The blooms on the plant are beautiful, white with a deep violet coming from the center. A very popular choice for a household orchid, offering soft and delicate features, romantic even. I've used them many times in my bouquets. I had planned to use them in my own, as well as in centerpieces for my wedding. Tall candelabras and orchids were going to fill the twelve plus tables of the room, and a single bloom pinned on each of the groomsmen and the groom—

Stop.

I immediately block that train of thought from going any further and bring my attention back to something that makes me less…vulnerable.

"You should move that orchid closer to the window. It will do better in more light," I offer Dr. Embry some advice.

She turns her head, following my gaze behind her. She gives a curt nod as if contemplating what I said and turns back to me. "You *are* the expert," she says smiling but leaves the orchid where it is.

I have been coming to see Dr. Embry for several months. It wasn't my idea and for quite a while, I fought against it. But several loved ones believed I needed someone to talk to, especially my mother. Looking back, I guess I can't really blame her. Unfortunately, she had a full hands-on experience to my breakdown, needing to move in after the accident to care for me.

For weeks, I wouldn't even get out of bed. All I wanted to do was hide under blankets with the blinds drawn closed, keeping the outside world as far away from me as possible. I would spend hours in my dark bedroom, Ben's pillow clutched to my chest, trying to inhale his scent, committing it to memory with every breath before it faded. I grabbed his clothes from the closet, even the dirty ones, and slept in his layers once his pillow lost all traces of him. I refused visitors, unable to hear more condolences or listen to another happy memory they had of him. Because that's all that was left. Memories. I also had those memories, my mind too full of them. They played on repeat in my head as if on a loop. I couldn't handle anymore.

My life was made up of sleep, an occasional meal, the even less occasional shower. Time ceased to exist for me anymore. I had no idea how much time had passed before my mother informed me that she had made some calls, inquiring about psychiatrists in the area.

"Rachel, you need this," she simply said, opening the curtains of my window, drawing day light into my bedroom. "Maybe she can help because I just don't know—" she didn't finish her thought.

I could see it in her eyes that she didn't know how to help me. Her fear was that allowing me to continue on like this would cause such damage that I would not be able to fix it. At the time, I believed this was a mild threat or an attempt to guilt me out of the bedroom. Bethany Miller had a knack for such deeds and it did work to some extent. A few days later, I woke up at a respectable time and took a shower. I went downstairs to the kitchen and started a pot of coffee. The look on my mother's face when she saw me in the kitchen pouring her a cup fell somewhere between relief and victory.

The next day started much the same. I got up, took a shower and this time even put product in my dark brown hair, making its natural waves come to life. I found some clothes that didn't include an elastic waist or flannel and went downstairs to make coffee once again. Later that morning, I was encouraged to help my mother wrap some Christmas gifts. Everything was going well until I found a gift I had bought for Ben. It was nothing extravagant, just something I thought he'd get a kick out of. A fun gift. Something we could laugh at and use after we were married.

Still neatly wrapped in their package were two matching pillowcases. Well not exactly matching. One, in elegant written script read *Mr. Right*. Mine, written just as elegantly read *Mrs. Always Right*. It was an ode to our stubbornness, a character flaw that had begun when we met and stayed with us throughout our relationship. A strange bond that continuously kept pulling us together instead of pushing us apart. As soon as I found those pillowcases, there was too much emotion for me to process and I excused myself, going back upstairs. I stayed in my room for three days.

After those few days, I began to feel a little restless which I suppose was an improvement. I'd start to get up, get ready and make coffee. I didn't notice at first, but as days passed, I would accomplish a little more. I began running small errands, I went to lunch with my mother and some of her friends and I even stopped by the shop a few times, showing interest in how my business was doing. Without recognizing how or when it happened, I slowly become more than just a woman in hiding, only finding solace in her bedroom.

Weeks later, I took a deep breath before meeting my mother downstairs in the kitchen for breakfast. Standing over the sink, her graying hair pulled up in a perfect French twist, she was a little startled when she saw me walk in, fully dressed, laptop bag in hand, ready to start my day. She handed me a cup of coffee, her eyes questioning where I was headed off to this early.

Putting my bag down, I leaned against the counter, inhaling the sweet scent of French Vanilla coming from my cup. I looked up at her and saw her eyes, brown like mine, waiting.

"I'm going to work," I said.

She tried hard to hide her surprise, masking it with a tight smile and a few quick nods. "Wonderful, Rachel."

But I could see in her eyes—the look of hope mixed with

concern that I'd be away from her all day. Half of me loved her more for it, appreciating everything she's given up for me these last few months, but the other half felt ashamed and guilty for the exact same reason.

Life after that day became a little more regimented. I continued to go to work. I even slowly started to enjoy it again. My best friend Tess would come over in the evenings and we would watch movies (all comedies of course), eat ice cream, and she would fill me in on the gossip surrounding our small group of friends. Slowly, I began to feel more like myself.

One night over dinner, I told my mother it was time for her to go home. She had been here long enough. She had been my live in support system too long. It was time I stood on my own again.

"Oh, honey, I don't mind. I'm sure your father loves having all this time to himself. He finally has some peace and quiet to build those ridiculous model ships. And it's nice here, just us girls," she said, sipping her evening tea.

I knew she was hesitant to leave me. I was an only child of a stay at home mother. I knew she worried that if she left, no one would be around to make sure I didn't revert back to my days of isolation in my bedroom. I also think a small part of her enjoyed having to take care of me again. But I needed this. I needed to learn how to be on my own again. I gave her a warm smile and simply said something she said to me when a change was desperately needed.

"I need this."

Before my mother left, she handed me an appointment card. *Dr. Sheila Embry PH. D – Psychiatry.* It confused me. I thought this was all but forgotten. I thought I was doing well. Didn't she notice the effort I was putting into living life again? I went to work every day, I saw Tess several times a week. I had a routine. Wasn't that what everyone wanted to see?

"I'm happy that you're back at work, going out, seeing

friends," she said. "But darling, you aren't living. Simply going through the motions of daily life isn't the same thing." She took both my hands in hers and squeezed. "She comes highly recommended. Please, just go and talk to her. Maybe she can help you figure out what's next for you. Ben would have wanted that for you."

My eyes began to sting. I could feel the tears burning at the mention of Ben's name. "What he would have wanted?" I repeated quietly, but inside my head, I was yelling.

WHAT HE WOULD HAVE WANTED!

I knew what Ben would have wanted and it would have been for me to deal with things in my own way.

What more could everyone want from me? Expect from me? My world had forever changed in a matter of a minute. Sixty seconds. How many people can say that? Be prepared for that? What I needed was more time to come to grips with this, not some woman I had never met telling me it was time to carve out a new life path. I canceled the appointment my mother made immediately after she left.

Dr. Embry's office proceeded to call me every week after, asking if I was ready to reschedule. After the fifth call, I finally caved and said yes to an appointment, thinking if I just went to one, they would then leave me alone. That was months ago.

"So, Rachel, how are you feeling today?" Dr. Embry asks. Her long blonde hair is tied up in a bun and she's wearing the navy pantsuit I hate. She always starts our conversations this way. *How are you feeling? How have you been sleeping? How have you been coping?* Those were the easy ones to answer. At first, I tended to keep my answer short and to the point.

Fine.

Well.

Fine.

After a few visits, I began to see that my one-word answers were no longer satisfying her.

I do believe that there are positives to therapy. Some people find the support they need and use it as an integral part to their healing process while others find inner courage to face the outside world again. For me, I'm not really sure why I continued to come. I haven't had any epiphanies or found a new inner strength to move on and start that new chapter of my life. Whatever insights therapy was supposed to help me accomplish, haven't happened. Most importantly, the pain of losing Ben hasn't lessened. I suppose a part of me continued to come to make my mother happy. I owed her at least that much. And, to the outside world, it looked like Rachel Miller was piecing her life back together. Moving forward, moving beyond her grief.

All lies.

But today when Dr. Embry asks me how I'm feeling, I'm tempted to give her an honest answer.

Anxious.

Pressured.

Angry.

Take your pick.

Instead, I repeat the same thing I do every visit.

"I'm feeling good. It's a busy time at work. Spring is here, lots of events!" I answer, raising my fist in the air. Even I know I'm coming off too strong. When I don't say any more, she looks down at the notepad in her lap and starts to write something down. She does this often and I can never tell what she's writing. I've tried many times. Staring at the way the pen moves, trying to make words out of the swirls and dots she just made. But it's always of no use. I move my eyes about the room, focusing on the orchid again.

"What about socially? Have you been out much since last time we spoke?"

I quickly wonder if grocery runs count, but somehow I know that wasn't what she was looking for.

"A new bar opened up downtown and Tess asked me to go

with her last week." I smile, hoping that will satisfy her to some degree. She nods but then looks at me, waiting for me to say more. I have no more to tell. I never went.

It's true that Tess had asked, *begged* even, for me to go check out the bar with her and a few of our friends. I had agreed to go. But that night, when I opened my closet to get ready, the only dress that seemed appropriate to wear was the one I wore to Ben's surprise birthday party—a royal blue tank dress with splashes of vibrant purple throughout. As soon as I put it on, memories of that night came flooding back. The look of surprise on his face when we walked into his favorite bar for what was supposed to be a quiet night out but instead turned out to be a room filled with all his friends, some co-workers and our families helping him celebrate turning thirty.

I remembered how we danced, moving together to the sounds of old eighties hits. I remembered how he whispered in my ear how beautiful I was, how thankful he was for the party, how he couldn't wait to get me out of that dress once we got home.

I quickly took off the dress and hid it in the back of the closet, shutting the door. Taking a few calming breaths, I called Tess telling her something had come up with one of my flower deliveries and had to go to the shop to straighten it all out. After assuring her that I didn't need any help and insisting she and the girls go ahead without me, I put on a pair of lounge pants and one of Ben's favorite old t-shirts and crawled into bed where for the first time, I dreamed of Ben.

APPEARING ALMOST LIKE a magic trick right before my eyes, he's wearing exactly what he had on the night of the accident. Blue jeans and his Police Academy sweatshirt under his black winter jacket. As soon as I see him, I jump into his arms, wrapping my arms and legs around his body. The firmness of his hard chest feels so real pressed against mine. One strong arm is wrapped around my back, the other under my backside, holding me up. I bring my face in front of his, taking him all in. He looks better than I remember—a bright smile, his eyes creasing a little reminding me of how I used to make fun of our five year age gap. I run my fingers through his sandy blond hair and kiss each one of those creases. I hold on to him hoping I never have to let go. I lower my face into the crook of his neck, inhaling his scent. I want to live in that scent forever. I want to bottle it up and spray it all over the house, keeping him with me.

As if nothing has changed, we talk like we usually do, we laugh like we always do, we kiss like we always want to. It's not until I start to randomly cry that I remember what reality is actually like. Several thoughts come to my mind, things I want to say to him. How I'm not sure I'll be able to move on without him. How much I miss him. How angry I am at him for leaving me.

"You promised me forever," I whisper.

He takes my face in his hands, his eyes scanning over me as if he were committing me to memory as well. Bringing us closer together, he rests his forehead against mine.

"I didn't leave babe," he says kissing me softly. When he starts to pull away, I quickly grab his hands, keeping him close, refusing to let him move any further. "I'm right here. I've been right here and I will always be right here."

His lips lingering on mine, tickling me as he speaks before bringing them right back down to my mouth, where I pray they stay. His tongue works its way from the outer edge of my bottom lip before slowly slipping in between. As soon as we connect through this kiss, a calm comes over me. A calm only Ben can give me.

I CAN'T REMEMBER how long we stood there, pouring every bit of loneliness and need into that kiss but when I woke up the next morning, I remember feeling more alive than I had in over a year.

I knew then I could still live my life with Ben. I knew it wasn't conventional or even real for that matter, but for me, it was enough. I didn't tell anyone about my dreams or my want for them to continue. They would only see it as regression. I saw it as a way of making my new life work for me. For me and Ben.

"Did you have fun?" Dr. Embry asks, shaking me out of my thoughts.

It was the first best night in a long time.

"It was amazing," I smile.

She smiles kindly, and then once again, writes something down in her notepad. I begin to feel like everything I say is being graded against some healing chart I wasn't made privy to. I watch as she scribbles down a few words and leans back against her chair. Behind her, one of the orchid blooms has fallen off and landed on the shelf. I glance down at my watch to see how much longer is left in our session.

Closing her notepad and resting it on the table, Dr. Embry takes off her glasses and looks up at me. "Rachel, I think it's great you're starting to reintegrate yourself into social settings. Being around people, meeting new people, these are all wonderful steps in regaining a sense of enjoyment and fulfillment back into your life. Little accomplishments can mean big steps in coping mechanisms. Be proud of those accomplishments."

A tight smile forms on my face at her comment. Perhaps the "coping mechanisms" I lead her to believe I was using were not exactly as she thought, but they were working for me. And wasn't that the point? To find a way, a reason, to make me want to start living again? Every day I now lived for the possibility of what night could bring.

"It seems as though you are making some headway in figuring out the next steps for yourself," she says, laying her glasses on top of her notepad.

"I think so." And I did. I found my way. I found Ben again.

"Well, you most assuredly look more rested. A good night's sleep will do that for you. You're starting to get your color back. Keep doing what you are doing."

My face breaks out into a smile. "I will."

LIKE CLOCKWORK, MY cell starts to ring the minute I exit Dr. Embry's office. Not even needing to look at the call display, I answer.

"Hi, Mom."

"Hello, darling. How is your day going?"

It's ten a.m., not much could happen in anyone's day thus far. This was her way of asking how my appointment went without seeming too intrusive. Walking out of the building and towards the parking lot, I wedge the phone between my ear and shoulder, looking for my car keys in my purse. "Just fine, like always."

"I'm happy to hear that."

After a few seconds of silence, I imagined my mother pacing back and forth in her kitchen, debating whether or not to say what's on her mind. Reaching my car, a red Volkswagen Jetta, I open the door and throw my bag inside. The late morning sun has warmed the air quite a bit since walking into Dr. Embry's office an hour earlier. Shuffling the phone again so I can take my jacket off, I hear my mother take a deep breath.

"I ran into Dorothy Perry at the tennis club last week. She mentioned that her son had just moved back to the city. You remember Jackson, don't you?"

Of course I remembered Jackson Perry. Every girl who went to my high school remembers Jackson Perry. Captain of the lacrosse and soccer teams. Honor roll. Too gorgeous for it to be fair.

"You two went to high school together, isn't that right?

Dorothy mentioned how many of his old friends no longer live in the city and I thought it might be great for him to have someone to show him around. What do you think?"

Confused, I start to fish around in my purse for my parking validation. "He's from here. He doesn't need a tour guide."

"Maybe you'd like to meet him for dinner? It might be nice to catch up."

"Mom, we didn't know each other in high school. He's a few years older than me. We have nothing to catch up on."

The last time I saw Jackson Perry was years ago, the summer before he left for college. He came into The Bloom Room to buy a bouquet of flowers, for whom, I didn't know. I watched him from behind one of the display cases as he placed his order. The rest of that day I spent wondering who the flowers were for. I thought of checking the receipts to see if the name of the recipient was written anywhere but decided against it, not wanting to appear like I had a schoolgirl crush on the prom king (which if I remember correctly, he was).

"Perhaps you'd like to get to know him."

I stiffen at the realization of what this conversation is actually about. This is the first time my mother has ever mentioned meeting other men or anything remotely close to dating. Not even Tess has broached that subject with me. I feel the heat of the sun directly on me now, and I know I need to stop my mom from going any further.

"No," I say.

"Rachel," she tries again. "Wouldn't it be nice—"

"Mom, I said no." I feel myself start to sweat, beads of wetness forming on the back of my neck, a few stray strands of hair now sticking to it. I turn the car on and crank the air conditioning to full blast. It doesn't take long to feel the cold air blowing as I point all the vents towards me, cooling me off from the sudden rush of anger I feel towards the direction of the current conversation.

"Sweetheart, it's just dinner. It could be fun."

Not only does my mother seem fixated on the idea that now is the time to set me up with someone, but of all people, she thinks Jackson Perry is that right person. Jackson is two years older than me and was a god in high school. Mr. Popular with a ton of friends, smart, athletic and always had a stream of girls following him. Dated quite a few of them too. But he didn't have the reputation one would think. Kind to everyone and never looked down on anyone even though he came from a wealthy family. Last I heard, after graduation he went off to an Ivy League College and then moved overseas to Europe.

"I'm not interested," I answer, stressing every one of my words.

Reluctantly, my mother gives up. "Fine. Just thought I'd ask."

Feeling a very strong urge to get off the phone, I let my mother know that I need to get to work. But after hanging up, I continue to sit in my car, my heart pounding. A reminder that it's already occupied and there is no vacancy for anyone else.

chapter 2

THE PERFUME OF roses, lilies and every other flower comfort me as much as the aroma of a mother's kitchen comforts others. While some yearn for the scent of Sunday dinner, sweet and fresh floral fragrances are what's heartwarming to me. It immediately puts a smile on my face. These are the scents that surround me on a daily basis. Walking into The Bloom Room, I take in the sight of all the fresh flowers before me. The floor is lined with buckets full of pink, red, and yellow roses, white and fuchsia lilies, and hydrangeas the size of a baby's head. It's the middle of the week and the flower delivery I was waiting for must have just arrived.

I've owned The Bloom Room for a few years. I started working here part-time in high school, then over the summers while home from college. After graduating with a degree in Business, Emily, the owner, asked if I would like a permanent position at the shop. She needed some help organizing orders, paying bills and issuing invoices as well as new marketing ideas to keep the business growing. Then, two years later, Emily informed me that she and her husband were looking to retire—and move out of the city. I was certain this was her way of telling me they were selling the shop. My devastation and shock quickly turned into surprise when she offered to sell The Bloom Room to me. I had just turned twenty-five, recently become engaged, and was in no financial position to even think about buying a business.

When I told Ben about the offer, he asked only one question.

"Is this something you want?"

I did.

I really did.

I loved The Bloom Room and the thought of it becoming all mine…it was a dream I never even considered but suddenly was all I could think about. I knew I could build the business and make it even better than it was. Ben knew my answer as soon as he saw the look on my face.

"Okay then. Let's figure out how to make it work," he said.

My parents had already paid for all of my schooling and were helping us with the purchase of our new home. I couldn't go to them again and ask for financial help. Neither Ben nor I wanted to depend on them as much as we already were. So several meetings with the bank, a loan, and one very agreeable seller later, The Bloom Room was mine.

The day the shop was transferred into my name, Ben and I celebrated by tearing down some of the existing shelves, repainting the walls a beautiful cream color and completely rearranging the flow of the store. My absolute favorite renovation was my office. We created a space where not only could I work but an area that I could meet with event planners and brides-to-be. The best part of my day was always the brainstorming sessions I would have with clients. I loved watching an event unfold right before my eyes by simply choosing what type of flowers and colors were going to be used.

After Ben's accident, my staff really pulled through for me. They kept the shop open, made sure that any events The Bloom Room was hired for were taken care of, paid the bills and kept my business alive. I was very lucky and grateful to them. Those first few weeks they really went above and beyond what any employee should. I would never be able to repay them for keeping my dream alive while I was living my nightmare.

Currently, Anna, my right hand, was in the middle of unpacking bushels of white tulips when she looked up and saw me walking through the front door.

"Morning, Rachel," she says smiling, brushing away some loose strands from her dark brown ponytail. Anna's sweet demeanor and kind face are an asset when dealing with customers. She points towards the delivery. "Looks like we have quite a day ahead of us."

"Looks like it." I mentally check off flowers from my order as I walk by them. "Has everything come in?" I gaze around, inspecting if anything is missing.

"All but the Baby's Breath, but it should be here by noon."

"Good. I'm going to get caught up on some invoices," I tell her, walking towards my office in the back.

"Tess is waiting for you in there!" Anna calls back.

Once inside, I see Tess sitting in my chair, her black patent heels resting on top of my desk talking into her cell phone—loudly.

"I don't care what he says. He was paid to stand there and look pretty, not give his fucking opinion on politics, PETA, or who played a better Batman. You tell him to go put on the stupid speedo and smile or be replaced."

I drop my purse on my desk, alerting her of my presence. She looks up at me, sticking a finger to her head and pulling the imaginary trigger. Giggling, I roll my eyes at her because I know better. Tess lives for bossing other people around. It's what makes her a great television producer for the city's local morning show.

"Call me if there are more problems—but there better not be," she says, finishing her call.

I feel bad for whoever was at the other end of that call. Being hit by a Tess backlash is like being slapped open handed all over and all at once. You don't know which direction it came from, but you feel it everywhere.

"Never work with models," she says to me as I come around the desk and usher her out of my chair, pointing to the one across from me.

"Work with them? I thought you only slept with them," I tease.

"Yeah, well, don't do that either," she mutters, scrolling through her phone.

Tess has a habit of mixing business with pleasure. Fortunately for her, she has no problems having sex with a guy one day and firing him the next. Separating the office from the bedroom is like some magical superpower she has.

We met in the high school lunch line on the first day of freshman year. She stood behind me, tapped me on the shoulder, and told me she hated my sweater and that she was doing me a favor in telling me so. My first reaction was to turn around and ignore this rude girl. But it was my second reaction that won out, as I looked down at my sweater and wondered if it was really that bad.

"It is. Trust me," she answered, reading my thoughts. Twelve years and a better fashion sense later, she's still my very best friend.

To look at us, we are complete opposites. Her blonde shoulder length bob to my long brown waves, her blue eyes to my brown, her A cups to my C's. She envies that I fill out dresses better while I envy that she never has to find the right bra for these dresses.

"This is a little early. It's not even eleven yet," I say, noticing the time on my laptop. We usually meet at least once a week for lunch, not counting all the other times we see each other in the evenings and on weekends.

"I've got a meeting uptown so I can't do lunch. But to make up for it, I brought these!" She holds up a paper bag from C'est Bon, a pastry shop a few blocks away. Tess knows my weakness for everything and anything sugar. Opening the bag and waving in front of my face, the sweet smell of baked goods has my stomach growling.

"Pastries… Are you trying to seduce me?" I ask, looking into the bag. Strawberry strudel. Delicious.

"Maybe."

Grabbing my piece of deliciousness, I sit back down in my chair ready to bite into strawberry heaven when I notice Tess is watching me, her expression easy to read. I know and am very familiar with this look. It's the same look she gives when she wants to borrow something or ask a favor. Her smile is yelling, *Do this for me! Do this for me, please!*

I put my strudel down on my desk, not even taking a first bite. "What do you want?"

"Me? Nothing." She shakes her head and presses her lips together.

Narrowing my eyes, I raise a brow, letting her know I don't believe her.

"Okay, you got me," she says, waving around an imaginary white flag. "I'm here to make plans with my best friend for Saturday night. And I'm not taking no for an answer."

In the grand scheme of things, that doesn't sound so bad. I pick up my pastry and take the first bite. "What kind of plans?"

"I'm so glad you asked!" she answers, her smile too wide. "A few of us are going to Martini's Twist and you *are* coming this time." I watch her pull a chocolate croissant from her bag and take a huge bite.

Tess has been trying for months to get me to go out to a bar with her and some of our friends. I know her persistence comes from a good place and she's been very patient and supportive of me, but my anxiety over atmospheres like this is hard to ignore. I think Tess sees herself as both my own personal cheerleader and bodyguard, encouraging me to jump high but always prepared with a safety net should I need one.

"You've been going there quite a bit," I say, trying to focus on something other than my anxiousness.

"Have I?" she questions.

I nod.

"Meeting one of your models perhaps?" I eye her suspiciously.

She scoffs. "Rachel, please."

But I notice that she doesn't look me in the eye. I watch her start to tear her croissant into tiny pieces. She's nervous about something and Tess is very rarely nervous about anything.

"Are you sure? Because your croissant thinks otherwise," I say, pointing to the pile of flaky strips that has now accumulated on my desk. She looks down and realizes what she's done. Brushing her hands together, she rids herself of the pastry and leans back in her chair.

"He's not a model," she mumbles, looking off to the side, continuing to avoid eye contact.

Her attitude surprises me. Tess has never been secretive or nervous when it comes to telling me about a man she's seeing. This new close-mouthed approach only indicates one thing—she may actually like this guy.

"Okay, so he's not a model," I say smiling, encouraging her to say more. She's still avoiding eye contact. "Are you going to tell me more or should I look into your pile of crumbs for the magic answer?"

"Paul." Her eyes meet mine. They are unmoving, waiting for my reaction.

"Paul?" I ask confused.

She takes a deep breath and says it again. It takes me a minute before I make the connection. She's talking about my Paul. Ben's Paul.

"Oh," is the only sound I make, my lips creating a perfect little circle.

"It's nothing serious! We just bumped into each other a few weeks ago and then again last week. We exchanged numbers and texted a few times. He's going to be there on Saturday with a few of his guys and I thought we could meet him. Them."

She says all this quickly and in one breath. I can tell she's incredibly uncomfortable though I'm not sure why. In all the years I've been friends with Tess, I've been there to witness her many ups and downs with different men, none of which have caused this much of a change in attitude from her. Regardless of how meaningful or meaningless each was, deep down I think Tess has always wanted to find a relationship that would last longer than an orgasm. Maybe that's why I'm so thrown when she mentions Paul.

"I had no idea you two were even talking," I say, perplexed.

"We aren't! Not really. You know, just texting."

I let out a small laugh. "Why didn't you tell me earlier?"

I also wonder why Paul hasn't mentioned anything.

"I don't know," she says, looking a little guilty. "I know how close you two are and I didn't want to upset you. You aren't upset are you?" Her face suddenly showing worry.

"Of course not," taken aback that she was worried I wouldn't be okay with this. "He just doesn't seem your type is all."

And he's not. I have yet to see Tess with anyone who couldn't be in a Ralph Lauren photo spread. Sure, Paul is handsome but in the same way Ben was. More rugged than refined, more muscular than lean, jeans and t-shirt over shirt and tie.

"He's not," she agrees. "But I don't know… he made me laugh."

I smile, understanding a bit more. "He's good at that."

Paul has been a constant in my life for years but more so after the accident. I think a part of him feels responsible for me. As though he promised Ben to always look after me. He took the time to check up on me, called to remind me when my car needed an oil change. When I mentioned how different and unnerving it was sleeping alone in the house after my mother left, he came over and installed new locks on the doors. When summer came along, I would sometimes come home to find him mowing the lawn. My first real laugh after the accident was with Paul. He came over to fix that leaky pipe in the kitchen. I was upstairs in the bedroom when I heard a scream followed by an exuberant amount of swearing. I rushed downstairs, taking them two at a time to see Paul soaked from the head down.

"I forgot to turn the water off," he said, wiping his face with his damp shirt. I watched him and started to laugh a deep belly laugh that I felt all the way back to my spine. Tears were running down my face. Paul stared at me, stunned at the sound of me losing control before finally joining in. We laughed for so long and it felt so good. The pipe never got fixed that day.

Looking back at Tess, I realize that she isn't asking me to go out on Saturday because she thinks *I* need it but because *she* does. Never one to admit nervousness, Tess finds other ways in seeking help. And right now, she's asking me to help her. If that means it's time for me to be her support for a change, how could I say no?

"Fine, but I'm borrowing something from your closet!" I tell her.

Relieved, she squeals and starts clapping her hands. Getting up from her chair, she rushes over and pulls me into a hug. "Anything you want! I'll bring over a bunch of choices and we'll get ready together." Seeing how happy she is even has *me* feeling a little excited.

"Sounds good," I reply, hugging her back.

Breaking apart, Tess moves back towards her chair and starts gathering her belongings. "So, since that's all covered, what about you? Anything fun and exciting to report?"

"You saw me yesterday. What could have possibly happened since then?" I ask as I start to arrange some invoices in front of me.

"Lots!" she snorts, rummaging through her purse.

I think back to my phone conversation with my mother, wondering if I should mention it. "Well, I guess one thing…" I start to say slowly. Tess looks up from her bag, waiting for me to continue. "My mother tried to set me up on a date today. Or a hangout. I'm not even sure."

Tess's eyebrows raise up high. "Wow," she responds, definitely surprised. "Bethany finally strikes. With whom?"

I shake my head. "Doesn't matter. It's not happening."

Tess nods twice before continuing to look for something in her purse.

I don't know why, but I have this sudden urge to say his name aloud, even if it is for no other reason but to hear it come from my lips.

"Jackson Perry," I state quietly.

"Hmm?" Tess mumbles, the sound of keys jingling.

"It was with Jackson Perry," I say again.

The purse drops from Tess's hand, only her keys remain, hooked to her index finger. She blinks a few times, staring at me.

"Jackson Perry is back in town? How the fuck did I not know this?"

I shrug.

"Wow. I wonder if he's still as hot as he was back when I used him in my spank bank." Her face in a state of serious concentration, indicating that she's really pondering about this.

And with that, I'm ready to end this conversation. "Anyways, I told her no thank you. Not interested."

Tess nods but seems like she's in a daze. After a minute, she bends down and starts scooping up her belongings. "Probably for the best," I hear her say. "If he's anything like I remember, I'd have to kill you simply out of jealousy."

I laugh. "Lucky for me then."

Tess stands, ready to leave. Before opening the door, she looks back, confirming our plans. "Saturday night?"

I smile, reassuring her. "Saturday night."

AFTER WORK, I head home to change into my running clothes. I live outside of the downtown core, and not too far from my house is a beautiful park with different trails and paths. A few months ago while I was getting dressed, I caught a glimpse of myself in the mirror. I could hardly recognize my reflection. I knew I had lost weight. My clothes hung loose, my bra had become too big, and some pants didn't even stay up. I'm not sure what it was about that day, but in that moment, I saw what the last few months had done to my body. My thighs didn't touch, my hip bones were jutting out at my sides and I was pretty sure I saw a few ribs. My reflection simultaneously scared and woke me up. I no longer wanted to be the sickly girl staring back at me in the mirror. Dr. Embry's words from a previous visit rang through my head just then.

"You should find something new, something different that has no association to your life before now. A hobby, something that is all yours. Find that break you need and just be Rachel for an hour. You may be surprised at what you find."

The next day, after eating a full breakfast of eggs, bacon and toast, I went and bought a pair of running shoes. I had never gone running before, at least not on purpose and the first few times, it showed. My legs felt like they were going to give out after five minutes and I could hardly breathe, my lungs burned so badly. But as the weeks passed, my legs started to take me further and my lungs started to adjust to the faster breathing. Steadily, one mile changed into two and then three. My body wasn't only adjusting, but changing as well. I slowly started to put on some of the weight I lost, and I was toning up. When I looked in the mirror now, I was happy with what I saw.

Locking my front door and putting the spare key in my jacket pocket, I pull out my iPod and find my playlist. Thirty Seconds to Mars starts blaring out of my earphones. Jared and I have a few miles ahead of us.

After a little warm up, I start to really push myself once I get to the park. Now that my running had surpassed its embarrassing beginning, I was excited to run the trails in the park. After a few weeks of trying different paths, I found one I loved. Surrounded by trees to protect me from the wind and the blinding setting sun, the path took me along the outside of the park, along the lakeshore where ducks swam and were fed by tossed pieces of bread. A little further down the path there was a small play area where families let their kids run wild while parents stood back watching. I couldn't hear the laughter or the small screams of excitement through my earphones, but I could see all the happy little faces as they went down the slide or made their way across the monkey bars.

But the best spot is where the path cuts across into the park and dozens of Magnolia trees line the trail. For a quarter mile, these trees take over the path, growing large enough that their branches reach over me, touching each other on opposite sides. Wooden park benches sit under them, giving people a place to sit and take in their beauty. The trees only bloom for a few weeks in late spring, and when they do, it will be like running through a pink cloud. I can already see the buds beginning to pop on the branches, knowing that in a few weeks, this path will look completely different.

I feel my heart beat fast and the back of my neck becoming drenched with sweat. I stop to take a short break, sitting on one of the benches that line the path, thinking about my day.

Over the last year, I've done everything in my power to keep my world as monotonous as possible. I no longer liked surprises. Lack of control over situations leaves me feeling powerless, defenseless against life's quick and unexpected turns. And today I've had two. Between my mother's new dating project and conceding to Tess's Saturday night plans, I'm left feeling a little out of control. Another reason why I needed this run—to try and regain some footing. These runs help clear my mind while I get the adrenaline rush my body craves. Every drop of sweat and stomp of foot releases a buildup of emotion, the stress and anxiety my mind has created, and after a day like today, there is a lot to unload.

The wind picks up and spreads goose bumps across my body. I shiver slightly, my body automatically turning away from the cold breeze. I fold my arms across my chest, rubbing my hands over my prickly skin. The music quiets in my ears, my iPod asking me to choose another playlist. Behind me I can hear the stomping footsteps of another jogger coming closer, his voice deep but out of breath as he speaks aloud into what I can only assume is his Bluetooth.

"Got it," he breathes, loudly. "Martini's Twist."

My head whips in his direction when I hear the mention of the same bar Tess has us going to, but all that's left to see of the runner is his back. Dressed in all black, his legs move him further away from me with every stomp. I don't know why I stand here, staring like I do, but only when he's no longer in sight do I feel the cool wind hit me again—a reminder it's time to get on the move. Exiting the park, I start to make my way back home.

I see my house in the distance and push myself into a full sprint. Reaching my door, I pull out my key and make my way inside. Kicking off my shoes and dropping my jacket in the middle of the floor, I make my way to the kitchen to grab some water and collapse on the couch. The minute I sit down, my body turns to Jell-O. I'm so exhausted the idea of getting up to shower is almost too much. I close my eyes, listening to my heart rate start to slow.

I hear the sound of my phone chiming, telling me I've received a text message. I reach for my cell that's sitting on the coffee table in front of me. Sliding my finger across the screen, I open my text window.

Paul: Saturday night. See you then.

I guess it didn't take Tess long to reach out to Paul, confirming our Saturday night plans. I quickly text back.

Me: Yup 

Putting my cell back on the table I get up and make my way to the shower. The best part about runs like this is that they exhaust me, and exhaustion leads to a deep sleep. A sleep where dreams can come and take me away to another place. A better place. A place where I feel whole.

chapter 3

I'M A FEW blocks away from The Bloom Room, the buildings and store fronts very familiar. The intersection is void of any passing cars or people rushing to their individual destinations. Considering this is one of the busiest intersections in the area, it takes me a minute to adjust to how quiet and calm it is. I look from side to side. It eerily reminds me of a scene from a movie where a zombie apocalypse or disease outbreak has happened, before all the carnage and looting begins. Everything is as it should be, only empty. But I know this isn't a movie and I know there is no outbreak. I'm dreaming, and this time, we are at the beginning, where we first met.

I close my eyes and take a deep breath. Memories of that day come flooding back, as clear as if it was just yesterday. My heart fills with warmth and excitement, as it always does when I think of Ben. Sometimes my dreams are simple flashes, momentary breaks where his face will flash before my eyes or I'll hear his voice echoing from some place far away. A face I can't grab quick enough or a voice I can't seem to hold on to.

But then there are others, just like this one, that are throwbacks to our past, a place with meaning, a time with a happy story. Dreams like these are when I know I'll have time with him.

Memories of this corner years ago on a sunny day just as it is now rush to my mind, cars and people hurrying by, the noise of a busy downtown core coming alive as it always does on a Monday. And a uniformed officer, stopping me on the side of the road.

When I open my eyes, Ben is standing in front of me. He looks younger dressed in his police uniform, his sandy blond hair cut short, his jaw clean-shaven as any young officer's would have been. His blue eyes are piercing against the navy of his uniform. He looks just like he did all those years ago when he first approached me.

Ben always used to say that it was my eyes that first caught his attention. It was sweet and romantic but a total lie. Ben first saw me from across a very busy intersection. I always knew there was no way he could have seen my eyes from that distance. As time went on, I learned Ben was more of a boob guy than anything else. I knew that's what got his attention, but I let him keep telling his version because sometimes, rewriting the details of history makes for a better story.

"We're going way back this time," he says, looking down at his attire. His hands pat down his chest, reminiscing of a time when he used to wear those clothes daily. His eyes come back up, meeting mine, and I can't help but bite my lower lip. I always loved seeing him in uniform. His broad muscular shoulders defined through the navy shirt, the shiny badge of authority pinned to his chest. I can't lie and say that the power that comes with the uniform wasn't a huge turn on.

"I guess I was feeling sentimental," I say, a little embarrassed. My stomach flutters as I eye the handcuffs strapped to his belt, memories of the night he used them on me coming to mind.

He takes a step towards me, using his thumb and index fin-

ger to lift my face up to his.

"I like sentimental," he says, smiling before lowering his lips to mine. His kiss is soft, and I immediately fall into his rhythm, like a choreographed dance we've perfected over the years. I open my mouth slightly, allowing his tongue to enter and meet mine. With a slow sweep, he kisses me like it's his only purpose. It's been over a week since we've seen each other. I wonder if he senses the lapse in time the same way I do.

Breaking away, he releases his fingers from my chin. "I've missed you, Rach."

"Me too," I answer back, slightly out of breath.

Ben has been the only man who has ever taken my breath away with a simple kiss. The boys from high school, the men in college, and even those who came after, none of them have ever come close. Taking his arm, we start to walk leisurely down the empty streets, as though we were going for a Sunday stroll. My arms wrapped around one of his, I rest my head on his shoulder. As we pass shop after shop, he stops us abruptly, my body falling back against his as I lose my footing at our sudden halt. He wraps his arms around me and looks around, his eyes scanning the area.

"Right here. This is where I stopped you," he says.

"You mean where you accosted me and then proceeded to lecture about road safety?" I ask, unable to keep the cheekiness from my voice. My eyes are glaring, but my inability to hide my smile isn't doing anything to conceal how happy this memory makes me.

"Jaywalking is *a serious offence," he answers back, his tone serious but his smile also showing his fondness for this memory.*

Following his gaze to the area around us, I see the sign for the dry cleaners run by a very sweet elderly couple. Mr. Sanchez comes in every week to buy a single rose for his wife. The sign reminds me of where I was heading that very day.

"I was late and needed to get back to the shop," I argue back, taking a stand. I straighten my body and cross my arms across my chest. I'm silently daring him to continue our narrative sparring match. "I ended up being twenty minutes late after your little power trip."

He laughs, his head falling back. "Power trip? Nah. I just couldn't let the prettiest girl I'd ever seen get away with breaking the law." He wiggles his eyebrows once, then twice, knowing I'm a sucker for it.

"Uh huh... sure." I shake my head, doing my best not to fall for it.

"Swear to God." He raises his right hand. "The minute I saw you walking down the street, I couldn't take my eyes off you. When Paul caught me staring and saw what got my attention, he got it...he knew. Why else do you think he stayed back while I stopped you?"

"To not be a part of a serious legal injustice?" I offer, shrugging my shoulders.

He barks out another laugh. "Not even close. He knew not to mess with my game."

"Handing me a forty-five dollar fine for jaywalking was part of 'your game'?" I looked at him disbelievingly.

"It worked didn't it?" His smile is cocky.

It *did* work. The entire time he stood there lecturing me on the dangers of walking across the street in a non-cross walked area, the more I noticed his eyes, straight nose, square jaw and of course, his mouth. His lips to be more accurate. The more he spoke, the more I stared and the more I wondered how they'd feel. I begin to feel my cheeks flush.

Ben smiles, watching me relive this memory. "You're blushing," he teases.

I roll my eyes at him. "Well, I knew something wasn't right when you started to fill out the form and asked where I worked and if I was married or single. I don't believe those are custom-

ary questions."

"Nope. But they got me the information that I needed."

"So smug. You're lucky I didn't report you." I playfully nudge his shoulder.

Reaching out and taking me in his arms again, he holds me close and kisses the top of my head. I rest my head on his chest, wrapping my arms around his trim waist.

"Smug? No," he says softly in my ear. "I was just planning my future."

I smile, knowing that not only was he planning his own future, but he had planned mine as well.

chapter 4

AFTER A VERY long and busy day at the shop, I'm exhausted and wanting nothing more than to curl up on my couch and watch reruns of *Criminal Minds*. Instead, just as discussed, Tess comes over with hangers of dresses for me to choose from. It's Saturday night and as much as I long to stay home, I did promise to be the Goose to her Maverick. This would be the first time since Ben's accident that I was going out to a bar, to socialize, with strangers—men. I can already feel my stomach clenching, reminding me of my anxiety.

"That one," Tess says, pointing to the black dress laying on top of my bed.

It's a fun flirty dress, cap sleeves with an A-line cut hitting the mid-thigh. I put it on and take a look at myself in the full-length mirror propped up against the wall. She's right. It fits me just right, and surprisingly, I like how I look in it. Tess pairs the dress with a pair of gold heels and a matching gold bracelet. The reflection in the mirror now showed two girls gearing up for a great night. A part of me worries that maybe the dress is giving off the wrong impression. A *single and ready to mingle* vibe, but when I see the look of excitement on Tess's face, I know I can't let her down. I try my best to relax, putting a smile on my face while Tess finishes getting ready, doing my best to ignore my nerves. I take deep breaths, counting backwards from ten, concentrating on inhaling deeply through my nose and exhaling slowly through my mouth, an exercise Dr. Embry suggested I use when I feel myself becoming anxious.

"Imagine you are inhaling hot fiery breath and releasing it as cold, icy air," she'd say.

I see Tess looking at me from the bathroom door, waiting for me to reply to something she just said. I realize I have no idea she had even been talking.

"I'm sorry, what?"

"How do I look?" she repeats, standing in front of me in her red stretch mini dress. She has black heels and large silver hoops in her ears. She looks great and I tell her so. I must not have been covering my nerves as well as I thought because she walks over to me and rests her hands on my shoulders.

"Rachel, this is going to be fun," she says. "Everything is going to be fine and tonight you are going to smile, laugh and have a few drinks. You are going to enjoy yourself and talk to people. But if you really need to, we'll leave. Whenever you want."

I take another deep breath and nod. I eye her from head to toe. "Paul's not going to stand a chance with you in that dress."

"That's the idea," she answers, doing a few last minute adjustments in the mirror. "If he knows what's good for him." She winks at me through her reflection. Taking one last look, she turns to me. "Ready to have fun?"

THIS BAR DEFINITELY seems to be the "it" place of the moment. I had driven by it a couple of times during the day while it was closed and there were no crowds outside its doors waiting to get in. Seeing it open tonight, I can understand why Tess has continued to come back. Black leather booths line one side of the room while high-top tables fill in the rest of the space. The bar itself is long and takes up the one side of the wall. Glass shelves are filled with liquor bottles, glassware of all different shapes and sizes are neatly lined directly above. The walls are painted a caramel color and beautiful red glass chandeliers hang from the ceiling. The lighting is dim and the music loud. Tess holds my hand as we make our way through the crowd to a table where two of our friends and girls she works with, Sophie and Lana, are already sitting with pretty purple drinks in front of them.

"Ladies!" Tess says hugging each one once we get to the table.

Taking a seat, I wave hello to both girls. Like Tess, both Sophie and Lana are beautiful and dressed to kill. Sophie has fiery red curls while Lana has her long, dirty blonde hair pulled up in a high ponytail. Both their outfits look like they've come off a runway.

"Hey, Rachel, it's good to see you." Lana smiles. She was definitely the more talkative of the two. It dawns on me then that it's been quite a while since I've seen her or had a girl's night out.

"You too," I reply.

Taking off my jacket, I take another quick glance around the bar. It definitely has more of a martini lounge atmosphere than one of a club. The music playing is a mix of electric and jazz, but there are people dancing as though Usher was playing over the sound system. A handsome waiter dressed in all black comes around to grab our drink order. Just seeing all the bottles lined up behind the bar overwhelms me.

"Two of those," Tess orders, pointing to the drinks Sophie and Lana already have. Nodding, he looks over to Lana and smiles before walking away. This does not go unnoticed by the table.

"Looks like someone started early tonight," Tess says, looking over at Lana raising her eyebrows.

"Yup, that's Brett," Sophie pipes in. "While you two took your sweet ass time getting here, I had the pleasure of watching Lana plan their wedding and name their two children."

"Ha ha," Lana says sarcastically, rolling her eyes as she sips her drink.

"I'm sure your children will be beautiful," Tess adds.

Lana takes the teasing in stride because we all know it's just a matter of time before one of us become the next target. Tess's attention moves quickly from us to scanning the crowd at the bar.

"I don't think he's here yet," I say, leaning into her. Her head whips back towards me, flustered I think at being caught looking for Paul. Brett chooses the right moment to come back with our drinks.

"Thank you," I tell him as he places my drink in front of me. He has spiky blond hair and is rather muscular. Not in a body builder way but he definitely looks like he spends a good amount of time at the gym. Before leaving the table, he turns towards Lana, his eyes not straying from hers.

"Another?"

Nodding her head, we all watch a little uncomfortably as these two play a game of sexual chicken, neither blinking nor looking away. Finally, Brett gives in, giving a quick nod and smile before starting to walk away.

"Brett!" Tess yells out, calling him back towards us. He rests his forearms on our table, standing right by Lana's side. "What time do you finish tonight?"

A little wide-eyed, he glances over at Lana before answering. "Eleven."

She claps her hands together. "Great! Lana here would love to buy you a drink once you're done." Looking between the two, she smiles mischievously as she sips her drink.

A coy, grinning smile slowly appears on Brett's face as he looks over at Lana. The flush on Lana's face is so apparent, even the dim overhead lighting does nothing to hide it.

"Is that so?" he asks her.

"Umm. Sure. I mean if you're available. I mean, not busy." I don't think her cheeks could become any more red.

Letting out a quick laugh, he smiles. "Definitely not busy…and yes, available." He winks once at her before stepping away from the table, heading back towards the bar.

"What the hell?' Lana whispers, her eyes narrowing on Tess.

"Relax, you'll thank me later," she answers, dismissing Lana's anger and taking another sip of her drink.

It was obvious to us that the rest of Lana's night would be spent looking at the time on her phone, waiting for eleven o'clock to come. I watch her take sip after sip from her drink, and I know if I don't slow her down, the poor girl may not even make it until then. I lean across our table so that she can hear me over the loud music.

"He likes you," I offer smiling, hoping to settle her nerves.

She glances in his direction. "You think?"

I nod once. "Totally. Couldn't keep his eyes off you." This seems to calm her and give her a little more confidence.

After a few minutes of listening to Tess and Sophie talk about work gossip, Sophie nods towards the door.

"Look who's here," she says smiling into her glass. We all turn to see Paul and two other men I don't recognize walk in.

"Don't all look together!" Tess chastises us.

The guys haven't noticed us yet, but I immediately feel a sense of comfort having Paul here. I look over again to where Paul and his friends are standing when he sees me. He smiles, acknowledging me before his eyes move to the woman beside me. He lifts his chin in greeting before bringing his attention back to his friends. I slowly turn back, nervous to see Tess's reaction to Paul's very casual greeting.

"Are you fucking kidding me?" I hear her say, her jaw rigid and hard. "That's all I get? A fucking chin pump?"

"He's with friends. Give him a minute. I'm sure he'll be right over," I say, hoping to diffuse a ticking Tess time bomb. Tess is the kind of girl that demands attention, but only when she's looking for it. Unfortunately, I don't think it worked as I watch her down the rest of her drink then use the back of her hand to wipe her mouth. I look back in Paul's direction, hoping to get his attention but there's no need. His eyes are back on Tess.

"Pretend I said something funny and start to laugh," Tess orders us.

"Could you be more obvious?" Sophie chimes in.

Tess's eyes move around to each of us, daring us not to oblige as she plasters a huge, rigid smile on her face. "Now!" she says through clenched teeth. The three of us look at each other and begin to laugh, mostly out of fear.

After a few minutes of awkward laughs followed by even more awkward silence, Sophie stands.

"I can't take this anymore. Lana, you're coming with me," Sophie begins. "Until eleven o'clock, you're mine and you're going to help me find someone to buy me a drink."

Lana casually nods and follows Sophie over towards the other side of the bar.

Leaving us alone at the table, Tess turns to me. "How do I look?" she asks, shaking her fingers through her hair.

"Still amazing," I assure her. I've never seen Tess act this way. She's always so calm and in control when it comes to men. Seeing her this way further adds to my suspicion that she likes Paul more than she's letting on.

A few more minutes have passed and Paul has yet to come by the table. I look back over and see that he and his friends are at the bar, ordering drinks. One of his friends has struck up a conversation with two women. I can feel the tension rolling off of Tess. I know she's watching this scene unfold. Turning back towards her, I see her try and take a sip from her drink before realizing it's empty. I watch as she takes the remainder of mine and downs that instead.

"He's just being polite," I tell her, again hoping to calm her down. "Look, he's not even talking to them. Probably just helping his friend out."

"Whatever." She shrugs. "Like I said, we only texted a few times."

I know she's trying hard to hide whatever it is she's feeling. Anger? Jealousy? She's sitting up so straight and stiff, I'm afraid that if someone bumped into her, she'd fall right off her chair. I look back towards Paul and see he is still at the bar with those girls. If my aim were better, I'd take the strawberry garnish from my glass and whip it at him to grab his attention.

Behind me, I hear a man's voice offering to buy Tess and me another round. Before I even have enough time to turn around, she's accepting and inviting them to join us.

Them?

I turn back towards the table and see one man sit across from Tess.

"Dylan," he says, offering his hand to Tess, shaking it. I can tell by his voice that he's the one that offered to buy us a drink. He then offers me his hand. I shake it but am distracted by the feel of his friend brush up against my shoulder as he walks past to take the other seat directly across from me. Once he does, my breath inadvertently catches. Sitting in front of me is undeniably one of the most beautiful men I've ever seen. A man I've seen before, years ago.

He extends his hand to me. "Jackson."

"Oh, fuck," I hear Tess whisper under her breath before letting out a small chuckle.

I'm frozen. Jackson Perry is sitting right across from me. I wonder if this is a strange coincidence or if someone is playing a joke on me. Could my mother have planned this? I disregard that thought quickly, knowing how ludicrous that would actually be. But I'm pretty sure that the chances of Jackson Perry's name being bounced around several of my conversations this week and him being here right now are the same odds as me winning the lottery, only then to be struck by lightning on my way to cash in the winnings.

After a few seconds, Tess kicks me under the table. Taking his hand, I shake it, hoping he doesn't notice that my hand is already shaking. "Rachel," I manage to say.

He smiles, taking his hand back. I can tell he has no idea who I am or any recollection that we went to the same high school. And the man sitting in front of me now is not the same teenager from the back then.

His hair is still dark, cut short on the sides, staying longer on top. His eyes are light, but it's hard to tell their true color in the dim lighting of the bar. His nose straight and chin slightly pointed. The short stubble of hair on his chiseled face only magnifies the fact that Jackson Perry is now *all* man. He's wearing a light blue checkered shirt, fitting him well enough to show that what's underneath is also all man.

Dylan's voice distracts my attention from Jackson's broad chest and back to the rest of the table. "So, ladies, what are we drinking?"

"Purple Hazes," Tess replies.

"Oh, no thanks," I interrupt. "I'm fine."

"We insist, right, Jax?" Dylan says, grabbing one of Jackson's shoulders.

My eyes shift back over to Jackson and he's looking at me with a kind smile. "Only if Rachel wants."

"She wants!" Tess says smiling, kicking me under the table again.

I give her a tense smile, one she is also reciprocating. I see her glance once more in Paul's direction then back at me. *Okay, Tess, message received. We are having drinks with Dylan and Jackson.* I turn back towards Dylan. "Okay, sure. Thanks."

Motioning to a waiter nearby, Dylan orders our drinks plus another round for Jackson and himself.

Tess leans in over the table, her arms folded in front of her. I see her eyes move from me to the man sitting directly across from me. "Jax? That's an interesting nickname. What ever happened to just 'Jack'?" She crosses her legs under the table, and I can feel her foot hit my shin every few seconds as she swings her leg back and forth.

He smiles and slightly shakes his head, amused. "Ask my parents. Last name as a first name. I hated it as a kid, begged to have it changed to Michael or Adam. Instead, they started calling me Jax. Name stuck. Now it seems like everyone's name is Jackson or Jax."

Even with the music being loud, the sound of his voice is all I can hear. It's strong and deep and sounds nice coming out of his mouth. My eyes remain on his lips as I think back to whether I knew about his nickname in high school. I think everyone who didn't know him always referred to him as Jackson Perry. First and last name at all times. But I like Jax. It suits him.

His lips quirk up a little, and that's when I know I've been caught staring at them. I blink a few times before raising my eyes, bringing them up to meet his. His lips form a smile that on anyone else would seem cocky, but on him it seems…kind.

His attention is swayed away somewhat when Dylan speaks. "So, what are our plans tonight?" he asks.

"Well, *we*," Tess points at me and herself, "are planning to have a few drinks, enjoy ourselves, and then head home."

"Sounds good. I'm in." Dylan grins.

"Cute." Tess narrows her eyes at him, but I can tell she's having a little fun.

I'm not naïve, nor am I oblivious to the bar scene. It's just been a while since I've been in it. I realize that most of the men are probably looking for a fun and easy hook up, but having it so easily put out there is a little surprising. Have things changed that much since I was single and going out? Since when were men that forward? Out of the corner of my eye, I can see Jackson looking at Dylan, taking a sip from his glass, quietly laughing and ever so subtly shakes his head. He catches me watching him again.

"Ignore him," he says to me. "I do."

He smiles again and this time dimples appear. *Has he always had dimples?* Or have I just never been close enough to notice? Right now, I'm close enough that I could stick my pinky in one of them if I wanted. I fist my hands together under the table, ensuring I don't.

"You know, Jax, we actually went to high school with you," Tess informs him.

"Really?" he looks at her and then me. I can see he's trying to remember us.

"We're a few years younger," I tell him. "You don't actually know us."

He keeps his eyes trained on me as I watch him wrack his brain, trying to come up with any memory he may have of us. His gaze is so intense I feel a shiver run down my neck and spine. Finally, he accepts that he truly has no recollection because one side of his mouth rises and he simply says, "Well, it's nice to finally meet you."

Still feeling the shivers from his stare, I'm unsure how to respond. So I smile then take a sip from my drink.

"Well that's too bad. I would have loved to hear some incredibly embarrassing stories about this fucker," Dylan nods towards Jackson. After downing his drink, he looks back between Tess and me. "How is it possible that two beauties such as yourselves are here all alone?"

"What makes you think we're alone?" Tess answers back.

"Well, I'm the one buying you drinks. I don't see anyone else rushing over. Call it male intuition," Dylan winks.

"Well what does your *male intuition* say about this?" Tess says, raising her middle finger.

Laughing, Dylan leans back.

"It tells me I should be talking to Rachel," he says, his attention now shifting on me.

"Oh, hell no!" Tess howls. "There's no way I'm letting her first pick up in over a year be from you with those kinds of lines." Finishing what's left in her glass she stands up and grabs her purse. Pointing to Dylan with her index finger. "You, come with me. We are going to work on making that guy over there jealous."

Getting up from his seat, Dylan smiles, loosening his tie a little. "Making other guys jealous is my specialty."

Rolling her eyes, I hear Tess mumble something under her breath before she looks at Jackson.

"Do better than your friend."

Looking at me, she only winks, then turns away and walks towards the bar with Dylan following right behind. My eyes are throwing daggers at her back. Not only can I not believe she left me alone with him but she made me out to sound like some kind of social pariah who hasn't spoken to a man in over a year. Technically, it's true but who knows what he must be thinking now. If anything, he must be trying to come up with an excuse to get away from me as soon as possible. I slowly turn back around, fully intent on saying goodbye. Instead, I see Jackson trying his best to hold in a laugh.

"I'm not sure who I should be more worried about—him or her," he says, light laughter escaping his lips.

I smile and within a few seconds of hearing him laugh, I slowly join in. "Him. Definitely him."

Leaning in closer, he slides his glass from hand to hand. I

watch the amber liquid swirl around in his glass. "I have to say, I kind of feel like an ass."

My eyes squint in confusion. "Why?"

"I don't remember you," he says, his voice hinting towards regret.

I wave off his comment. "Please, don't. I'm two years younger. You wouldn't have noticed me."

I watch him scan my face, moving from my eyes down to my mouth then back up again. "I don't understand how I could not."

If this is what Tess meant when she told him to do better, he's doing it. It's been a long time since I had a man flirt with me and I have no idea how to react. Should I say nothing, taking the chance it will only encourage him more? Or should I kindly say something, discouraging him from continuing? I wish I could say I felt the same way Tess did when Dylan gave his one-liners, but Jackson's words feel different. They seem genuine and sincere.

Realizing I shouldn't encourage him, I become more rigid, trying to convey how uncomfortable I am with the attention. Noticing, he steers the conversation in another direction.

"So, Rachel…" he looks slightly embarrassed when he realizes he doesn't even know my last name.

"Miller," I help, taking a sip from my drink.

Thankful, he smiles.

"So, Rachel Miller, what have you been up to in the last—" he glances down at his very expensive looking watch, "five to ten years?"

The last thing I want to do is talk about my most recent years. I don't want to watch him mentally picturing the word *widow* written across my forehead like so many others do. I glance upwards, thinking about what to say and what to leave out. "Well, after college I moved back here and now I own my own business."

"Really?" he seems impressed. "What kind of business?"

"I own a flower shop."

His eyes slightly widen in surprise. "Which one?"

"The Bloom Room."

He laughs. "Incredible. I walk by your store almost daily. My office is in the Brooks Building."

I picture the Brooks Building in my head. A large glass building whose tip seems to meet the clouds. I know from previous deliveries made to the building that there are a lot of corporate and bank offices in that building.

Right as he is about to ask another question, we are interrupted by someone approaching our table. I look up to see Paul standing beside me, possessively placing an arm around my chair.

"Hey, Rach, who's your friend?" Paul smiles, his lips stiff, nowhere near reaching his eyes.

"Paul, this is Jackson," I introduce them. "Paul is an old friend."

Jackson smiles and offers his hand to Paul. "How's it going?"

Watching them shake hands, I can see tension appear in both sets of arms. Jackson's hand seems strained, his knuckles popping out slightly from the grip Paul has on him. Hoping to smooth the situation and let Paul know I'm not in need of rescue, I nudge his shoulder and nod my head in Tess's direction. We both shift our eyes towards her and watch as she laughs at something Dylan has just said. Her hands reach out and rest on his chest, playfully pushing him away. Turning back towards Paul, I watch him stand straighter, his shoulders shifting back.

"Maybe someone else is waiting for a hello," I tell him.

Paul blinks a few times before returning his focus back on me. "Looks to me like she's doing just fine."

My eyes move back to Tess who is now looking back over towards us. "Go over there and say hello. Trust me," I tell him.

Looking between me and Jackson, Paul's hesitant to leave.

"GO!" I push him towards the bar. Lifting his hands in defeat, he starts to walk over to where I know Tess is going to make him work for her attention.

"I think I was I just put in my place," Jackson says, grinning. With every smile, it's becoming increasingly harder to ignore how attractive he is.

"Just a little over protective." I feel my face start to flush, unsure if it's due to my slight embarrassment over Paul's big brother behavior or my continued awareness of how good looking Jackson Perry is.

"Well, I can't blame him for that." He cocks one side of his mouth up.

I blink a few times.

He's flirting again.

With *me*.

"So, what about you? What have you been up to in the last five to ten years?" I ask, changing the subject.

Inhaling, he leans back in his chair. "After college, I was offered a position overseas—Switzerland. I thought it was a great opportunity. Great chance to travel, learn international business firsthand, so I took it. I stayed there for a few years, learned to snowboard," he states proudly. "Then after a while I missed being close to my family. Started looking for opportunities back here in the city, something came along and now here I am."

Even though I already knew about his years of being overseas, I decided to keep that to myself. "Business opportunities in…?"

"Investment banking."

I raise my eyebrows. "That sounds…"

"Boring?" he offers.

I let out a small laugh. "No…smart. I was going to say smart."

Jackson gives me a light chuckle in return. Neither of us

says anything for a minute as we stare at each other. I break eye contact and scan the room, mostly in effort to put a little space between the two of us. I notice quite a few sets of female eyes looking this way. *His way*. I'm sure they are all just waiting to take my place the minute I leave. And then it occurs to me that one of these other women *should* be sitting here instead of me. Any one of these women would be a better choice for him to get to know than me. I'm about to thank him for the drink and nice chat when he begins to speak.

"We should—" He stops, his attention now focused on the seat beside me. Looking over, I see Sophie has magically appeared and has sat down at the table.

Extending her hand to Jackson, she cocks her head to the side and grins. "Sophie."

His eyes move from Sophie back to me before he graciously takes her hand. "Jackson."

I smile awkwardly, feeling a little relieved to have the distraction but also a little annoyed at Sophie's sudden presence.

"Where's Lana?" I ask, trying to mask my confused feelings.

"Eleven o'clock," she simply replies, her eyes still on Jackson. I nod in understanding, remembering that our waiter friend has now finished his shift. Turning towards Jackson, I see his lips are pressed together and he's watching me. I think he's also a little thrown by Sophie's appearance, but I realize this is exactly what was needed. Sophie is an available, beautiful woman. I should bow out and give Jackson a chance to mingle with someone other than me.

I look down to check the time on my phone and stand up from the table. Jackson immediately follows, standing, rushing to pull out my chair further. He's close enough that I can feel his body softly brush against mine as he moves to stand behind me. The slightest hint of his cologne, spice mixed with masculinity, floats around me, and I feel lightheaded, finding his scent more intoxicating than my drink.

"Thank you for the drink, but I've got to get going," I say, trying to regain my balance.

"Oh," he says with a hint of disappointment, his eyes slightly squinted.

"Don't worry, I'm sure Sophie can keep you better entertained than I can," I tell him jokingly but feel slightly disappointed to be leaving. But it's because of that disappointment that I know I should.

Leaning in closer, I can feel his breath against my neck as he speaks directly in my ear. "Let me at least walk you outside, get you a cab," he says.

"No need," I wave him off and take a step back. I glance back towards the bar, seeing Tess and Paul each drinking a shot and laughing. Not wanting to interrupt, I look towards Sophie. "Let her know I left?"

She nods. "Sure."

Looking back at Jackson, not sure how to end our evening, I awkwardly stick out my hand. Looking down at my offering, his mouth quirks up. He takes my hand in his and instead of shaking it, he lifts it to his mouth. His lips softly brush against my skin. A quiver of surprise runs through my body, causing me to tighten my fingers around his hand. My reaction causes him to smile, before he releases me. "It was a pleasure, Rachel."

Frenzied, I nod. "Good night."

I turn and make my way towards the exit. The cool night air hits me as soon as I get outside. It's been years since I've felt the touch of another man's lips. It's only been Ben for so long. My head is spinning and I realize I'm fighting to catch my breath, chasing after every inhale. *How did this happen?* Only minutes ago I was calm and resolute in my want and need to leave. Ready to forgo this night and let Jackson go flirt with someone else. Then with one brush of the lips, I'm cemented outside the doors to the club with my back pressed against its brick wall, disappointed to be leaving.

But even more terrified to stay.

A cab pulls up to the curb and the driver asks if I'm leaving. I nod, finally able to move, getting in the car. I work on my breathing techniques.

In like fire, out like ice.

It's not until I reach home that I realize my breathing has finally slowed.

chapter 5

LOOKING AROUND THE dimly lit bar, everything looks just the same as the last time I was here. The only time.

The word "dive" gives this place too much credit. The dark paint is peeling, revealing the cement walls behind it. The floors are uneven and sticky under my feet. I'm sitting at a table that has carvings engraved all over it. Initials promising true love forever are mixed with stick figures giving provocative gestures. Only one of these seems to fit the atmosphere of this place. Without reason, I would never have come in here on my own. But that evening, years ago, I did have a reason.

Just as I remember, the pool table still sits in the corner, right next to the restrooms. Behind the bar are two beer fridges, both lined with only two options—cheap and cheaper. But I know somewhere hidden at the bottom there is a box of red wine. Above the bar is a chalkboard highlighting the menu. In scrawny writing, only one item is listed.

To look at this place, you'd think it needed to be con-

demned. There was absolutely nothing appealing about it except for this memory. And because of that, it will always hold a special place in my heart.

The first time I walked in here, I took one look around and was ready to walk right back out. In fact, I did. I couldn't believe this was where Ben chose to take me for a first date. Having decided to meet him there, I was certain I had walked into the wrong place. I turned back to read the sign over the door.

The Crown and Anchor.

I was at the right place. When I walked back in, my eyes found Ben sitting at a table near the side window, his face red from holding in his laughter at watching my reaction.

"Don't be scared. This place has the best crab legs in town," he said back then, pulling out my chair.

And now, I was sitting back at that same table. Daylight flooded in through the grimy windows, casting a glow over our table. It's then something new catches my eye. Fresh initials are carved into the table. B+R. *I run my fingers over the new addition, little splinters sticking out from the carving. I look around to see if I can notice anything else different before twisting back around to find Ben sitting across from me just like he did on our first date.*

"You're late," I scold him.

"No, you're just always annoyingly early," he winks. He looks just like he did that night. Dark jeans hanging off his hips, a black button up shirt untucked with the sleeves rolled up. A chain carrying a small silver cross hanging from his neck, hidden by his shirt.

"Best crab legs in town," he says, taking a look around the empty room.

"So I've heard," I giggle.

Looking back towards me, he shakes his head and rubs his hands against his thighs. "I said it before and I'll say it again: none of that was my fault. How was I supposed to know you were allergic to shellfish? You should have said something as soon as you sat down," he accuses.

Covering my laugh with one hand, I can't help but feel a little sorry for how badly his plans had gone that night. Not that I didn't go out of my way to make them harder for him, but he deserved it. After showing up at The Bloom Room a few days after our first run-in, I almost didn't recognize him out of his police uniform. And when he asked me out, I was most certain he was joking.

"You had it coming. I actually had to pay that fine you gave me, you know," I scowl.

Cocking his head to the side, he shrugs. "Don't do the crime if you can't do the time."

"Thinking about it now, I actually think you deserved worse than you got that night." I point my finger back at him. "You're lucky I let you off that easy."

He snaps his teeth, attempting to catch my finger, but I'm too quick.

Okay, maybe I didn't let him off that easy. But it could have been much worse. All I did was point out what a health hazard this place must be, wonder how the hell a shithole like this gets fresh seafood every day, ask the bartender for a glass of his driest Pinot Noir, which left him scratching his head and sending his line cook to the nearest liquor store, and left Ben to do all the talking.

"Easy?" He throws his head back and laughs. My heart clenches at the sound. I miss that laugh. I miss the feeling of complete happiness that laugh gives me. "I sat here, a bucket of delicious crab in front of us, ready to dig in and you just sat there." He pauses, thinking back to that exact moment. A slow grin forms across his lips.

"Then you crossed those great legs of yours." His eyes dip under the table, and I feel his leg come between mine, resting against my thigh. "You crossed your arms, pressing them

against your tits." His eyes move up from under the table, pausing on my chest before reaching my face. "And you had that look of disgusted horror on your gorgeous face." His eyes meet mine. My breath quickens. "I knew you liked me the moment you didn't get up from this table and walk out," he says confidently. He rests both his hands up in front of his face, almost like he's praying. I can see him trying to hide his smile.

"There's that smugness again," I tell him, raising an eyebrow.

He leans over the table like he's about to tell me something private. "I could see right through the attitude you were giving me." Taking a strand of my hair, he places it back behind my ear. I lean my cheek into his hand, holding it there with my own.

He's right, even with all the attitude I threw his way, he remained unfazed. He just kept coming back at me with a smile, a joke, or a simple look that told me I had no chance, he was going to win me over. And he did.

"I miss you," I say quietly into the palm of his hand.

"I know," he whispers back. Taking a deep breath, he looks to the corner of the room. "Come on," he says standing, nodding towards the other side of the room. He takes my hand and leads us to the corner where the pool table sits. But it's the jukebox beside it that Ben stops at. On our first date, it had an out of order sign on it, but right now it's lit up and working.

He looks through the song list and smiles, finding what he was looking for. "I knew you were a keeper when you didn't leave. You stayed and ate three loaves of bread while I ate the crab."

I pinch him hard near his ribs and he winces.

"Ow!" He rubs his injured side.

"I did not eat three loaves," I hiss at him.

"Could have fooled me," he teases.

I come at him again, ready to do more damage than a simple pinch when he catches my hand with one of his and presses a few buttons on the jukebox with the other. I recognize the song immediately. It's almost impossible not to when you've seen the movie a hundred times. It was Ben's favorite.

"I've always wanted to live out my Top Gun fantasy with you," he tells me, taking me in his arms and dancing with me to the words of the Righteous Brothers.

Placing my arms around his neck, I bury my face in the crook of his shoulder. This is where I'm the most content, feel the safest, the most loved. His hands move slowly up and down my back. It's such a familiar and calming feeling. It feels more real to me than anything else.

Then I'm reminded of a few things that are going on in my life and I giggle. Ben pulls back and looks at me, curious.

"Guess who is hooking up as we speak," I taunt.

"Don't know, don't care," he answers.

"Oh, you'll care about this one," I assure him.

His eyes open slightly. "Okay...who?"

"Tess—"

He snorts. "There's a surprise."

I ignore his insult. "And Paul."

He looks at me like I've just grown a second head. "Are you serious?"

I nod, barely containing my laughter. Ben just shakes his head.

"She's going to eat him alive," he says disbelievingly.

I shrug. "I don't know...I think she really likes him."

"Yeah, for how long?"

I scoff. "Don't be mean. Who knows, maybe it's true love."

His eyes meet mine. "I know true love and it's hard to match." He raises his hand, caressing my cheek softly with his fingers. "Some just aren't as lucky as us."

I smile before bringing my face back down to his chest. We continue turning in circles slowly, and I hear him whispering the lyrics in my ear. Listening to him, I realize how sad the song ac-

tually is. Pulling back, I look at him.

"I promise to never lose that lovin' feeling," I tell him, trying to lighten up the mood.

He stops us from spinning, scanning my face for a few seconds, his demeanor changing slightly. He looks skeptical, almost hesitant to say what's on his mind, but before I can question it, he smiles. His forehead comes down and rests against mine before he kisses me. His lips resting on mine softly, unmoving. He stays like that for a minute before pulling away and moving us in circles once again.

chapter 6

"I SWEAR, I work with idiots—all of them!"

Tess's miffed voice is exceptionally loud and clear over the phone. I'm positive I'm not the only one who's hearing how she's really feeling. She's been away on location for most of the week and this is the first time we've had a chance to touch base since the weekend. "Not one person bothered to show up on time today. How are these people surviving life?"

I attempt to cover up my own laughter by shuffling papers around on my desk. This week has gone by rather quickly, and I've been busy with meetings for upcoming events. Within the last couple of days, I've been hired for two large corporate events, and the prep work alone has filled my days. Most nights I haven't gotten home until after ten o'clock. The days were long, but I didn't mind. Keeping myself as busy as possible is exactly what I need right now. When I have time to slow down and take a breath, my mind inevitably starts wandering places I don't want it to…thoughts of lost breath and strange lips.

"I'll be back tonight. Let's have a wine tasting on your

couch," comes Tess's voice, steering me away from my overrun thoughts.

"How about tomorrow? I may be here late getting things sorted for an event tomorrow," I tell her, referring to the thirty small bouquets I had to have ready for a corporate luncheon.

"Shit," she says. I hear an overhead speaker alerting everyone that they have five minutes. "I have a date," she whispers.

"A date?" I ask smiling. I lean back in my chair waiting to hear more details.

"Yes. He finally got his shit together."

Between being so busy at the shop and Tess leaving for her business trip, we haven't had a chance to discuss what happened between her and Paul after I left the bar, but hearing that there is now a date happening leads me to believe the night ended well for them.

"Are you going to make me beg for the details?" I ask. I realize that perhaps I've been thinking a little too much about the outcome of Jackson's night and not nearly enough about my best friend's.

"Well, let's just say things moved along after you left."

"Moved along?"

"Yes…moved along. He felt me up outside in the alley."

I barked out a laugh. "Felt you up? Are we back in high school?"

"Trust me, no high school boy I knew could do what Paul did."

Whatever it is that she may be hinting at, I don't need to hear, but the excitement in her voice makes me smile. The beginning of every new relationship can be as exciting as it can be scary. All the *what ifs* are so easily mixed together with thousands of possibilities. The rush you get with that first phone call, a first date, the first kiss. For the first time in a long time, I can hear that rush in Tess's voice.

Many of her past relationships barely breached anything

past physical. That choice has always been hers. I'm sure plenty of men would have loved to have spent more time with her, but she always said an emotional relationship was her nemesis, a burden she didn't need. Maybe she just never met someone worth the effort. Hearing her now, I think maybe she's ready for the "burden."

"Did he ask you out before, during, or after he felt you up?" I tease her, unable to give up this opportunity after the years of taunting I've had to endure from her.

"Before," she answers matter-of-factly. "I barely had a chance to answer before Sophie literally came falling over me. That girl cannot hold her liquor. Paul helped me put her in a cab. Then he pulled me into the alley and we started making out like two horny teenagers. It was all very cliché."

One part of this statement stands out to me more than the rest and I inwardly cringe because of it. I try my hardest to not sound too interested, but my mouth is moving faster than my brain.

"Sophie left alone?"

As soon as the words are out, I want them back. The seconds that pass in silence feel like minutes. I can practically hear the wheels in Tess's head turning.

"Yes. She did," she finally says.

Then, more silence. My free hand comes up and starts massaging my temple where a sudden pounding pain has just started. It's one thing for me to keep my curiosity about Jackson to myself, but now I've put it out there for Tess to dissect like a frog in biology class. And I remember how Tess was in biology—painfully slow and thorough. I quickly try and come up with anything to distract her. *Maybe I should ask her for some more details about the alley?*

"So… Jackson Perry?" She sounds awfully amused. "He looked fucking amazing." I can hear the hint of triumph in her voice as if she's been waiting for me to ask about him. "He asked about you after you left," she casually adds.

My hand drops down on the desk with a loud thump, my body now on high alert. "What did you tell him?" I hear my voice raise several octaves.

"Nothing really."

"Nothing?" I question her, but it sounds more like an interrogation.

"Yeah."

Her nonchalant tone irritates me.

"I hope you didn't give off the wrong impression," I accuse her.

"And what impression is that?"

"That I'd be interested."

She laughs. "Aren't you?"

The bluntness of her question surprises me. Of course I'm not interested. I *can't* be interested. I've spent over a year trying to figure how I could ever move on from the love of my life only to have him come back again.

"No," I say definitively.

"Are you sure? Because it's okay if you *are*. It's been over a year and I know Ben would want you to—"

"I said no," I interrupt her. My voice is firm but on the inside, I'm shaking. Shivers are attacking all my internal organs and even though I do my best to ignore it, I know something inside, something I haven't felt in a long time, is trembling.

"Okay," she concedes, sounding apologetic.

I hate confrontation with anyone, let alone my best friend. I want to bring the conversation back to something safe, something happy. Something not about me.

"So, where is Paul taking you?" I change the subject.

She knows I'm doing this on purpose, but she follows along. "We're going to dinner, then maybe for a drink or two. Maybe you could meet us after?" she offers.

The last thing I want to be is a third wheel, a pity invite, especially on a first date. "Thanks, but I think I'll sit this one out. Just be sure to give me the details later."

"The first call I make," she promises.

Once I hang up, I try to take my mind off everything Jackson related. I rearrange invoices by payment dates, reprint the event schedule, reply to emails and get started on those bouquets. After several hours, I've accomplished three things. One, my office is the most organized it's been in months. Two, half the bouquets for the luncheon are made and ready to be packed for transit. And three, I've run through every possible conversation scenario that could have happened between Tess and Jackson. Each one leaves me feeling exposed and bothered, wondering what he possibly could think of me now. But it's my incessant worry over *his* thoughts that worry me the most.

A DAY LATER, it's late afternoon by the time I get home. I think of Tess getting ready for her date with Paul. I hope it goes well, for both their sakes. Tess may be my best friend but Paul is also very important to me, and I want him to be happy. I remember Ben telling me several times that he wished Paul would find someone for himself to make him as happy as I made him.

The afternoon air is still warm and at a perfect temperature for a run. I grab my running gear and make my way to the park, passing by many others who have the same idea.

With my earphones blaring music, my hair knotted on top of my head and sweat seeping through my shirt, I push myself to run further and faster. I love the feeling running gives me. Like nothing can catch me. I can leave everything behind, choosing when and if to look back or slow down. When I push myself harder, run faster, I feel like I have control over when real life gets to catch up with me.

After my running app tells me I've run nearly four miles, I feel both exhilarated and exhausted. I circle back around, heading towards my favorite spot. As soon as it's in view, I slow my pace, now walking towards the benches under the magnolia trees. They are just starting to bloom, the buds of last week now popping open with a hint of soft pink. It won't be long before the branches will be filled with flowers, completely covering the path.

Taking a seat on an empty bench, I reach around for the water bottle that's strapped to my hip. Several gulps later, I lean my head back and let the soft breeze soothe my overheated body.

After a few relaxing moments, I sense someone take a seat beside me on the bench. Opening my eyes, I see a man's back, shirt stretched along the muscles of his shoulders, a line of sweat following the length of his spine. His arms are resting on his legs, his muscular thighs straining against black shorts as he takes deep breaths. He leans back against the bench and looks over at me. Sitting beside me is a very sweaty—and still very handsome—Jackson Perry.

I'm so stunned to see him here that it takes me a minute to even register that he's talking to me. I squint my eyes, watching his lips move but hear no sound coming out.

My face must convey how confused I am because he starts to laugh. His chest and shoulders shake lightly, and his eyes crinkle a bit with his smile. Shaking his head swiftly, he lifts his hands and brings them up to my face. My breath catches and my heart skips a beat as the back of his fingers graze my cheeks before moving further, pulling my earphones out of my ears.

"Maybe now you can hear me," he says grinning.

If my face wasn't already flushed from the run, I'm sure it is now. Jackson Perry's sudden appearance after a week of him remaining somewhere in the corner of my mind has left me baffled. I take a moment to appreciate the sight of him here beside me. He's wearing a gray short sleeve running shirt with the words *Don't Give Up* written across his chest. Earphones are hanging from the neck hole of his shirt. His hair is a mess, the kind of mess one would spend time in front of a mirror trying to achieve. My eyes move to his face, day old stubble perfectly outlining his strong jaw. When I see him raise an eyebrow, I realize he's just watched me slowly check him out. Again.

Finally, I find my voice. "You surprised me," I tell him.

I take a sip of water hoping the cool liquid will ease some of the heated blush covering my neck. Inwardly I pray it's not as apparent to him as it to me. *How is he here right now?* Hours of my day have been spent thinking about him and now here he is, smiling at me, seemingly amused at my shock.

"How did you find me?" I ask, a slight tone of accusation present.

Now it's his turn to look surprised, both his eyebrows shooting up at my words. After a few seconds, he lets out a hearty laugh, his head falling forward. I catch a glimpse of the back of his neck, a small drop of sweat slowly making its way from the edge of his manicured hair, down underneath his shirt. The need to catch that drop is so strong I fist my hands together to keep them from reaching out. Jackson sits back up and leans against the bench, crossing his arms over his chest.

"I'm not stalking you," he says, his voice laced with amusement.

My blush runs deeper. "Of course… I-I just meant…"

He leans sideways, coming closer to me. "Maybe it's *you* who's stalking *me*." He smiles then returns back to his original spot.

God, I hope I'm not that transparent. There is no way he could know how disgustingly often he's come into my mind today.

I hear him chuckle. "I'm kidding," he says watching me.

His eyes scan my face before looking past me, pointing in the direction behind me. "I live on the other side of the park. I saw you a little while back. Thought I'd come by and say hello." His eyes are dancing with delight. "Hello."

For someone who looks like they've just run several miles and out of breath a moment ago, his voice is incredibly smooth. My head turns and I look over to the other side of the park at the tall buildings cutting into the blue skyline. Embarrassment creeps over me. I can't even say this is a coincidence. He lives right over there, a stone's throw from the park. I'm practically in his backyard. I feel like such an idiot. I turn my head, facing him again.

"Hello," is all I can manage to say back. My embarrassment overshadows my ability think of anything else to say.

"Great day for a run." He looks up at the magnolia trees and takes a deep breath. Not wanting to get caught staring at him again I also look up at trees.

"Wow. These trees are beautiful," he says.

I nod in agreement, hoping to shake the Jackson shaped cobwebs out of my head.

Pull yourself together, Rachel.

"Yes, they are. This is my favorite place in the park. They only stay in bloom for a short time so I like to come here as much as possible." Finally, I'm able to string a few sentences together.

His mouth cocks up to one side. "That's right…florist." His eyes move back to the trees. "I can see why you like it here. I've only been out running a few times so far. Mostly, I've been using the gym in my condo building. I'm glad I found this. Now I'll have to keep coming back."

There is a sound of promise in his voice, and a small part of me hopes to be here again when he comes back.

"Well, you have another few weeks to enjoy it," I tell him.

He smiles.

My eyes fall back to his rising chest. I'm hypnotized by its rhythmic movement. Swallowing, I force my eyes away from him.

"So, how have you found being back home? Happy to be

back or wondering if you've just made a huge mistake?" I ask, half joking.

He lets out a small laugh and turns his head towards me. "Happy. Most definitely happy."

The smile on his face is very sincere and he looks a little relieved even. I wonder if there was another reason for his return other than wanting to be closer to his family. Maybe a woman was involved. Looking at him, it would be stupid to think there wasn't. He's gorgeous, and I can only imagine how many beautiful, blonde, Swiss ski bunnies caught his attention. And from all the looks I saw coming his way at the bar, I'm sure there are plenty on this side of the pond wanting his attention as well. *I wonder if Sophie caught it last week.*

"It was definitely an adjustment, but luckily things have fallen into place rather quickly. A few weeks before I moved, I flew back here and found a condo, bought a few basics—a bed, couch, TV. Arranged for it all to be delivered as soon as I arrived. At least I had a home waiting for me. And everything at work so far has been very smooth. I met Dylan my first day. Most of the guys I grew up with have moved away or are out in the suburbs raising families. My options were lacking in the friend department," he says with a wink.

"Dylan's not that bad," I say smiling. "He definitely helped Tess out."

"No, I guess he's not," he agrees, with a laugh.

"Well, your mother is happy to have you home," I say, taking a sip of my water. I see him look over at me, his eyebrows drawn together, confusion written all over his face. I realize what I just said and how it sounded. I try and backtrack. "I mean, I'm sure she's happy to have you back. What mother wouldn't be? Her only child back home. She must be ecstatic."

I beg myself to shut up.

"Yeah, I'm sure she is," he says suspiciously. "Do you know my mother?"

Shit.

"No!" I say. "I mean, not really. She belongs to the same tennis club as my mom and I think she mentioned it to her." I take another drink from my water bottle just so I don't have to look at him.

"And your mother then mentioned it to you?" His voice is skeptical but then turns teasing. "Rachel, have you been talking about me?"

I choke on my water before I look over at him. He's grinning, taunting me. And from the looks of it, he's enjoying it too.

I calmly clear my throat. "It may have come up in conversation that you had moved back and your mom thought maybe you might need someone to hang out with, that's all."

He freezes for a moment before letting out a few small coughs of his own. He takes a sip from his own water bottle.

"Christ, that's embarrassing. Only a few weeks in and my mother has already tried pimping me out," he says, shaking his head and looking out towards the park. If he *is* embarrassed, he hides it well, because from what I can tell, he just seems a little amused by all this. I, on the other hand, wish I could swallow back every word and rearrange them all, using a very thick filter.

"Oh, I'm sure that's not what she meant! I'm sure you have no problem meeting women and have no need to be pimped out," I assure him.

He whips his head back towards me and blinks a few times. "Thanks. I think."

"I mean…" I trail off, my cheeks on fire. I take a deep breath, starting over. "I just meant I'm sure you don't need any help. Look at you!" I say, gesturing up and down, showcasing him like a model from *The Price Is Right*. "I'm sure you have girls lined up. Maybe you even had a few last night."

His eyes pop open wide.

Dear God, please swallow me whole.

Did I just call him a slut? A man whore? Someone shut me

up now!

"I'm just going to stop talking now." I wipe my hands over my face, keeping them there, hiding me. After a few seconds, I hear him start to laugh a deep belly laugh. I feel his hands wrap around my wrists, pulling mine away from my face.

"Please don't stop talking," he says between breaths. "I like listening to you. It's…refreshing."

His hands are still wrapped around my wrists. They're warm and big, and for the first time in a long time, my stomach flutters. It's a nice feeling. A *familiar* feeling. A feeling I've missed having while not asleep. A feeling I shouldn't be having while awake.

I give him a small smile and slowly remove my wrists from his gentle grip. He lets go, choosing to ignore my sudden discomfort with his touch and sits back against the bench.

"Well, maybe I *could* use someone to show me around. Show me the new hip places that have popped up since I've been gone."

"Oh, I'm sure there are better people than me to show you around. I hardly go out as it is.

I wouldn't really know of any trendy new places," I tell him waving my hand, completely aware of how boring I must sound.

His eyes dart to my lips for a brief second before they meet mine again. "Even better. We can discover them together," he responds, his head cocked to the side, watching me.

Maybe this is the time I should be honest with him. Tell him I'm flattered but… "Jackson, I'm not really looking for—"

He interrupts me. "Jax."

"What?" I ask.

"Call me Jax. Only my grandmother still calls me Jackson and it's usually only after I've done something really bad," he winks.

I laugh and shake my head at his small confession. His playful demeanor makes it even harder to turn down his offer. "I'm not sure I'm the right person for—"

"What?" He raises an eyebrow. "Making a new friend?"

Clapping his hands together in front of him, he starts to rub them together as though he's concocting a plan. "The way I see it, after having met Dylan, it's your moral duty not to leave me stranded with him as my only friend."

This makes me laugh once more. "Moral duty?" I ask.

"Absolutely," he answers. I know he can see I'm hesitant, and I hate how uptight it makes me look. He nudges my shoulder. "No strings."

I'm not sure what it is about him but he can make me feel completely on edge and totally at ease all at the same time. It's both terrifying and thrilling. Most of all, confusing.

"Sure. Okay. Friends?" I strain the last word, making sure we are on the same page.

He nods once before standing. "Friends." Pulling his cell from a strap around his bicep, he hands it over to me. "Put your number in there."

Taking the phone from him, I enter my number. He looks down at the screen to make sure it's saved and then smiles back at me. "I'll call you soon," he says.

Nodding, I gather my things off the bench and watch him start to jog away. Moving in the opposite direction, I don't even make it two steps before my cell is ringing.

Unknown Caller.

"Hello?" I answer.

"I did say soon," I hear Jax's voice on the other end. I quickly scan the park to see if I can spot him. I do. His shoulder is leaning against a tree, one leg crossed over the other, watching me. It's hard to see because of the distance, but I know he's grinning.

I fight my own urge to grin back. "Yep, this is pretty soon."

He laughs.

"It was good to see you again, Rachel. I'll talk to you tomorrow," he says coolly.

"Tomorrow?" I ask, but he's already hung up.

I watch him give a small wave and jog away for the second time. This time he doesn't stop, but my eyes stay glued to him until I can't see him anymore.

chapter 7

I'VE BEEN AWAKE since six, my brain in overdrive. There is a weight pushing on my chest, making it impossible to relax or settle. Even breathing is hard. I wonder if I'm having a panic attack which in turn has me panic even more. Sweat is dripping down my back, causing me to shiver. *Is it normal to have such anxiety over making a new friend?* Tossing and turning and punching my pillow isn't giving me any answers. Frustrated, I bring my pillow to my face, screaming into it.

I need to do something, *anything*, to take my mind off the sudden chaos I feel my life is now in. It's times like these I wish I wasn't so efficient at work. Everything went great at the luncheon yesterday so there is very little I have to take care of this morning.

Raising up on my elbows, I take a look around my room. For every ounce of organization I have at work, I lack at home. Clothes are tossed on every inch of my bedroom floor, the amount of laundry needing to be done daunting. Swinging my legs off the bed, my feet touch the ground as well as some shoes.

Looking down, I see two separate shoes that do not match.

"Well, Rachel," I speak out loud to myself. "You wanted something to do."

After a quick trip to the bathroom, I tackle the chaos that is my bedroom.

Two solid hours of doing laundry, hanging clothes and organizing shoes, I'm pretty impressed with what I've accomplished. It's almost enough to motivate me to clean the rest of the house. Almost.

When my landline starts ringing, I drop the rest of my laundry, thankful for the distraction. Glancing quickly over at my alarm clock, I know it can only be one of two people calling this early on a Sunday—my mother or Tess. I'm praying for the latter.

"Hello?"

"Good morning, sunshine!" Tess answers, sounding awfully lively so early in the morning. I take this to mean her date with Paul last night went well.

"Well, don't you sound chipper." I hear her giggle on the other end. "Okay, give it to me. How was it?"

"Let's just say I wouldn't mind if the date was still going on."

"Wow, that good?" I laugh.

"That good," she repeats. "This one feels different." Her tone has also changed. More serious than ever when talking about a guy.

I take a seat at my kitchen table, waiting to hear more. She fills me in on some of the details. Where they went to dinner, where they went for drinks, the drive home, walking her to her front door. The good night kiss.

"Do you think that's weird? Only a small kiss? I mean, we made out at the club," she asks.

"Not at all. He was being a gentleman," I reassure her.

Tess snorts. "I've never had one of those. Maybe I didn't

recognize the gesture," she says. "How was your night?"

I take a sip from my freshly poured coffee and choose my words carefully but rush through them at the same time. "Nothing special. Went for a run in the park after work. Ran into Jackson Perry. Came home, watched TV and went to bed. Got up early. I'm planning on cleaning the house. I also think I'm finding a new love for doing laundry. There's something so rhythmic and repetitive about it that I like. Wash, dry, fold. Wash, dry, fold."

Five Mississippi's go by before she says anything.

"Okay, two things. One, I'm totally calling your bullshit on your sudden love for doing laundry…"

"Untrue—" I try to argue.

"And two," she continues as though I've said nothing, "you just happened to run into Jackson Perry in the park?"

"Yes, in the park. A chance meeting."

"A chance meeting?"

"Yes."

"Interesting."

"No, not interesting. It just so happens that he lives on the other side, in one of those condos. He was out running and saw me. Stopped to say hello. Completely a chance meeting." I don't know why I keep repeating the words "chance meeting."

"Let's pause for a minute so I can picture this right: he was out running—hopefully shirtless—saw you, then just waltzed over to say hello?"

"Are you planning on repeating everything I say?"

"Was he?" her voice pitches.

"Was he what?"

"Shirtless?" she asks as if it was the most obvious thing.

"What! No!" I almost yell. "He had a gray shirt on that was damp with sweat. Clung to him like second skin. He must have been running for a while," I say, thinking back and picturing him sitting on that bench.

She giggles.

It's that sound that makes me realize how I just sounded talking about him. I straighten in my chair. "Nothing to giggle about. He was running. Obviously he's going to get sweaty." I know she can tell I'm getting flustered.

"Sounds like your night was almost as exciting as mine," she teases.

"Hardly," I lie.

I choose not to tell Tess about my restless night because I'm sure all that will do is goad her, adding fuel to her fire while I feel mine slowly burning out.

"Okay, so then what?"

"Then nothing," my voice falters. I know she's picked up on it.

"There's something you're not saying."

I exhale long and loud. "We exchanged numbers so we could…hang out I guess. *As friends!*" I stress that last part maybe a little harsher than needed.

"You gave him your number?"

"Yes, as friends," I reiterate.

"Interesting."

"Not interesting! He was just being friendly. I bet he doesn't even call," I stubbornly argue. But then I remember that he has in fact, already called me. Not even a minute after I gave him my number. I keep my mouth shut on that one.

She laughs loudly into the phone. "Oh, I bet he does! And I bet you've been up for hours waiting for it!"

Her accusation silences me. *Is that what all my restlessness has been about? Have I been subconsciously waiting for him to call again?*

"Not even close," I answer, but even I can hear the waver in my voice.

As if on cue, not far from where I sit, I see my cell phone vibrate and light up. My fingers shake as they slide across the screen.

Jax: Hello, friend. You awake?

I stupidly flip my phone over on the table, as if hiding from the text. A rush of nerves runs through my body.

"You should, you know," Tess's voice surprises me, momentarily forgetting I'm already having one conversation.

"What?" I ask a little breathless.

"When he calls. You should hang out with him."

I open my mouth, ready to disagree, but she doesn't give me the chance.

"I know, I know. Friends." She renders silent for a few seconds. "I just think it would be good for you. Make a new friend, Rachel," Tess urges me, eerily beginning to sound like Dr. Embry.

I hesitantly pick up my cell and turn it over, his unanswered text staring back at me. Before I can even comprehend what I'm doing, my fingers are moving over the screen.

Me: Yeah. For a few hours now.

The dots on my phone tell me he's writing back.

Jax: Plans for today?

"Tell me you'll at least think about it," Tess nearly begs.

I don't know why I don't tell her I'm texting with him as we speak, but I keep it a secret, only promising to think about it as we hang up. My phone dings again.

Jax: I hear there's a great outdoor market down by the docks. Up for it?

I know the exact market he's referring too. I've never been.

Me: Shouldn't I be the one coming up with things to do? You asked ME to show you around after all.
Jax: Is that a yes?

I take a minute to reply, wondering if Tess and Dr. Embry are right. *Maybe making new friends would be good for me.*

Me: Okay. I can meet you there.
Jax: I'll pick you up. Address?

Having him come pick me up feels a little strange, a little personal, but I give him my address anyway. He lets me know he'll be by in an hour and asks me to wear jeans, which I think is a little odd. I go back to my room and try to find something to wear. I settle on a pair of skinny jeans, a black knit sweater, black boots and a jacket. I put a little makeup on and brush out my hair, letting the waves cascade down my back. As I leave the bathroom, I remind myself that this is simply two friends hanging out, so it really shouldn't matter how my hair and makeup looks. I hate myself when I turn back and do another once over in the mirror.

Exactly an hour later, I hear a knock at my front door. Opening it, I see Jax standing there wearing dark jeans and a brown leather jacket. Sunglasses are covering his eyes, but his smile is full and bright. His face looks like it's been kissed by the wind, leaving a slight pink blush across his cheeks. But what really catches my eye is the motorcycle helmet in his hand. I point towards it.

"What's that?" I ask.

He smiles and offers me the helmet. "Have you ever ridden on one before?"

I look behind him and see the bike parked on the street. It's black and shiny and looks a little sporty. I'm unsure how two people are supposed to fit on it. I shake my head, a little nervous.

"Perfect. Another first," he says, grinning. He cocks his head towards the bike, encouraging me to follow.

With every step, the bike looks bigger and bigger. Some thought I may have a fear of any kind of motor vehicle after the accident, but I don't. In actuality, I love driving, but a motorcycle is a whole different ballgame.

Turning towards me, Jax takes the helmet out of my hands and places it firmly on my head, buckling the strap under my chin. He looks up from his squatted position and smiles.

"Are you sure this thing is safe?" I question, my eyes looking at this beast parked a few feet away.

He smiles as he nods. "Absolutely. I'll get on first, and then you sit behind me and put your feet here," he says, pointing to the little pegs.

I watch him put his helmet on and sit on the bike. He starts it up, the roar of the engine loud even with the helmet on. He looks back at me and offers his hand. Taking a deep breath, I place my hand in his and he helps me up onto the bike. Sitting behind him, I put my feet on the pegs as instructed, and then I realize I don't know how else to hold on.

"Wrap your arms around my waist!" he yells back at me.

My arms hang at my sides for a few seconds, unmoving. It's a simple task. *Wrap my arms around him. Like a hug.* My breath stutters when I feel my chest rest against his back. I'm sure he's able to feel my heart start to pound too.

"Ready?" he yells, looking back.

I nod and he starts to pull away from the curb. Instinctively, I grab a hold of him tighter and crush my body harder against his back. I feel his stomach shake and I know he's laughing at me.

After a few minutes of riding and taking some turns and corners, I get more comfortable and start enjoying the ride. The wind is loud and feels cool as it whips past us, my hair blowing behind me. The roar of the engine is not nearly as loud as I anticipated once on the bike. At a red light, Jax turns his head to the side. "You all right back there?"

"Yes!" I yell back. "This is fun!"

Nodding, he turns his head back to the road and we continue to ride.

As we approach the docks, I start to really like being on a bike. The crisp spring air is so refreshing, brushing against my cheeks, leaving them burning but cool at the same time. It's similar to the way I feel after a run, only I don't have to work nearly as hard for this feeling. This adrenaline comes easily and quickly and stays the entire ride.

Jax pulls into a parking lot and turns off the ignition. I hop off and unbuckle my helmet, the feel of the ride still rushing through me so fiercely that my legs feel a little unstable. Jax swings one long leg over the bike, standing and sees my smile.

"Fun?" he asks, his smile lighting his face. He takes our helmets and pulls out a fancy looking lock from the inside of his jacket pocket, attaching them to the handlebars.

"Yes!" I take my sunglasses off, running my hand through my hair. I can feel my fingers getting caught in all the knots. "But I think I paid the price," I say, using my fingers to comb through the mess.

Jax chuckles. "Yeah, sorry about that. Probably should have warned you to tie it back."

I'm still fiddling with the knots when his hands stop mine and bring them back down in front of us.

"It looks perfect," he says, squeezing my hands lightly before letting go.

I bite my lip, distracting myself from the warm feeling left from his touch and put my hands in my jean pockets. I take a look around us. The parking lot is full, a good indication that this market is worth seeing. We make our way towards the entrance, and the moment we turn a corner, I'm taken aback at what I see.

Rows of booths are lined together, filled with everything from fresh fruit and vegetables, jars of jam and honey, natural soaps and so much more. A sweet aroma of baked goods and coffee is mingling in the air.

"Wow, I can't believe this is my first time coming here. It's kind of embarrassing," I say as we walk by the booths. There are lines of people at almost every one.

"I guess it's a good thing we came," he says, nudging my shoulder. "The thought of you living the rest of your life in shame is simply unacceptable."

Smiling, we walk around and look at what some of the booths have to offer. "Did they have these kinds of markets in Switzerland?" I ask.

"Probably. If they did, I didn't go to any," he says, stopping to look at some fresh fruit. "I didn't have too much free time while I was there. Except for some snowboarding, I was a pretty bad workaholic. I didn't make much time for anything else," he admits.

I frown while picking through some lemons. I think back to how I've spent my last year. I too haven't made much time for anything other than work and…dreams. The fresh citrus scent from the lemons is a reminder of how much I've missed life's simple little pleasures. Of how long it's been since I could enjoy them.

"That's too bad," I utter.

He nods in agreement. "Too career driven back then, I guess."

"Not anymore?"

He turns a quick glance my way, a smile cocked to one side. "Oh, I'm still very driven. I've just changed some of my objectives."

Another shiver runs across my body, something I'm getting accustomed to since being around him. "What kind of objectives?" my voice coming out more breathy than I hoped.

He quickly scans over me before leaning in closer. "Making new friends for one." He backs away smiling.

My curiosity is peaked. "How do you think you've done so far?"

His eyes dance with amusement. It's the only way I can think of to describe it. A boyish charm sweeps over him, and it's impossible not to notice.

"So far, so good," Jax winks.

I look down, pretending to be interested in the tomatoes in front of me. "So, you didn't have a girlfriend?"

I want to slap myself as soon as the words are out of my mouth. I refuse to look up at him, too mortified, so I have no idea what his reaction is.

"Nothing serious," he replies, but I can hear an edge to his voice, unease perhaps.

I sense I've touched upon a sore subject, so I let it go quickly. I turn away and start to walk toward another booth, hearing him thank the vendor before following. I stop us in front of a booth selling fresh juices.

"What do you think? Care to try something made from aloe and beetroot?" I ask, scanning the ingredient list, hoping we forget my last comment.

"Well, it's a day for firsts. You choose."

"Anything you hate or are allergic to?" I ask.

"Nope. Open to anything."

After looking over all the choices, I opt for the two drinks that have the least amount of odd combinations. I reach in my bag to grab for my wallet when Jax stops me, placing his hand over mine.

"Let me," he says.

"Thanks," I say, putting my wallet back in my bag. Our drinks are handed to us, both of them a deep green color. "This looks interesting…"

He laughs and takes the first sip. "Not bad," he says, urging me to take my own.

It isn't that bad actually. Much more fruity than I expected.

We continue walking around, floating from booth to booth, checking out all the local goods. I'm quite surprised to see all the local vendors and even some from further away who set up at this market. I store it in the back of my mind to look into marketing The Bloom Room here. With the amount of people walking around, I'm sure it could bring new business to the shop.

When Jax sees a baked goods stand, he starts pulling me towards it.

"Now we're talking," he says, his eyes wide as he looks at all the cookies, brownies and fruit squares in front of him.

"I didn't peg you for a sweet tooth kind of guy," I laugh.

"We all have our vices," he scans the table. *A vice I completely understand.* "My turn to choose. Anything you hate or are allergic too?"

"Just shellfish."

"I think we're safe here," he smiles.

He chooses a chocolate brownie and a pecan tart—both look delicious. He offers them to me, and I immediately go for the brownie. As soon as I take a bite, I close my eyes, knowing it may possibly be the best thing I've ever tried. It's soft on the inside with a harder crust on the outside. *Just how I like them.* I'm delightfully surprised to find a dark chocolate filling in the middle, a small moan escaping upon the discovery.

When I open my eyes, I see Jax watching me. "Whatever is in that brownie, I think I need some," he grins. I blush and he starts to laugh. "I've never met someone who blushes so easily. You're good for the ego."

I've never met someone who could say something so cocky yet be so charming while saying it.

"Trade," he says, holding the rest of his pecan tart out to me. Looking down at his outstretched hand, I shake my head.

"No way! This is too good," I say, taking another bite. He

watches me for a few seconds before a wicked gleam appears in his eyes. The second I see movement from him, I stuff the rest of the brownie in my mouth. The piece is so big I can hardly bring my lips together. Chewing through the final little bites, I stifle a laugh.

"I don't share chocolate," I say, swallowing the last little bit.

Jax's surprise turns into a boisterous laugh. "You're something else, you know that?" he says. His laugh is a mix of boyish fun and manly tone. I smile, knowing I want to hear it more.

"You've got a little..." He brings his hand up to my mouth, his fingers under my chin while his thumb brushes a few crumbs away. The minute he touches me, my face stills but my heart jumps. My breathing becomes fast and labored, and I know he can feel it. Strong, short bursts of air are hitting his fingers as he gently holds my face. Without noticing, I rise up on my toes, closing the distance between us. My body seems to completely have a mind of its own, yielding to his touch.

A small smile plays at his lips, and he leaves his fingers resting under my chin for a few more seconds before pulling away. "There's that blush again," he says softly, teasing.

I fall back on my heels, becoming rooted where I stand, my eyes glued to his. In this light, I can see how blue they are. They remind me a little of Ben's, only not quite as dark. Jax's could look like crystal in certain light, but right now, they are as blue as the sky.

It's the thought of Ben that wakes me up from my daze. Taking a step back, I let out a small embarrassed laugh.

"Never get between a girl and her chocolate."

"Lesson learned," he says grinning. He cocks his head towards the end of the aisle. "Come on, I think there are some local artists over this way."

When we arrive at the artists' area, I am floored at the displays in front me. There are sculptors, photographers and spray paint artists. But what seems to catch both of our attention is a rack of paintings a few booths away. We walk towards it, examining all the work from this artist. Some are of landscapes, others are still life, but what I love about them is the use of color. The paintings are intense, using bold colors such as reds, blues, purples and grays. You'd think they would come off as angry, but it's quite the opposite. These paintings are so full of expression, a strong bright presence that leaves you smiling.

"What do you think?" Jax asks, nodding towards the work in front of us.

"I think they are amazing!" I tell him, walking around to the other side of the display.

One painting immediately grabs my attention. It's a landscape scene with trees lining a narrow path. It reminds me so much of the park. The bold and bright color choices are the exact opposite of what you'd expect. Various shades of purple are used for the leaves and flowers, strong strokes of red are brushed horizontally, making the sky look on fire. There's a dark shadow of a person sitting on the bench along the path.

"You like this one," Jax states, his eyes moving between the painting and me.

I nod. "It reminds me of the park."

"Do you have a place to hang it?" he asks.

I snort. "No, but even if I did—" I look at the price tag and my eyes widen. "Is that the price?" I whisper, aghast.

I'm shocked considering these paintings aren't even in a gallery. They are being sold on a sidewalk! A middle-aged man with a long beard tied by an elastic band comes up to us. He has paint drippings all over his clothes, his jeans and shirt covered in splashes of color.

"This is one of my favorites," he says, wiping his hands on a cloth. I look behind him and see a workstation he has set up.

"It's beautiful," I tell him, looking back at the park painting.

The artist bows his head in gratitude. "A beautiful painting for a beautiful lady."

I chuckle at his sales technique. "Thanks, but we are just looking."

Resolute, he starts to walk away.

"We'll take it," Jax says out of nowhere.

I snap my head towards him, unable to hide the stunned shock from my face.

"What are you doing?" I whisper through clenched teeth, the artist walking back towards us. He's now sporting a huge, victorious smile, a gold tooth glinting in the sunlight.

"You're right, it is beautiful," he whispers back.

"You can't buy me art!" I argue.

"I'm not buying it for you," he corrects me, reaching for his wallet.

Confused, I blankly stare at him for a few seconds. "Then…?"

"I'm buying it for me. My walls are still pretty bare." A wicked grin appears. "And now you'll be able to see it whenever you want."

He pulls out his wallet and I catch a glimpse at the several hundred dollar bills inside. He pulls out five of them, handing them over to the artist whose name I make out to be Redd Capser based on the signature on the painting. "Can you do us a favor and take it out of the frame? We're on a bike."

Redd happily complies and why wouldn't he? He just became five hundred dollars richer. Within minutes, Redd is coming back with the canvas wrapped and rolled up in a clear plastic bag. I'm still a little too stunned at what just happened to say anything. I can't believe he just spent that much money on a painting because I said I liked it. And who carries that kind of spending cash on them? I'm lucky if I can scrounge up enough for a sandwich at C'est Bon on a good day.

Jax shakes me out of my shock when he wraps an arm around my shoulders. It's hard not to notice how our bodies seem to align seamlessly, my shoulder perfectly snug under his arm, the curves of my body filling the curves of his. A terrifyingly perfect match.

"You're cute when you're speechless. Let's go get some lunch," he smirks. "After watching you with that brownie, I'm sure you can handle a burger."

Jax moves away from me, taking a few steps ahead when he turns and sees I haven't moved.

He cocks his head, urging me to follow. "Come on!"

THERE ARE A few restaurants along the water and he leads me into one called The Burger Barn. We are welcomed by a hostess who I notice does a double take at Jax.

"Welcome to The Burger Barn," she greets, looking directly at him. "For two?" she asks, my presence finally being noticed.

"For two," Jax repeats, smiling.

"Right this way," she says, giving him a once over before turning and leading us to our table.

I wonder if I should be insulted that this woman is openly ogling him right in front of me. I quickly scan the crowd, wondering if others are doing the same.

"Let me know if you need anything," she tells him. He smiles politely and opens up his menu. I watch the hostess slowly take a few steps backwards before fully turning around and walking away.

"Must be exhausting always attracting such attention," I say, looking at my menu.

Jax looks up from his own.

"What do you mean?" his cocky smile tells me he knows exactly what I mean.

"You're the guy who gets free pie everywhere he goes aren't you?" I raise my eyebrows.

His laugh wraps around me like a happy blanket, the corners of his eyes creasing with his smile. "Okay, maybe I've gotten some free dessert once or twice in my day."

"I find it very hard to believe that Dylan has been the only 'friend'," I use my fingers as quotation marks to emphasize my point, "you've made since you moved back."

His face becomes serious. "He's not," he says slowly. "Not anymore."

His eyes meet mine, but this time it does something to my heart. It doesn't beat faster or pound harder in my chest. This time it feels like an elastic band is being tied around it, squeezing too tight. My hand rests on top of my chest, massaging the area above my heart.

Before I have a chance to analyze this feeling, our waitress comes by looking to grab our orders. Even though she looks to be in her fifties, she also seems to have fallen prey to Jax's presence like the hostess. After placing our order, she leaves, giving Jax a smile before he coyly winks back.

"You know exactly what you're doing," I accuse him, half smiling. "Now I understand why all the girls in high school were crazy about you."

"Were they?" he questions, suddenly very interested.

"Oh please, you knew! Girls would wait for you by your locker, by your classroom. The whole female student population would come out to watch you play whatever sport you were team captain of. I mean you were voted best smile, for crying out loud," I say exasperated.

"And were you one of these girls?" he says, wiggling his eyebrows.

I roll my eyes, feigning its unlikelihood but I have to bite the inside of my cheeks to keep the truth from being written all over my face. Tess and I may have gone to a few of his lacrosse games.

I lean back against the booth, Jax mimicking my movement. We sit and stare at each other, waiting to see who cracks first. He does. He comes in closer, leaning his arms on the table.

"I win," I say.

"I didn't know we were competing," he says, a knowing look coming over his face.

"Yes, you did."

His smirk is arrogant but playful. "Maybe I let you win. But just this once." He sits back and rests an arm on the back of the booth. "So tell me more about this shop of yours."

He changes the topic quickly but thankfully it's one I feel comfortable with and can go on and on about. I tell him how I used to work there as a teen and throughout my college years. I explain Emily's wish to retire and how I then bought the shop. I express to him how much I love it, even more so now that I have complete control over everything. He seems interested enough, even asks about some of the corporate events I was involved in. When our food comes, we continue talking right through our meal.

"I'll have to stop by, put your artistry to work," he says, smiling before popping a French fry in his mouth.

After our lunch, we head back towards the parking lot. From under the bike's seat, he pulls out a backpack and puts the rolled up canvas inside, half of it still sticking out.

"You don't mind, do you?" he asks, offering me the backpack. "Precious work of art in there."

"Of course," I tell him, strapping the backpack on my shoulders.

Riding back towards my house, I'm much more at ease and am able to enjoy the entire ride. When he pulls up to my place, I'm even sad the ride is over. He turns off the bike, and I reluctantly hop off. Undoing my helmet, I pass it over to him and he secures it behind him.

"So, *friend*, that wasn't so bad, was it?"

Taking his sunglasses off, he half leans against his bike, his helmet in one hand and running his fingers through his hair with the other.

"No, it wasn't." I quickly cast my eyes downwards, uncomfortable with how easily I can get absorbed in watching him do simple things like…stand. But the truth is, I had a great time. "Next time it's my turn to come up with something to do."

"I look forward to it." He gives me half a smile before standing upright. Again, I'm unsure of how to end this, I give an awkward half wave before turning and making my way to the door.

"Aren't you forgetting something?" I hear Jax call from behind me.

I turn around, eyes squinting into the sun. "Sorry?"

It only takes him a few strides to reach me, his hands coming up to my shoulders. Smiling down at me, I feel him grip the two straps, carefully pulling them down. The backpack falls, and Jax steps in closer as he reaches around to grab it. Our close proximity causes my heart to do a miniature version of that same squeeze from earlier. I still don't know if I like how it makes me feel.

After what seems like hours, he takes a step back, the backpack hanging from his hand, and a flirty grin gracing his lips.

"Shit. Sorry. I forgot I had that."

Chuckling, he places his sunglasses back on and turns towards his bike, strapping the backpack over his shoulders.

I stand there like a statue watching him. He looks over at me and gives a small wave before taking off. It's not until I can't hear the roar of the motorcycle anymore that I realize I'm still standing in the middle of my driveway, staring off into the direction he went.

chapter 8

THE ROOM IS only lit by the glow of the hallway light. It slices an off angled rectangle across the floor. Not too far away lies a bed, its comforter and pillows thrown on top, suggesting it was made very quickly and without much attention. The room is a step up from a college dorm in that it has a much bigger bed and there's no desk, but there are few similarities I find amusing. The framed autographed jersey that hangs proudly on the wall, a roughed up looking chair which has a pile of semi-folded laundry sitting on top, and—my personal favorite—the Sports Illustrated poster of girls in bikinis on the back of the door. I suppose I should be somewhat impressed that they weren't topless.

There is one thing really stands out though. The one lone candle, sitting on the dresser, lit and mixing with the glow from the already existing hallway light. The smell of cranberries floats through the air, reminding me of Christmas. But it's not Christmas time. It's the beginning of summer, and this is the first time I was ever in Ben's bedroom.

He's standing right behind me and my body begins to become aroused. Is it by his presence or was I already in this state before the dream started? I can't tell, nor do I care at the moment. His voice sends a chill down my spine.

"I remember this night." He steps out from behind me, circling me as he walks around the room.

I watch as he takes in the contents of what used to be his bedroom before moving towards the candle. His face glows from the light of the flame. "Do you?"

I take a deep breath. "Of course."

"I remember every moment," he says, looking at me. "I remember where we went for drinks, I remember what wine you drank. How many glasses you had," he smirks. "Were you nervous?"

I don't answer because he already knows. Was I nervous? A little.

"I remember you suggesting we come here," he continues.

I remember that too. It was maybe our fourth or fifth date. We met at a bar, one near Ben's apartment. I knew our relationship was about to get more physical, both of us wanting it to. Until then, there had only been groping and petting and kissing. Lots and lots of kissing. But we weren't teenagers anymore. We weren't virgins waiting for the perfect moment. We were adults who both wanted the same thing—each other.

Ben takes a few steps, making his way over to where I've stood since this dream started. Once in front of me, he brushes some of my hair off my shoulders, revealing my open collar. I take a glance down and see I'm wearing the same dress I did that night. The only reason I remember it is because Ben had broken the zipper trying to get me out of it. We laughed about it then, but our laughs quickly turned into moans once the dress fell to the floor.

"Why here? Why tonight?" Ben asks, his fingers tracing along my shoulders and neck.

"I-I don't know," I answer breathlessly.

"I think you do," he says, circling me, pressing his chest to my back. "Something has you...worked up."

I try to make sense of what he's saying but the minute his lips are on my neck, all previous thoughts disappear. His fingers glide up my arms, brushing my hair aside.

"Something has you needing," his lips move against my skin. "Do you remember when I found this spot?"

His tongue slips out and circles the sensitive area just under my ear. My body shivers, my arm rising up and wrapping around his head, holding him there.

"I remember how you squirmed the first time I kissed you there," he whispers.

I try hard not to squirm this time, cementing my feet to the floor and pressing my behind into him. I feel him laugh silently.

His lips stay on my neck, moving slowly while one hand comes up and palms my breast.

"Ben..." I moan.

"What, baby? What do you need?"

"You know what," I whimper.

He breathes out. "I do. But do you?"

I exhale in frustration. Why does he keep talking in circles? Why isn't he already ridding us of our clothes?

"You're driving me crazy. What are you waiting for?" I say, nearly begging.

His lips leave my neck as he circles around to my front, scanning my face. His lips quirk up slightly. "You're in control here, babe. This is all you. You decide when we start, when we stop."

"I don't want to stop," I say hurriedly. "I want you."

He says nothing, like he's giving me a moment to reconsider. But I'm flush with need, with want.

"Don't you want me?" I ask.

A small rush of uncertainty runs through me, wondering if

maybe, after all this time, he doesn't need me like he used to. He sees my concern and immediately lifts his hands, cupping my face.

"Always," he says. "I wanted you so bad that night and every night after. Days too," he smiles.

I smile back, feeling a little relieved. "So then what are we waiting for?"

His expression changes, becoming serious. "Are you sure it's still me you want?"

His words stun me, and I step away from him, almost as if I've been slapped.

"What?" I ask. My voice shakes from shock and...anger, I think. "What is that supposed to mean?"

Ben lifts his hands in surrender, apologetic as soon as he sees the hurt on my face. "Nothing. It meant nothing. I'm sorry."

I'm still too shaken to move so Ben takes a tentative step towards me, slowly placing his hands on my hips. Our bodies align and press against each other. He nudges his head against mine, encouraging me to look at him. When I do, the lust in his eyes from earlier is back.

"I'm sorry," he repeats. His fingers press harder into my skin. "I know what you need, and I know why we're here. Let me give it to you."

He slowly lowers his face, waiting to see if I'll object. I don't. When our lips meet, I open my mouth and let him take control. He guides me to the bed, laying me down slowly and with care. I feel his body come rest on top of mine.

"You and I both know this isn't real, but when you wake up, you won't be able to tell the difference," he says between kisses to my neck and chest.

"When I wake up..." I repeat quietly.

"You won't be able to tell the difference."

His hand reaches for the very zipper he broke years ago—this time it comes down easily. He slowly peels off the dress, ex-

posing first my shoulders, then breasts and then my stomach. He takes the time to kiss every freshly revealed area of skin.

"You're still so soft," he says.

I squirm under him, working the rest of my dress off and down my legs. I remove my bra and go to take off my panties, but Ben's hands stop me.

"Me," he interrupts. "This has always been my favorite part."

His fingers dip inside the band and brush my sensitive skin. I can hear myself moaning, panting, and waiting for more. His hands pull at the material, taking what's left of my clothing off.

He looks at me, a smile I can't quite figure out gracing his lips. It's lustful but sad too. He repeats his earlier words to me. "You won't be able to tell the difference."

Then his head disappears between my legs.

chapter 7

I'M FIGHTING FOR every breath I take. My inhales are short and rapid, my lungs burning from the blunt force of oxygen they're getting. My heart is beating at a rate I've never felt. Sweat is running from my temple down the sides of my face. I can feel the beads running down my neck, getting lost under my shirt. My legs feel like they are on fire. My body is telling me I should stop, but my brain has so much adrenaline pumping through me, it refuses to slow down.

The evening sun has started to set, a haze of purples and pinks are lighting up the sky. The magnolia flowers are now in full bloom, pillows of pink found on every branch. New life, new beginnings, new beauty. I wish I could be looking at it all, but I'm not.

The only thing my eyes are focused on is Jackson Perry running a few steps ahead of me. His long lean body moves so effortlessly, his arms swinging softly in rhythm with every running leap he makes. A sheen of sweat covers his arms, and in this light, makes his skin glisten a bright color of gold. The back of his gray shirt is damp, creating a V from his shoulders down to the middle of his back. My eyes continue to move downwards where I can see the outline of his boxer briefs against his thighs each time his shorts stretch against the back of his legs. A few times, this view has distracted me enough that I've tripped over my own legs.

Two weeks. It's been two weeks since our trip to the market, and Jax and I have been in contact almost every day since. Some days it's a simple text, others are phone calls filled with funny retellings of Dylan's attempts at charming new clients. And then there are days like this one that I look forward to the most. The days we actually meet. Each time has only been to go for a run, but I've never looked forward to my runs as much as when Jax and I do them together.

He's definitely in better shape and can go faster and longer than I can, but that hasn't stopped either of us. He's been great at going at my pace, sometimes pulling ahead, motivating me to go harder and faster. The problem with this type of motivation is that I'm often distracted by him being in front, my concentration wandering from the workout.

Jax turns to face me, running in place and waiting for me to catch up. His hair is damp and his bangs are falling over his forehead. The front of his shirt is also wet with sweat, a matching V darkening his chest.

"Let's go!" he yells before turning back and moving ahead once again.

His shouts are enough to get my legs to move harder. With every step, the distance between us gets smaller and smaller until I'm right back beside him. With a slight turn of the head, he watches me and grins.

That grin.

I know I'll never be tired of seeing it, but sometimes I wish I had never seen it at all.

I start to move faster and harder still, pulling a bit ahead of him, my ponytail whipping across my back, strands getting stuck to my neck. I hear him let out a quick laugh, between his hurried breaths. Speeding up, he's beside me again, and it pushes me to move on. I've been chasing after him as much as I've let him move ahead, leaving me behind. I get comfortable in my slower pace until he turns and looks at me. Then I can't help but start to run to him, like he's the finish line off in the distance I've been running towards this entire time.

Sprinting, I pound my legs into the cement, moving past him, not ready to cross the finish line side by side.

"Oh, no you don't!" His voice is full of laughter and it's all I hear before he runs past me and crosses first, a few good lengths ahead. He's bent over, hands on his knees, taking deep breaths when I finally meet him.

"You could let me win once," I say between my own staggered inhales. I rest my hands against my hips and look up to the sky, taking long deep breaths.

"Never," he answers back.

I bring my head back down and see he's no longer bent over but standing straight, watching me. His eyes are focused on my bared stomach, the cropped tank I'm wearing raised from my earlier movement. I watch as his gaze travel upwards towards my chest, freezing for a fraction of a second. His eyes are more gray than blue today as they finally make their way up to my face. His look is intense, pensive. He takes a step closer to me.

"I always win," he says softly and without apology.

Goosebumps prickle my skin, a shiver running down my spine. "I'm starting to get that."

Over the last two weeks, I've become more aware of the reactions my body has when he's around. I wish I could control it, ignore it, pretend it has no effect on me. I wish it wasn't becoming a reason my need to stay connected to Ben was more important than ever.

I rub my hands over my arms, trying to ward off my physical reaction. Taking a step backwards, I reach my arms over my head and Jax does the same. We stretch in silence, letting the warm air cool our overheated bodies.

"You should come over to my place. I have something waiting for you," he says breaking the silence.

I freeze, my arms extended out in front of me.

His eyes widen slightly, realizing how that sounded. "Umm, that came out sounding…"

I watch him as he struggles to find his words. His mouth is open, his eyes shy. I think this is the first time I've seen Jax come anything close to embarrassed. It's fun and a part of me wants to continue to play it out. It seems only fair considering how many times I've been flushed in front of him.

"Don't worry. I know what you meant," I shrug, waving my hand, letting him off the hook.

After a second, he smiles but it doesn't quite reach his eyes. "You ready?"

"Now?"

"Sure. Unless you have some other plans?" he asks.

I look down at my sweat drenched clothes. "No, no plans. But maybe I should change? I'm a little wet."

Now I realize how that just sounded and so does he. His eyes scan over me, the shivers tracing down my spine once again.

"I'm not worried." He smirks and cocks his head in the direction of his condo, questioning.

After a moment, I nod and begin walking with him towards his home.

JAX'S CONDO BUILDING is one of the newer ones built in the city, along the lakeshore. The outside looks to be made of glass with thick silver plates running up along all the windows. Huge urns sit in front of the doors, filled with large green bushes that have been perfectly manicured into spirals. The revolving glass doors are big enough to fit at least four people in each quarter. A doorman is posted in front as we approach.

"Good evening, Mr. Perry," he says, opening the door for us. "Miss," he acknowledges me, tipping his cap.

Inside the lobby, the floors are a beautiful cream and gold marble, the walls painted to match. There is a cream leather sofa and a couple of chairs arranged around a dark coffee table. The concierge desk is manned by an elderly gentleman whose attention is focused on a small TV.

"Jimmy! What's the score?" Jax asks walking past him as he leads us towards the elevators.

"It's the damn coaching," he answers, shaking his head.

"Maybe next time," Jax says, laughing then leaning in towards me. "Cubs fan. It's a struggle."

I nod as if I understand what he's talking about, watching Jax push the call button for the elevators. "Do you ever worry that anyone could walk in here when he's so wrapped up in a game?" I ask curiously.

"With Jimmy? No way. He's got eyes in the back of his head. No one gets past him. Plus, if I'm running late in the morning, I can always rely on him for the sports scores."

The elevator arrives and Jax swings out his arm, inviting me to go in first. The elevator walls are mirrored, including the inside doors. Once they close, I see my reflection. My hair is a mess, my clothes still have sweat stains and my makeup looks like it's three days old.

Oh God.

I try to discreetly wipe away the raccoon eyes as Jax presses the button for his floor. I look down and see which button is lit.

I raise a brow. "Penthouse?"

Looking over at me, he shrugs. "Just a nicer way of saying *twenty-seventh floor*."

"Funny, I don't see the other floors having nicknames," I

tease.

"Touché."

He takes a step back, bracing his arms behind him on the railing and crossing one foot over the other. I turn to face the front again, watching the numbers above the door slowly light up. Every few seconds, I let my eyes move down to Jax's reflection. I hear his fingers strumming against the railing, slow and rhythmic. Being enclosed like this, with very little else to distract me, is unnerving.

When we reach his floor and the doors open, I sigh in relief. I follow him towards the door at the end of the hall, PH 3 written just below the peephole.

Jax unlocks the door, allowing me to walk in first. I feel his arm brush against me as he reaches for a light switch. Light illuminates the condo and I'm taken aback by the space in front of me. A small hallway leads to a very open living space where floor to ceiling windows takes up an entire wall, giving off a beautiful view of the city skyline.

"Wow."

"That's what I said when I first came to look at the place. After this, how could I say no?"

"You can't! Not to this!" I say as I walk towards the windows, taking in more of the view. The sun has not completely set and beautiful rays of light are shining between buildings. Directly below, I can see little dots of people walking on the sidewalk. Just how small they appear reminds me of how high up we really are.

Turning back around, I take in the rest of Jax's home. The living room is still quite bare, the walls a light cream color, a nice contrast from the dark oak floors. I can picture him relaxing on the chocolate brown leather sofa with his feet up on the wooden coffee table, watching the flat screen—the only thing currently hanging on his walls. I walk by a beautiful gas fireplace with a wood mantle. Only one picture sits on top with an image of his parents. Just standing in the living room, I know this place is huge.

"I'm just going to go change. Make yourself at home. Would you like a fresh shirt or something?"

He's standing in front of another hallway which I assume leads to the bedroom, or bedrooms in this case.

"No, I'm good, but maybe I could use your washroom?" I ask. Although I wouldn't mind freshening up a little, wearing some of his clothes feels way too personal.

"Sure, I'll give you a quick tour." He waves, urging me to follow him.

The first door he leads us to is an office. A mahogany desk with a black chair sits in front of more floor to ceiling windows. Another flat screen is hanging on the wall off to the side of the desk. Built-in shelves with rows of books are neatly and strategically arranged on the opposite wall.

"Very nice," I say appreciatively.

"Thanks. Helps me get work done when I'm in a comfortable space," he smiles.

The next door is a spare bedroom. It has nothing in it but unpacked boxes.

"Still a work in progress," he says, moving along to the next door.

"My room," he says quietly as he opens the door. I don't know why, but this is the only room I walk into. He flips the light switch and two bedside lamps turn on.

His room is exactly what I pictured it to be. Like the rest of his apartment, the furniture is dark wood against cream walls. The king-sized bed is accented with a navy comforter, neatly made. Aside from the dresser and yet another flat screen, there is nothing else in the room. I see two doors—one closed which I assume to be an ensuite bathroom, and the other I can tell is his closet. His penchant for tidiness includes his closet as all his suit jackets and shirts are aligned, organized by color.

"OCD?" I ask, cocking my brows and pointing towards the closet.

"I like things to be organized," he replies.

Taking another look around the room, I nod. Although most of Jax's place is still empty, it's masculine and tidy. The only thing that seems out of place is the pair of jeans haphazardly left lying on his bed.

I feel Jax step closer to me, and I realize that I've been staring down at his bed for a little too long. Blinking rapidly, I fiddle with strands of my hair, pushing them back behind my ear.

"I'll let you change," I say, quickly heading towards the door and out of his bedroom.

"Bathroom's on the left," I hear him call out.

Before I reach the bathroom door, I turn my head back towards the bedroom and watch as Jax pulls his shirt over his head. His back is to me as I watch the muscles along his shoulders ripple with the movement of his undressing. His body narrows towards his hips, and I can see the band of his boxer briefs peeking through the waist of his running shorts. My eyes become glued to the area right above the band where there are two back dimples. I remember Tess once reading an article about *Men's Sexiest Body Parts* and back dimples were on that list. I never understood why. Until now. Now they look like perfect little divots that palms of hands or heels of feet could fit into.

Then Jax turns, and I'm faced with hard abs. Not overly sharp ones, but defined. A small line of hair gets lost beyond the band of his shorts. Without thinking, my eyes follow that line down…until Jax's voice snaps them back up to his face.

"Everything okay?" His voice is different, a little breathless and husky. He's looking at me with an intensity I've never seen before as he takes a step forward. "Rachel?"

Embarrassed, I nod quickly and point to the door in front of me. "This door, right?"

I open the door and swiftly close it right behind me before

he can even answer. Leaning against the door, I close my eyes. I'm both humiliated at being caught blatantly watching him undress and feel awful for how much I…enjoyed it.

I take a few deep breaths and make my way over to the sink. The bathroom is free of any clutter and looks spotless. He must use the one attached to his bedroom because the bar of soap resting by the faucet looks brand new and the towel hanging from the rack is still perfectly folded. I splash cold water on my face over and over, bringing my cool hands to my neck, hoping to relieve the flush of red. Grabbing the unused towel, I pat my face and neck dry while looking at my reflection in the mirror.

"Get it together, Rachel," I whisper to myself.

A knock at the door startles me. "Everything good in there?" Jax asks.

"I'll be right out!" I answer back.

Taking one final look at myself, I summon the courage to go out there and face him.

I walk out towards the living room and see Jax has changed into a long sleeved black cotton shirt and is wearing the same jeans that were on his bed. He hears me walk in, clapping his hands together in excitement and ushers me to the couch. I sit down as he heads towards the front entryway closet, relieved that my earlier peeping tom moment seems to be forgotten.

"Like I said, this place is still pretty bare…" He grabs a large item wrapped in brown paper from the closet, carrying it back to the sofa. "But, I hope this helps change that."

Looking at the wrapped item, I know exactly what it is. Eagerly and without hesitation, I start to pull at the brown paper like a child on Christmas morning. I can see Jax smile as loose pieces of paper start to fly and fall off the package. Once all the paper is gone, I see the painting Jax bought a few weeks ago in a new beautiful dark wooden frame.

"It's beautiful," I say smiling up at him.

"Looks good, doesn't it?"

"Where are you going to hang it?" I ask.

"That's what you're here for. I figured you'd have a better sense of where it should go than me." He sweeps his arm around the room. "So? Where should we hang it?"

I look around the room and see that there are several different options. It could hang in the entryway. It could also go in the small alcove beside the TV where a nice chair and small table could fit. But I know there is only one place this painting should be hung. I take the painting out of Jax's hands and walk over to the fireplace.

"Here. It should go here," I say, holding the painting up in the spot where I think it should go and looking over my shoulder.

Standing with his feet apart and arms crossed, he looks at the painting being held over the center of the mantle and nods once. He briefly disappears down the hallway, returning moments later with a hammer and nail.

"You be the eyes, I'll handle the labor." He winks and takes the painting from me.

I laugh silently, moving to stand by the couch. After a few *little to the left* and *up a little more*, Jax hammers the nail into the wall. He picks the painting up and hangs it where it now rests, perfectly straight and centered. The splash of color the painting brings to the room makes an instant difference.

"I like it!" I say enthusiastically.

Smiling, he comes to stand next to me, admiring the new addition. "Me too."

We both stand there for a minute side by side looking at the painting. "With a few throw pillows and maybe a bookcase, this place will actually look like someone really lives here. Like a real home," I tease.

"Throw pillows? You're not one of those women are you?" he jokes back, nudging my shoulder.

The friction our bodies make sends a small jolt through me.

I think Jax feels it too because he looks down at where our bodies are connected.

"I guess it's a start," he says softly. He gives a small smile then goes back to looking at the painting.

I can't seem to look away from where our bodies are touching.

chapter 10

"I MET SOMEONE."

Dr. Embry stops her pen mid-motion, caught off guard. We are in our normal spots, me sitting on the couch, her in her chair across from me.

"Someone?" Dr. Embry repeats with a very small and surprised smile.

I nod once, slowly, fiddling with the hem of my shirt. Unsure if I want to say more, or if I even have more to say, I dart my eyes around her office. I notice that the orchid plant that used to sit on the shelf behind her is now gone. A crystal figurine now sits in its place. A brand new orchid is now sitting by the window.

"Rachel?"

Dr. Embry's voice brings my attention back towards her where she's waiting for me to follow up, but I'm not even sure what to say. My new friendship with Jax has left me…confused. About a lot of things.

"A man…" I start.

Dr. Embry tilts her head, interested. "I see. And this relationship is—"

"We aren't in a relationship," I quickly cut her off. Her brows jump up at the abrupt interruption. "What I mean is we aren't dating. We're friends."

An understanding look sweeps across her face. "I see. So this friend, do you see him often?"

I think back to the last few weeks. "I don't know. Maybe."

"More than others?"

I'm about to say no but stop myself before answering. I can't think of a day where Jax and I haven't spoken or seen each other. Without realizing it, he has become a part of my daily routine.

"Yeah, I guess so."

Dr. Embry watches me for a minute before continuing. "So, what is he like?"

"What do you mean?"

If she's asking about him physically, after last night, watching him change out of his running clothes, I could give a very detailed description. But I'm fairly certain that's not what she means.

"His personality. Is he outgoing? Funny? A good listener?" she asks.

"A good listener?"

She nods. "Yes. Is he someone you could confide in?"

I think about it for a moment. "Probably, but I wouldn't."

One of the great things about my friendship with Jax is that I don't have to think or talk about anything I don't want to. Things that are so embedded in all my other relationships that it's impossible to escape from. Our friendship is a blank canvas, and the last thing I want to do is paint it with sad stories.

She raises a brow but doesn't question my meaning any further. Instead she takes a different approach, almost as if she had read my mind. "How do you feel when you two are together?"

"How do you mean?"

She smiles as though she may already have the answer. "Is it nice being 'Just Rachel' again?"

The question seems simple enough to answer, the words on the tip of my tongue.

Yes, it is. It's nice being…

Happy.

Carefree.

Alive.

But the consequences of saying them aloud frightens me into silence. It's been a long time since I've been "Just Rachel." For years, my name has been connected to another. Never would I have ever thought that I could feel content not having Ben's name attached to mine. It was only a few months ago that I needed my nights with Ben to get me through the days. Now, my days don't seem nearly as daunting to get through, and in some ways, it feels awful.

"Rachel, there is no judgment. What I'm trying to achieve here with you is a safe place to discuss your feelings. More specifically, your feelings about where your life is headed, how you plan to get there. A lot of the time, it's the people around you that will help you the most in getting there. From what little you've said, it seems like this new friend of yours is someone you want to be a part of your life moving forward. And there is nothing wrong with that. It's great to meet new people, especially if they are people who bring you happiness. So, what I'm asking is whether this person is helping you get to where you want to be. Are you happier with him in it?"

"If I say yes," I say quietly, "does that make me an awful person?"

Taken aback, Dr. Embry's face shows some concern. "Why would you think that?"

"Ben and I were together for years and we planned for so many more together. My love for him hasn't gone anywhere. If anything, I feel myself trying to hold on to it more than ever. But something happens when I'm with Jackson. When I'm with him, I feel my hold on Ben slipping. Like I'm being pulled in another direction. One I wasn't expecting."

"And which direction is that?"

I take a long breath, admitting out loud for the first time what I've known to be true for weeks. "I'm attracted to him."

I feel the weight of relief at my confession leave one shoulder only to be matched by the weight of guilt on the other. "I did mean it when I said we're just friends. Nothing's happened. But, I am attracted to him." I cross my arms over my chest as though I'm protecting the love I have in my heart for Ben from the words that are now floating around outside it.

A sympathetic look comes over Dr. Embry's face. If she's surprised to hear my sudden outpouring of feelings, she hides it well.

"Men and women are constantly attracted to one and other. It's only natural to notice those around us. It doesn't mean that we have to act on it if we don't want to or if we aren't ready," she responds.

"Once I met Ben, I didn't really notice anyone after that. He completely filled my line of vision when I was with him. I'm scared the more time I spend with Jackson, I'll lose sight of Ben."

"It sounds like you are placing a lot of pressure on yourself. That you're placing the sole responsibility of Ben's memory on your shoulders."

Am I? Am I afraid that if I don't keep him alive, no one else will?

"It's natural that you would want to do everything in your power to continue to pay tribute to your relationship. It can be hard to let go of some of that responsibility. Maybe the best way of paying tribute to that relationship is to live your life to the fullest. There is nothing wrong or disrespectful in finding happiness again."

I know these words are meant to be comforting and reassuring. I know that no one in my life would question the love I felt and still feel for Ben. But my greatest fear is that if I move forward, I'll lose what links me to my past. That I'll lose Ben all over again.

"Concentrate on taking it one small step at a time. There's no rush, and you aren't on any timeline," Dr. Embry says, closing up her notepad, indicating our time is nearly up.

One small step at a time. Baby steps moving me towards something. A direction. A decision. A choice. A fork in the road where one day, I *will* have to choose which path to take.

I shudder at the thought.

"HI, MOM," I answer my phone.

It's late into the evening and I'm the only one left at the shop. It's the perfect time to get caught up on invoices, orders and emails.

"How nice that you answered," she responds, sarcasm laced through her tone. I roll my eyes and lean my head back against the chair. "You haven't called me back or answered any of my texts."

"Mom, I've been busy, and I just talked to you two days ago," I reply.

"Well forgive me for wanting to hear from my daughter a little more often. Perhaps to hear how her appointment was today or if anything new has been going on in her life that I should know about."

Inquiring about my appointments with Dr. Embry is nothing new, but it's the rest of what she says that catches my attention. "No. Nothing new," I say.

"Really? Nothing? That seems strange since I ran into Dorothy Perry at the club and she mentioned how nice it was that you and Jackson *did* end up meeting."

Crap.

"Imagine my surprise since you seemed *so* against it when I mentioned it a few weeks ago. I must have looked a fool."

She sounds more hurt than angry, and it does make me feel a little guilty. But I know my mother and if she knew about my friendship with Jax, I'd be facing an inquisition every time we talked. And considering how confused I am over this new friendship, I can't even imagine trying to explain it to her.

"Mom, you're making it seem like I'm keeping some big secret from you," I tell her.

"Well aren't you? You've begun a relationship—"

"We aren't in a relationship," I interrupt. Why is everyone so quick to label? Unless… *Has Jax maybe said something?*

"Fine. Friendship then."

"Is that what Mrs. Perry said?" I ask, now curious. It dawns on me that I'm now relying on the gossip of our two mothers to help me understand what exactly is happening in my own life.

"No. She just mentioned that Jackson said he did, in fact, run into you a few times. A little information I thought you might have shared with your own mother," she scolds.

I lean back in my chair, running that sentence over and over in my mind.

Run into each other a few times.

Run into each other a few times.

That's all he's said. I don't know why those seven words stick out in my mind so strongly. There is nothing untrue about it. Nothing inaccurate. But it also sounds like he could be talking about running into his mailman. I feel a small pang of disappointment rest on my shoulders.

And then I feel foolish. Foolish for stressing over my growing attraction for Jax and what it could mean when this could all be for nothing. When we first met, I told Jax I could only be a friend. I was even reluctant to give him that. Now look at me.

Disappointed that that's all I am to him? That I'm something as simple as *someone he's run into*?

"I guess because there is nothing to tell," I say, aware of the hint of disappointment in my voice. "Just like Mrs. Perry said, we ran into each other a few times."

"Perhaps if you saw him again? Got to know one and other…"

The last thing I want is for her to know is that we have gone out and all he's had to say about it has been that we've "run into each other."

"Mom, I know you are trying to be helpful, but I'm fine. Really."

"I just thought—"

"I know what you thought. But I mean it—I'm fine," I say with determination. "Like he said, we just ran into each other a few times."

SITTING ON MY couch in a pair of pajama pants and an old t-shirt, I try not to keep fixating on those seven words. Unfortunately, not even *The Mindy Project* can help me turn off my brain. My earlier conversations with both Dr. Embry and my mother keep replaying in my mind, for better and for worse.

A soft knock on my front door finally gives my brain a small reprieve. Glancing at the clock, I see it's past ten, wondering who could be stopping by this late. I hear another knock followed by a voice I recognize all too well.

"Rach, it's me," Paul says from the other side of the door. I unlock the two deadbolts and see Paul standing there, hands in his jacket pockets and an apologetic smile on his face.

"Sorry. I know it's late, but I just finished a shift and thought I'd stop by." He quickly glances behind me and surveys the inside of my house. He pulls his hands out of his pockets and points over his shoulder to his parked car. "I can stop by another time if you're busy."

"Don't be ridiculous," I say, opening the door to let him in. The cool air of the night hits me reminding me that I'm only in my pj's. Thankfully I still have a bra on. "I'm just gonna go and throw on a sweater," I say heading back to my bedroom. "I wasn't really expecting anyone."

"Yeah, sorry about that. I probably should have called," he yells back.

I can hear him moving around in the kitchen, the refrigerator door opening. For years, Paul has come over to this house and made himself at home. The fact that he still does is comforting. Old habits unbroken—regardless of changing circumstance.

When I make my way back to the living room, Paul is sitting on the sofa, a can of Diet Ginger Ale in hand.

"Really? This is all you have?" he asks, lifting the can.

"If I would have known, I would have been better prepared," I lightheartedly scold. I take a seat beside him on the couch. "So, what's up?"

Paul shakes his head. "Nothing, just thought I'd stop by. Make sure the house was still standing," he says playfully.

"Well, as you can see, the house *is* still standing, the roof is still overhead and I'm using both deadbolts you installed," I say pointing to the door.

"Good," he says sternly. "Always double lock. Even in the daytime."

"Yes, Lieutenant," I answer, saluting him. His eyes glare, but his lips quirk up into a smile. "So, is that the only reason you stopped by? Or was it for my diet soda?" I joke.

Paul laughs, running one hand over his mouth and chin. "Definitely not for the soda. But it's been a little while since we've just hung out, talked. Just missed ya, I guess."

"Yeah, it has been a little while," I say sadly. I really do need to make more of an effort to talk with Paul. "But I hear lots of your free time is now tied up elsewhere," I tease, nudging his leg with my foot.

"Oh, here we go," he huffs, tilting his head, looking up at the ceiling.

"What? Go where?" I say innocently.

Paul turns his head towards me and gives me a *you know where* look.

"Oh, come on, you could not have expected me to not ask!" I say through my laughter.

Paul straightens, leaning his body forward. He puts his soda down on the table before intertwining his fingers together and resting his forearms on his thighs. "Fine, ask away," he resolves.

"You tell me! Tess says you two have been hanging out," I say, not wanting to breach any confidentiality I have with Tess.

"Oh, I'm sure that's all she's said," he says sarcastically, taking a sip from his can.

I laugh. "Well, what do *you* say?"

He inhales heavily, his shoulders lifting. "Yeah, we're hanging out," he repeats my words.

"And?"

"And we're having fun."

"That's all?" I ask.

"What more do you want me to say?" he asks smiling.

"I don't know! Details. Where you think this might be going, where do you want it to go?" I offer.

"Whoa," he says, lifting a hand, stopping me. "I didn't come here to paint toenails and cluck like chicks in a henhouse. You want that, go see Tess."

"But I already know what she thinks!" I immediately close my mouth, knowing I've just given away that Tess has already talked to me about him.

A knowing smile comes over his face. "I knew it. Cluck, cluck, cluck." He crosses one leg over the other. "So what did she say?" he asks, semi-interested.

I shake my head and press my lips together, locking them

and pretending to throw away the key.

"Mine too," he answers smugly.

I frown in disappointment. "Fine. Keep your secrets."

Paul chuckles, once again leaning back against the sofa. His eyes start to roam around the room. I'm certain memories of Ben are running through his mind.

"I wasn't sure if you needed me to stop by and check up on the house anymore," he says quietly, his tone changing drastically.

"What do you mean?" I ask, confused.

"Tess mentioned you were seeing quite a bit of that guy..." he tapers off, scratching the back of his neck. He seems uncomfortable, like even mentioning another man in this house is breaking some kind of allegiance to Ben.

"Jackson." I nod slowly. "Yeah, we're just friends," I tell him.

Paul looks down at his can of soda and nods once. "Okay."

"We've hung out a few times. Nothing like a date or anything," I say, a strange need to defend myself rising. "Mostly we just run together. I mean, I'm not looking for... He's not interested..." I falter, finding it very hard to come up with the right words.

Paul squints, confused. "If he's too blind to see how amazing you are, then it's good that you aren't—" He stops, unable to finish the thought aloud. "It's better. I don't have to worry about you dating someone who's too stupid to know your worth. You deserve better. You deserve someone like Ben."

The mention of Ben's name brings a sad smile to Paul's face. "He knew you were the one the minute he saw you. I know he told you that but the look on his face that day, I'll never forget it. I knew it was game over for him before he finished crossing the road."

A lump forms in my throat, and I can feel tears building behind my eyes, but I do everything I can to hold them in. Paul sees me struggling, and his face immediate becomes apologetic.

"Shit, I'm sorry," he says quietly.

"No, no, it's okay." I wave it off, looking down in my lap. "We should talk about him more."

He nods, agreeing.

"He just loved you so much. I used to think he was a total pussy about it. Ragged on him about it all the time," he says quietly. He seems lost in thought, a small smile I don't think he's aware of forming.

"I miss him," Paul whispers.

"Me too."

"He didn't deserve this. Neither did you."

"Or you," I say. "I know how close you two are…were. I know I'm not the only one who lost him."

I watch Paul as he acknowledges his loss as well. I knew that it helped Paul cope with losing Ben by coming over here and helping me with things around the house. It made him feel useful and maybe even closer to Ben being here, being around some of his stuff. A few months after the accident, I gave Paul Ben's badge. I had enough personal belongings of his to help me get through the hard times, things that were sentimental to us as a couple. But his badge, that was something I thought Paul should have. They became brothers in the force first, brothers in life after.

After a few minutes, Paul rubs his hands over his face a couple times before standing. "Okay, enough of that," he says, extending his hand out to me, pulling me up from the sofa and wrapping his arms around me, holding me close for a minute.

I now know the real reason he stopped by. I'm the closest connection Paul has left to Ben and tonight, he needed a little piece of his best friend. I hug him tighter, hoping he's getting what he needs.

Once he lets go, he turns and walks towards the entryway.

"Thanks for the soda," he says, opening the door.

I smile, understanding that's not what he's really thanking me for, but I just nod. Once he's outside, he turns.

"Use all the deadbolts," he says seriously.

I promise and watch him walk towards his car. As soon as he's pulling out of the driveway, I close the door, using all the deadbolts as told. I sit back down on the sofa and think about what Paul said about how much Ben loved me, and it reminds me of how much I loved him. *Still* love him. It reinforces my belief that you only get one true love in your life, one soul mate.

Ben was mine.

I grab my cell phone and hit speed dial. After two rings, and before a hello can even be uttered, I rush out, "I need you."

"Twenty minutes," is the only thing Tess says before hanging up.

She gets here in fifteen, at my door with two bottles of wine, a tub of ice cream and an awful Adam Sandler movie. I hug her as soon as she walks in, because even though I know that's what friends are for, only your best friend will know that you only eat Rocky Road with your red wine.

chapter 11

IT'S SO CALM here. I can hear the sound of small waves hitting the shoreline, frogs and crickets chirping away into the evening darkness. A bonfire is burning in the distance, crackling and hissing, sucking out any moisture left from the wood. There is something so familiar and comforting about the sound of bonfires. Whether it reminds you of your childhood or something different, the comfort it brings warms me from the inside.

I used to love coming here, to Ben's family cabin. Steps away from the lake, the small three bedroom cabin was a perfect mix of modern and rustic. The entire home was made up of wood, but it was insulated. There was no television but a full kitchen. Horrible cell service but a complete bathroom. It was the perfect blend of getting away from it all without having to rough it too much. I remember being pleasantly surprised when Ben brought me here for the first time.

Our days were filled with canoeing, swimming and jumping off the dock. Early evenings were spent lounging on the ham-

mock with a good book. Nightfall would bring the bonfire and roasting of marshmallows. Perfect days of summer were had here, great memories were made, and right here on this dock is where I fell in love.

Wrapped in a blanket, I breathe in the fresh air. It's hard to see anything with how dark it gets out here, but when I look up to the sky, the moon and stars are so bright that their reflection on the lake is enough to create a white glow, illuminating the area around me.

"Nice night," Ben says.

I look over beside me as Ben leans back in his lounge chair. He's wearing that ratty plaid flannel shirt over a white t-shirt, his baseball cap sitting backwards on his head. He grabs two bottles of beer from the cooler by his feet, offering me one. I happily oblige, clinking it with his in cheers before taking a sip.

"Every night is nice here," I answer him back, sinking deeper into my chair and wrapping the blanket around me tighter. "I always loved this place."

Ben coughs. "You weren't too sure about that when I asked you to come out here the first time," he says grinning.

He's right. When he first mentioned going away for the weekend to his family cabin, I envisioned four walls surrounding a few cots, a table with some chairs and only a wood burning stove to cook on. This would be the first time we went away together and images of using an outhouse on our first getaway infiltrated my mind.

"You could have painted a more accurate picture of where we were going. The way you made it sound, I thought we were going to be fishing for our dinner and gutting them over our cots," I argue.

Ben laughs. "We did catch our dinner," he reminds me. "I thought it would be fun to scare you. Test you. See if you were woman enough to rough it for a few days."

"Woman enough?" I scold. "As in others you asked

weren't?"

Ben smirks and takes another sip from his beer. If he weren't so cute, I'd smack him. But it does leave me wondering how many other women he's brought here. I can't believe after all these years, it isn't something that's ever come up in conversation. Ben and I aren't prudes. I obviously know I'm not the first woman in Ben's life just like he wasn't the first man in mine, but the idea that he's asked other women to come here with him…irritates me.

I narrow my eyes at him. Sensing my glare, he peeks over and almost chokes on his beer when he sees the look on my face. Wiping the liquid that's dribbled down his chin, he groans. "Oh, come on! NOW you want to hear about all the chicks that have been here?"

That comment irritates me even more.

"Wow. That many?" I take a long sip of beer and look out over the lake. If my arms weren't trapped inside this blanket, I would have pushed him.

"Well, let's see," he starts, counting with his fingers. "There was Chrissy Whittsley, but her parents and mine were friends so she came with them. We were both ten. I kissed her over there behind that shed." He nods towards the small structure holding all the firewood. "Then there was Dorothy Lesser, and believe me, the lesser of her the better. She was the most annoying girl I've ever met. But my brother dug her so she doesn't count." He lifts a third finger. "I did ask this girl I was seeing for a few months if she wanted to come up. Made sure no one else would be here so we could be alone. I went out and bought all her favorite foods, even these gross old lady candies she liked so much."

I look over at him, watching as he digs into the front pockets of his jeans and pulls out an individually wrapped black licorice candy. I try very hard to hide my smile, biting the insides of my cheeks. Taking a candy, I unwrap it and pop it into my mouth.

"I'm really the only girl you've ever brought here?" I ask, my voice soft and cheeks hollowed from sucking on my candy.

"I don't willingly spend forty-eight hours straight with just anyone. They've got to be special." He winks, giving me another wrapped candy.

"And I was special?" I raise an eyebrow, popping the next piece in my mouth.

Ben turns towards me in his chair, leaning in closer and grabbing a fist full of the blanket, pulling me towards him.

"Absolutely," he whispers before bringing his lips down on mine.

I can taste the beer on him just like I'm sure he can taste licorice on me. When I open my mouth to let his tongue sneak in, his hand comes up, getting lost in my hair.

I've always been able to get lost in Ben's kisses. I no longer hear the bonfire crackling in the background or the small waves hitting the side of the dock. All I can hear is the sound of Ben's breathing becoming more ragged and the soft moans I'm making. Ben's tongue softly massages mine, then he gently pulls his head back and licks the outside of my lips, before kissing them sealed.

When he pulls away, I contently open my eyes. He's brushing my hair back behind my ears, his eyes following his hand with each stroke.

"This is where I fell in love with you," I confess quietly.

He raises an eyebrow. "Was it my mad fishing skills that finally had you falling over the edge?" he jokes.

I bark out a small laugh. "No. It wasn't on that first trip." His eyes lock on mine, intrigued. "I mean, after that weekend I knew you were worth holding on to for a little longer," I tease.

"I'm so flattered," he feigns sarcasm.

"Will you let me finish?" He nods once, blinking slowly. "It was a few weekends later. We came here and I met some of your

family for the first time. Your mom was so welcoming and sweet, and your brother and sister-in-law were so nice. Your family was amazing! But it was when I saw you with Lauren and Lindsay."

*Ben seems surprised. His nieces were only two and four when I first met them that weekend, but the way their faces lit up when Ben arrived, that stunned me. The minute they saw him, they both came barreling towards him, grabbing his hands, fighting for his attention. He gently explained to them that he had to first introduce me to everyone but promised to come back out and play. Later that day, watching Ben play with those two little girls from this very dock, lifting them up on his shoulders, chasing them around on the beach, threatening to throw them in the lake, listening to their squeals of delight...*that *was the moment I fell in love.*

"You weren't just Ben, the man I was dating anymore. You became Ben, the man I was in love with."

Ben furrows his brows, taking his time to find his words.

"It took you that long to figure it out?" he finally asks in disbelief. "Good God, woman! After all those dates and the flowers and the candy? The mushy texts I wrote? If any of the guys ever saw those they would have kicked my ass! After all that, it still took you that long to figure it out?" he nearly screams in insult.

"Shut up!" I laugh, reaching over and lightly shoving him with my shoulder.

Ben catches my hands and pulls me towards him. I almost spill my beer all over him with the sudden movement but once he plants me onto his lap and wraps his arms around me, I couldn't care less about the beer.

I rest my head against the crook of his neck and shoulder, thriving in the feel of his lips kissing the top of my head. Sitting here with him like this, it feels like the past year and a half didn't happen. It feels just like another weekend at the cabin, where the realities of real life can't reach us.

"I wish we could stay here forever," I tell him.

I feel him take a long deep breath, his chest rising against my back. When he doesn't say anything, I shift my head to the side and look up at him. "Don't you?"

He keeps his head straight, facing forward. I can see his eyes staring off into space, his mind thinking of what to say.

"Ben?"

"I wish lots of things," he says.

"Am I included in them?" I whisper.

"You are included in all of them." He looks down at me and smiles, but it doesn't quite reach his eyes the way I'm so used to seeing from him. He's holding something back, keeping some thoughts to himself.

"What are you thinking about?" I ask, looking back out over the lake.

"Just you," he says into my neck.

His voice carries a hint of worry. I want to assure him that he has no reason to.

"You don't need to worry about me. I'm perfect right now. I'm here with you. I don't need anything else."

I bring my hand up through the blanket, reaching the back of his neck, tilting his head so he can look at me. His eyes scan my face before he nods once and kisses the tip of my nose. I cuddle into him, wrapping the blanket and Ben's arms around me. Closing my eyes, I listen to the sounds of the night echoing across the lake. But it's Ben's almost inaudible muttered whisper that I hear the loudest.

"That's what worries me."

chapter 12

I WAKE UP the following morning to the smell of freshly brewed coffee. Even though my mouth is a little dry and it's taking me a few extra seconds for me to peel my eyes open, I feel pretty good. At least I think I do. The room isn't spinning and both my head and stomach are at peace which is surprising considering how much wine I had last night.

As soon as my best friend arrived, I opened the first bottle of wine, drinking half a glass before Tess even had her first sip.

"So it's that kind of night," she said, watching me take another large sip.

I could only nod, my mouth full of Merlot. Picking up the bottle, I started to refill my glass when Tess took it away from me mid-pour.

"I'll be in charge of distribution," she said, taking a seat on the couch. "Okay, start from the beginning."

And so I did. I told her about my mother's call. I told her about those seven little words that alone mean nothing but together were driving me crazy. I told her about Paul's impromptu visit and even though I know it was killing her not to grill me on what he may have said about her, she sat there and continued to let me unleash. I told her how my talk with Paul brought up memories of Ben, how much we both still missed him. I told her everything Paul said about my friendship with Jax. After that, the second bottle was opened and Tess didn't say a word while I refilled my glass.

Really, I'm pretty lucky I'm feeling as good as I do.

When I can't ignore the aroma wafting into my room any longer, I head to the kitchen where I find Tess. It didn't even register that she brought an overnight bag with her, but here she is, freshly dressed, makeup and hair done, ready for work.

"Good morning," she sings, pouring me a cup of coffee.

"Morning," I say, accepting the steaming cup.

I take a seat at the kitchen table, Tess following me with her own cup, humming to herself.

"Are you always this happy first thing in the morning?" I ask her, inhaling the steam rising from the cup.

Smiling, Tess looks at me over her coffee mug. "Not always, but if I'm told a sexy bedtime story, it usually helps me get a very restful sleep."

Confused and a little disturbed, I look her over then my eyes gaze down the hallway to the spare room where she slept. "I'm not sure I even want to know what that means."

Putting her mug down on the table, Tess sits back in her chair and crosses her arms. A sly smirk plays at her lips. "After you went to bed, I called Paul."

I put my mug down, waving my hands in surrender. "Okay, that's enough. I don't need to hear about the weird kinky things you guys did over the phone—which, by the way, you did in *my* spare room while I was home. Ever heard of boundaries, Tess?"

"Firstly," she starts, pointing one finger in the air, "they weren't weird."

I roll my eyes.

She lifts a second finger. "And secondly, I called with the intention of seeing how he was doing. After what you said last night, I thought maybe he needed someone to talk to. I wanted to be sure he was okay."

Knowing someone else is looking after Paul gives me a sense of comfort. Even though it's been a while since Ben's accident, after last night, it's clear to me that Paul still has some healing he needs to do as well, and having a support system is critical. "And how was he?"

She shrugs, sitting back in the chair. "He said he was fine. When I tried to get him to say more, he just changed the subject. He obviously did not want to talk about it. At least not with me."

"Don't take it personally," I say, trying to help.

She brushes off the comment, but I can tell her feelings are hurt by Paul's reluctance to open up to her. "He's a man of few words. Unless they're dirty, then he's a fucking thesaurus."

"Okay. Gross," I say, getting up to refill my mug.

"That wasn't the only reason I called Paul," she says behind me. "I also wanted to tell him to think twice before he speaks."

Turning back around, I raise an eyebrow. "Think twice?"

"Yes. About you. About your life. About Jax," she says, her tone suddenly serious. "It wasn't fair of him to make you feel guilty. I'm sure it wasn't his intention, but maybe he's being a little overprotective of you. And of Ben."

I can feel a prickle of heat run up my neck, the reality of everything I said last night hitting me smack in the face. Embarrassed, I look to quickly change the subject. "Like I said before, we are—"

"Just friends," Tess says with me. "Yes, I know. Just friends. But you should know that if you wanted to be more than friends, it's okay. You *are* allowed to feel things again, have fun, be available. And you're blind if you think Jax is not interested."

"Even if he is, maybe I'm not." Even I could hear the waffling in my voice.

"I don't believe that," Tess argues back. She rinses her mug out in the sink before turning towards me. "Let's not pretend that you haven't noticed how delicious he is because we know that's not true. Aside from how fuckable he is," I give her a snide look, "he's smart, successful and after what he did with that painting, *is* very into you. If you don't snatch him up, someone else will."

A new feeling starts in the pit of my stomach. A feeling I haven't felt in a long time but recognize immediately. It's the stirrings of jealousy at the thought him dating someone else. I have no business feeling possessive over Jax, especially when I've been doing all I can to hold on to Ben. But the feeling is there, and it's hard to ignore. *I'm such a hypocrite. He would be better off staying away from me period.*

"No guy spends that much time with a girl if he's not interested. And I hate to break it to you, but that works both ways."

THE MORNING HAS flown by at the shop. The store busier than usual for a midweek morning, the hours lost in flower orders, walk-in customers and two bridal appointments. It's not until I hear my stomach growling that I realize it's past lunch. I head over to C'est Bon looking to grab Anna and me a couple of wraps.

There is quite a line at the counter, a late lunch rush arriving at the same time as me. I'm reading the menu board over the counter when I hear my cell chirp.

Jax: For my sake, I hope they have brownies.

I look up, scanning the restaurant. My eyes are automatically drawn to the front door when the bells above it ring, then to the man walking through it. I know mine are not the only ones either.

He's dressed in a full three-piece suit the color of midnight.

It's so dark, it's almost black but paired with the crisp white shirt and ice blue tie, you can see the navy in it. The fitted vest and jacket contours his body just right, showcasing his broad shoulders and trim waist. Flashes of seeing his bare chest automatically run through my mind. My palms begin to sweat at the memory. I try as inconspicuously as I can to wipe them against my jean clad legs.

Seeing me in line, he smiles, taking off his sunglasses and closing the gap between us with determined steps. I watch as every single woman whom Jax passes keep their eyes glued to him—including the one who just walked right into the closed door.

"Hey," Jax says, slipping his phone into the inside of his suit jacket.

"Hi," I say.

Tess's words from early this morning decide now is the right time to start replaying in my head.

Are we becoming more than friends? Does he want that? Do I?

The line starts to advance and we take a few steps forward.

"What are you doing here?" I inquire.

Even with the aromas of the bakery all around me, it's Jax's clean, fresh scent that invades my senses. He smells faintly of laundry and a light mist of cologne.

"We were in the area for a lunch meeting. Happened to walk by and see you in here," he says, nodding towards the outside. Through the glass window, I see Dylan talking on his cell. He glances my way, gives a quick smile and wave before focusing back on his phone call. I return the wave before looking back at Jax. "A nice surprise," he adds.

I feel my heart jump at his words. Like a reflex after a doctor hits your knee, I can't stop it or control it. It has a mind of its own, and I'm powerless against it.

"How was your meeting?" I focus on the menu board ahead

of me, hoping to regain some control.

"Good. Prospective new clients for the firm. I think my charm won them over," he says.

I smile. "Good of you to stay humble."

He lets out a small laugh. "Always."

The lady at the counter yells for who's next and I realize it's me. Jax extends his hand out and I place my order of two chicken wraps and two iced teas.

"And a chocolate brownie." Jax points to the delicious desserts on display. I look over at him as he leans his head down close to mine. "I remember exactly how they make you feel," he says, glancing quickly at my mouth.

I stay still, not wanting either of us to back away for just a little while longer.

But the woman ringing up the order ruins the moment, insisting I pay. I pull my wallet out, but Jax has already handed her some cash.

"Wait, no! You aren't paying for my lunch, or Anna's for that matter," I start to argue but it's no use. Change has already been handed back to him, which he drops into the tip jar.

"Even though I have no idea who Anna is, it was my pleasure," he says smiling. It's so hard to stay focused on anything other than that smile when it appears. "I was actually going to stop by the store today. Hoping you could help me out with something," he adds.

Peeling my eyes away from his charming grin, I blink a few times and nod. "Sure, what do you need?"

He looks at me like the answer is obvious. He even chuckles a bit. "Flowers."

I swallow the small lump in my throat, instantly angry that it's there. "Well, you've definitely come to the right person," I say, forcing a smile, not finding the humor in my silly question.

"I thought so," he answers, smiling. "Something classic. She likes white, I know that."

She.

"Sure, no problem. When do you need them by?" I ask, turning so I'm not facing him. My eyes stay trained on the man behind the counter making my lunch, willing him to go faster so I can escape having to hear Jackson talk about buying another woman flowers. And also elude my jealous racing heart.

"Her birthday is Thursday. I was hoping I could pick them up that afternoon."

I feel him take a step closer to me, his chest dangerously close to brushing against my back. I nod several times, keeping my eyes focused on the slowest sandwich maker I've ever seen.

"Sure, no problem," I say again.

He doesn't offer any more information.

I hate myself for asking, hate myself even more for needing to know the answer, but I can't help myself. "Do you need a card filled out? Who should I make it out to?"

"No, thanks. My mother hates them. She thinks that whatever the card says, you should be able to say yourself."

Mother. They're for his mother.

The lump that was in my throat disappears, and a weight I didn't even know I was carrying lifts off my shoulders. But then my own mother's words come rushing back to memory.

"Speaking of mothers, I was busted by mine," I say. I know I'm broaching a subject I've been actively working to avoid. Approaching the line I myself have drawn, but it doesn't stop me. I can't seem to stop myself when around him.

"Busted? For what?" he asks, interested.

"Your mother told mine that you mentioned we bumped into each other a few times," I start. I try to sound nonchalant, but even I can hear disappointment. "A total betrayal on my part for not telling her first in her eyes." I look away, telling myself it's to gauge how much longer my lunch is going to take, but I know that's not the real reason I can't face him.

"Should I have said nothing?" he asks.

I shake my head. "Not at all," I say, still looking ahead.

I pick up some packaged nutrition bars and start reading the ingredient listings just to have something else to do. But when Jax's hand appears from behind me and takes the bar away, I have no choice but to give him my attention.

"So, is it that I mentioned to my mother that we've seen each other or is it how I said it that's upsetting you?" he asks, a hint of concern lacing his voice.

"I'm not upset."

He nods his head, but I know he doesn't believe me. "I don't usually tell my mother much about my personal business. I like to keep my private life private."

His words cause my heart to beat a little faster. And before I know it, I'm crossing the line. "I'm a part of your private life?"

He gives a knowing smile. "Aren't you?"

I know my next few words are going to put that line so far behind me I won't be able to see it. And I don't care.

"Do you want to do something tonight?" I say before I second-guess myself.

Jax raises his eyebrows in surprise, probably because this is the first time I've initiated us getting together.

"Okay," he says, lifting the right side of his lips into a half smile. "Should we meet in the park? Run the usual—"

"Not for a run," I interrupt. "I thought maybe we could…"

What? What am I asking?

The silence when he doesn't respond makes me very uncomfortable. I quickly start thinking of any excuse to get both him and me out of this, but somehow, I don't think *just kidding* would work.

"I'll pick you up at seven," he states.

I look back at him, our eyes meeting. I know I should say something in return since I *did* ask him out, but all I can manage is a nod. I hear someone start to annoyingly shout "forty-two" over and over. I'm about to tell them to shut up when Jax starts laughing.

"That's you," he says.

"Oh, shit!" I quickly turn and face the rather irate sandwich maker. I smile apologetically, grabbing my sandwiches and hastily making my way to the exit.

Outside, Dylan finishes his call and walks towards us.

"Hello, gorgeous," Dylan says, taking his sunglasses off and openly leering at me.

Amused, I give him a small smile. "Hi, Dylan."

"You know, we should ditch this guy." He nods towards Jax. "Blow off the rest of the day and give in to this undeniable attraction we have going on."

Pretending to consider his offer, I glance towards Jax who doesn't seem to find Dylan's approach as funny as I do. A small thrill at the thought of Jax being jealous runs through me. "Sorry. I already have plans."

"Probably for the best. It would never have work between us." He nods. "I need someone a little more…malicious. Speaking of, how's Tess?"

I bark out a laugh. "I'm going to pretend I didn't just hear you call my best friend a bitch. But from what I understand, your services at the bar did the trick. Sorry."

He waves it off. "All my talents, wasted."

His cell rings and he excuses himself to answer it, leaving me and Jax alone. I'm finding it hard to say goodbye even though I know I'll be seeing him in a few hours.

"So…tonight then," I say, cradling the lunch bag in front of me like a shield.

He nods once and smiles. "Tonight."

IT'S TEN TO seven and it looks like my closet has thrown up all over my bedroom. Every single top I own has been dropped haphazardly onto my bed or the floor. Dressed in only a pair of light blue skinny jeans and a bra, I've tried on every single top before discarding it for another. I know I shouldn't be nervous. We never said this was a date. We're just two friends hanging out like we've been doing for the last few weeks.

That's a lie and I know it. This time feels different.

A black top is half way down my arms when I hear the sounds of a motorcycle come up my street. I run to my bathroom, taking one last look. My hair is tied in a low ponytail having learned my lesson after the first bike ride and my makeup is minimal. I spritz a few sprays of body mist when I hear my doorbell ring.

I take a final look in the mirror, urging myself to act normal. Not to over think this. I walk calmly to the door, taking my time. In part, it's to give myself a few extra seconds to compose myself, but I know it's also so I don't look so anxious.

Stupid hidden teenage immaturity.

Taking a deep breath, I open the door and find Jax waiting. His face looks perfectly smooth, thoughts of him in his bathroom shaving enter my mind. My eyes drift lower to his wool hooded sweater and dark denim jeans. He's the perfect blend of classic and casual.

He straightens and smiles, his eyes moving the length of my body. He extends the helmet out to me.

"Ready?" he asks, seemingly not even interested in coming inside—which is probably best since my living room could use a little cleaning.

I nod, grabbing my purse and locking the door behind us.

"So, where to?" he asks as we walk towards the bike.

My body stills as I realize that in all my haste thinking about tonight and getting ready, I haven't actually made any plans. Jax halts, looking back at me when he realizes I've stopped following him. He sees my hesitation in answering and lets out a small laugh.

"Didn't think that far ahead?"

"I… I thought maybe we could…" I stutter, trying to think of something quickly.

Jax walks up to me. Taking the helmet from my hand and sitting it on my head, he buckles it in place. His smile shows he's taking pity on me.

"Have you eaten since lunch?" he asks, giving the helmet a little tug ensuring it's on tight.

I shake my head. "No."

"Good," he says with a nod, leading us to the bike. He cranks the bike once I'm seated snug behind him, looking back just before takeoff to say, "Hold on tight."

JAX PARKS OUTSIDE a red brick building with the sign *8 Ball* overhead. The windows along the front have neon signs advertising BEER, NFL, and BILLIARDS. I take in my surroundings as we walk inside, counting ten pool tables; half of them are already in use. The room has dark walls but the lights hanging from each table brightens up the room. There are TV's hanging in every corner, each playing a sports game. Jax heads to the bar, orders us a couple of beers, wings and nachos. He also grabs what looks like a small briefcase.

Walking towards a table, he nods to a stand holding cues. "Grab two. Make sure they're straight."

I do as he says, grabbing two cues before we grab a table and settle in. He opens the small briefcase, a set of billiard balls neatly arranged.

"Hope this is okay. I didn't really have time to plan anything," he says pointedly. I know he's poking fun at me, but I do feel bad about not having made plans on what to do.

"Yeah, sorry about that," I say shyly.

"I'll try not to take your lack of thought over this personally." He grins as he racks the balls on the table.

I want to tell him that he's wrong, that I've been thinking

about it all afternoon, but I keep my mouth shut. Instead, I grab my cue and start chalking the tip.

"Do you play?" he asks, grabbing his own cue.

Shaking my head, I tell him, "No, not really. You?"

"A little," he smiles devilishly.

"Really? You wouldn't be trying to hustle me, would you?" I glare at him.

I bend over the table, ready to break. As soon as my cue hits the white ball, it slides to the left and slowly rolls a mere foot away. I scrunch my nose in disappointment, grabbing the ball again and placing it back to the starting point. "Redo," I say.

He chuckles. "Absolutely."

I try again and this time the ball veers to the right and goes straight into the side pocket. Jax puts his beer down on the table, grabs the ball and comes over to my side.

"Maybe, you should start by holding the cue properly," he says.

He puts the ball back down and comes around behind me. He takes my hands in his and places them on the cue. His hands are much larger, completely covering mine. His body is lined up directly behind me as he bends us over the table. I can feel his chest lightly grazing my back and my right leg is flush against his right thigh. I inhale deeply and his now familiar scent of laundry and cologne washes over me, only this time it has the smell of the wind from our ride mixed in. I try and focus on what he's saying, lips so close to my ear, but all my other senses seem to be reeling.

"Aim to hit the center of the ball, keep the cue straight and follow through," he says calmly, so close I can smell a faint hint of beer on his breath.

He pulls our right arms back and with a quick flick, we hit the white ball dead center and break the balls apart. Two of them even go in. When he releases me, he stands and takes two steps back, leaving me bent over the table alone.

"Perfect," he says.

I stand, my legs trembling. I know it's not the victorious feeling of making those shots affecting me either. Never before has so much of Jax's body touched mine at one time. I'm overcome with need for more.

And just like that, he's back behind me, helping me align two more shots. Both times I'm dizzy by his closeness and both times, balls fall into their pockets. After that, he lets me play on my own and even though my aim and strokes are better, I'm still terrible. Jax, however, continues to get every single shot. I watch him from across the table, lining up each one, his long torso and arms covering the table. I distract myself from watching him by glancing at the television screens to see the scores of games I don't care about, but my eyes always go back to following his movements.

After we finish two games—me losing both—the food he ordered is brought out. Jax orders me another beer and a water for himself.

"So, Mr. 'I've only played a little', where did you learn to play so well?" I ask, grabbing a chicken wing.

Jax smiles as he bites into a nacho chip. "I don't know what you mean."

I look over my beer bottle and raise my eyebrows.

He laughs. "I may have played a game or two in my day. A friend in Switzerland was a bit of a pool player. Taught me a few things. Thought it would be a great way for us to make a few extra bucks. Place some friendly wagers," he says, grabbing another chip.

"Friendly wagers?" I ask amused.

"Well, *we* thought they were," he adds. "Worked out quite a few times until one guy caught on and didn't take it so well. We left with no money and a black eye for Stefan."

My eyes widen. "That doesn't sound friendly to me. More like you were a troublemaker."

His smile is playful and big enough to meet the corners of his eyes. I know it's easily becoming one of my favorite things to see.

"Hardly. Like I said before, I mostly worked. The firm I was with had some pretty big clients that demanded lots of attention. Didn't leave too much free time."

"Yeah, you mentioned that before," I say, remembering our previous conversation. "What about now? Finding time to make trouble?"

There's a glint in his eyes as he answers. "I'm trying."

I grab another wing and focus on pulling the meat off the bone with my fingers.

"What about you?" he asks.

I swallow the chicken, looking at him. "Me?"

His grin is off to one side. "Yeah. Are you finding time to make trouble?"

I feel like every minute spent with him is trouble for me.

"Well, I spend most of my free time with you so…" I reach for another chicken wing, peeking back up to see he's smiling, seeming happy to have heard that.

"I'm honored," he says, grinning. "So, that other guy?"

I swallow the sip of beer I just took. "Other guy?"

He nods. "From the bar."

"Paul?"

Another nod.. "He's involved with your friend?"

"Yeah, sorta. I hope so."

"So he's not…" he looks at me expectantly.

Oh my God. Does he think Paul and I may be…involved somehow?

"No!" I shout, almost too loudly. "No," I repeat softly. A terribly slow, quiet minute passes before I ask him the same. "Are you?"

"I'm not involved with him either."

I bark out a laugh, spitting beer across the table. I immediately cover my mouth, trying to swallow the rest. “Sorry,” I say after it all goes down.

I should be mortified but the smile on his face is too big, making me forget that I just showered him and the food with beer.

“Don’t be sorry. Never for a laugh strong enough to spit beer across the table,” he says, taking a napkin and wiping the dark spots on his sweater.

I follow suit, grabbing napkins and cleaning off parts of the table.

“No,” I hear him say.

I look up.

“To your question. It’s a no for me as well.”

My heart reflexes like a knee jerk once more. He knows it too.

“Ready for another game?” Jax asks, standing, changing the subject.

“You know, the gentlemanly thing to do would be to let me win,” I say, repeating my words from when we were running in the park.

Jax nods once, contemplating. “The hustler in me just can’t allow it.” He walks around to the other side of the table, bends and winks at me.

I watch him bring his arm back from behind him, swinging the cue perfectly straight and fast. The sound of the white ball smacking into the rest is loud, and so is the sound of three balls falling into their pockets.

chapter 13

I'M STANDING OVER a bouquet of white roses and peonies. They are sitting in a simple square vase with a sheer cream bow wrapped around it. I've spent two hours working on this bouquet. Two hours of adding less and taking away more. Two hours trying to make this the most beautiful arrangement anyone has ever seen. In the time I've spent on it, Anna has arranged four large vases for delivery.

"Relax," Tess says into my ear as I hold my cell between my head and shoulder, trying to work and talk at the same time. I add another large green leaf, then immediately take it out. "So what? He didn't text yesterday. Not a big deal. You even said everything went great on your date," she tries to assure me.

"It wasn't a date," I correct her. At least, I don't believe it was. Even so, not hearing from him yesterday was…unexpected.

After a few more games of pool, Jax took me home. He helped me off the motorcycle, walked me to my door, waited until I unlocked it, then simply smiled and said good night. There was no awkward moment, no uncertainty of how the night would end. It seemed like it wasn't even something he contemplated.

"A wave Tess. That's it," I mumble into the phone. I can hear the sounds of traffic in the background. I've caught her between meetings, moving through the city in a taxi.

"You know, to be fair, you haven't been the easiest to read. Maybe he's just trying to follow your lead, which as far as I can tell, has been a circle. Excuse me, sir, could you possibly go any slower? I love showing up to meetings twenty minutes late."

Her voice oozes sarcasm and annoyance. I feel bad for the driver.

"You know what you should do. Go over to his office. Bring those flowers you've been fidgeting with," I immediately pull my hands away from the arrangement, "and surprise him. Take the *lead*!" she emphasizes.

"Go to his office? Isn't that a little bold? He said he'd stop by the shop. Doesn't going there look a little…desperate?"

"No, it looks like you're an independent woman who doesn't wait around for a man to come to you. Stop driving yourself crazy, and go see him!"

"But I'm not an independent woman who doesn't wait. I'm the complete opposite in fact."

"Just do it!" she screams, startling me.

"Okay, fine! Geez." I hang up and stare at the bouquet, convincing myself that this is a good idea.

Just go.

Independent woman.

I repeat the mantra to myself over and over.

I'll simply say hello, drop off the flowers, and leave. No big deal.

I add two more roses to the vase and stare at it.

"I need to start over," I mutter.

JAX'S OFFICE BUILDING is located in the downtown core, not terribly far from the shop, but I don't want to carry the heavy vase all the way so I opt to take a cab—much easier than trying to find parking at this time of day.

As soon as I pay the driver and step out onto the sidewalk, I begin to rethink this whole thing. Millions of reasons why this is a bad idea rush through my mind. *He could be busy or in a meeting or not even here for that matter. I should have just let him come pick up the flowers himself.*

I'm about to hail another cab when I hear my name being called. I turn and see Dylan walking up the sidewalk towards me.

Dylan's eyes fall to the bouquet and he cocks a grin. "For me?"

"For Jax," I answer with a smile. His eyebrows raise slightly. "His mom actually! They're for his mom," I quickly add. "It's her birthday."

Dylan smiles, his eyes becoming small devilish slits. He nods towards the entrance of the building. "Come on then, I'll bring you up."

I follow him inside, security letting us through easily once Dylan states I'm with him. Once we're in the elevator, my earlier nerves start to resurface. I tap my nails against the glass of the vase, my eyes locked straight ahead.

"I'm sure Jax will mention it, but a bunch of us are going out Friday night after work. I just closed a huge deal for the firm. It was a bitch of a time, but negotiations are all done, papers are signed, and it's time to get fucked up. You should come."

I nod, not paying any attention to what he just said.

"Cool," he says. "We're going to Vice."

"Okay."

Wait, what? Before I can ask what I just agreed to, the elevator doors open and Dylan ushers me out.

The fourteenth floor is impressive. A large reception desk sits in front of the elevators and a young, very pretty blonde sits behind it. She smiles politely towards Dylan before bringing her eyes over to me. "Delivery?" she asks.

"Umm, yes," I nod awkwardly.

"It's okay, Kelly. This one can be hand-delivered," Dylan interjects.

Dylan leads us past the desk, and I follow him to a set of glass doors. As soon as we enter, I feel like I'm on the set of a legal drama. Office doors line the hall on one side with small cubicles on the other. We walk along the open hallway, and I can't help but peek into every office. Most have their doors open, but every one of them has a giant glass window so you can easily see inside. Some people are working furiously on their computers, others are speaking on the phone. Everyone looks very busy. Even though I have a business degree, I've never pictured myself in a work environment like this. I'm actually a little intimidated by it all.

We walk into a corner area of the floor where four office doors are manned by another reception desk. This time a man sits behind it. He has a short haircut and a very young looking face. He looks like he's playing dress-up in his dad's suit.

"Jax busy?" Dylan asks baby face, walking past without waiting for an answer.

"Mr. Perry is in a meeting with Ms. Vasquez," he responds. "I can take those," he offers, standing to take the flowers.

I realize with the way I'm dressed, black leggings and a loose purple blouse, everyone must think I'm a delivery girl. Which technically, I suppose I am, but a small hint of embarrassment starts creeping up my neck. I must really stick out here.

"That's not an important meeting," Dylan says, walking towards the first office door. "Come," he tells me.

He knocks twice and opens the door. "Delivery," he nearly sings out loud.

I step into Jax's office right behind Dylan. I see Jax immediately, seated at his desk, but that's not what keeps my attention. It's the redhead standing beside his chair, leaning over his shoulder and pointing to something on his laptop that my eyes are now focused on.

Oblivious to what we just walked into, Dylan moves to the side and leaves me standing in the middle of the office, completely exposed.

"Look who stopped by," Dylan says, smiling.

"Rachel!" Jax says, surprised to see me in his office.

"Hi," I say.

I look past Jax to the bombshell behind him. She slowly rises and I'm able to fully take in her appearance. If Sofia Vergara has a younger, red-headed sister, she must be it. Not only is she gorgeous in a very exotic looking way, but her white pencil skirt is not shy about showing off her curves and her open blouse most definitely highlights her assets. Jax's eyes follow mine and he quickly stands, coming around the desk towards me.

"Let me take those," he says, taking the vase from me and sitting them on the small coffee table in the corner.

"I thought I'd save you a trip and drop them off," I say, still unable to tear my eyes away from this woman.

I feel him come stand close to me. "I'm glad you did," he says quietly.

Finally shifting my gaze from Vergara's little sister, I look up at him, his eyes focused solely on me like I'm the only one in the room. I glance down, breaking some of the intensity of his stare. It also gives me a minute to appreciate seeing him in another suit. Gray slacks and vest over top a baby blue shirt with a white collar. *GQ* should really track him down if they want to increase magazine sales. This man definitely knows how to wear a suit.

The sound of a throat clearing shakes us both back into reality and towards the woman who just pulled us out of our small bubble.

"Jessica, maybe we could finish this later?" Jax says.

A small, immature thrill at her being dismissed comes over me. I watch her as she comes around Jax's desk, grabbing a few papers and folders along with her. She stops in front of him, brushing her long hair off one shoulder, exposing her neck and collar bone.

"Sure, I'll come back later." Her eyes meet mine and she gives me a curt smile, silently letting me know that she'll be back, just as soon as I leave. It's amazing the words women can say without uttering one syllable.

In instances like this, I wish I was more like Tess, confident and self-assured enough to give the same kind of smile back. One that says, *Give me your best shot, I dare you!* But I'm not like Tess and I know my smile comes off looking weak.

Thankfully, Dylan comes to my rescue. "Jessica, why don't you buy me lunch?"

She turns, the sound of her heels clicking against the floor as she walks towards Dylan is almost deafening. "I'm not hungry," she says dryly.

"Then don't eat," he answers, closing the door behind them.

Alone in the office, Jax steps in front of me, his hands planted in his pant pockets. "They're beautiful. Thank you," he says looking over the bouquet.

"I hope your mom likes them."

"Impossible not to." He smiles. "I'm really glad you stopped by. I want to apologize for not calling yesterday."

I try and dismiss his apology, shaking my head as if to say not to worry about it, but he stops me.

"No. I should have. I wanted to," he stresses. "A work issue came up, and my day was monopolized by meetings and conference calls. It was close to nine o'clock before I even had a chance to look at the time, and I was still in a meeting. But still, I should have called."

He seems apologetic and it makes me feel foolish for over thinking it as much as I did. When his eyes meet mine again, he smiles. "Thank you for bringing them by. I needed the distraction. Even better that it was you."

A shiver runs down my arms. "You're welcome."

I look down at my leggings and ankle boots. "Although I do believe everyone thinks I'm a delivery girl. A little underdressed for the office I think," I laugh nervously.

The wall of windows along the side of his office allows for a lot of natural light to come in and in this brightness, his eyes match the color of the cloudless sky.

He shakes his head slowly. "I think you're a breath of fresh air."

He makes it so hard to breathe when he says things like that.

"So, what are the plans for tonight?" I ask, pointing to the flowers.

He blinks a few times before looking over at the bouquet. "My dad and I take her to her favorite restaurant. She doesn't like to make a big deal of it. Not anymore at least." He takes his hands out of his pockets and ushers me towards the small black leather couch against the far wall of the office. He takes a seat beside me, his arms resting on his thighs, hands held loosely together.

"When I was younger, my mother loved birthdays—especially hers." He smiles pointedly at me. "Planned a big party every year. Had it catered, invited all her friends. Every year, they popped champagne at ten seventeen, the minute she was born. I used to think those parties were so lame. I'd stay in my room and play video games until bed and when I was older, I made sure I was out with the guys, but she loved it."

A look of fondness for the memory comes over his face as he talks about his mother. It makes my heart beat a little faster.

"Why no party this year?" I ask, craving to hear more details, learn anything I can about him, his family.

He tilts his head my way, but his eyes don't meet mine. "My mother had a cancer scare a few years ago. Thankfully, the doctors caught it early enough that a few surgeries did the trick."

My heart slows, compassion and comfort taking over. Without hesitation, I move closer and cover both his hands with one of mine. He smiles at the gesture, and I feel him interlace his fingers with mine. I look down at our connected hands, surprised at how natural it feels, how natural being with him is. This feeling has been developing and as much as I've tried to ignore or label it as something different, in this moment, it's staring me in the face, unwilling to go away.

"After that, she said she didn't want the parties or the champagne anymore. She just wanted to celebrate life with the two people who meant the most to her."

I understand all too well the want to spend important days with the ones you love. They can be taken away in a blink of the eye.

"I think I'd really like your mom," I say quietly.

"I think she'd really like you," he utters back.

He lifts his free hand and brings it to the side of my face, his fingers brushing gently against my cheek. "I think *I* really like you," he says.

My breath catches and I can only hold it in, afraid of what will happen next. It reminds me of the feeling you get right before you're about to rip off a Band-Aid. A seemingly simple act yet it can cause a small stir of fear in the pit of your stomach. I don't know why but for whatever reason, before that rip happens, I've always gone through a routine to help try and prepare myself. I hold my breath, close my eyes and count to three. I know the pain will be minimal, but my body will still react—a small shake or convulsion as though I'm in shock it actually happened. Even with all my preparedness, I'm never ready. That feeling, the shock, the involuntary body jerk, is happening to me right now.

With those few words, Jax has ripped off the Band-Aid that's been covering my heart for close to two years. I wasn't prepared. I didn't even have a chance to count to three.

"Mr. Perry, your two o'clock is here," his assistant's voice echoes through the room. I let go of the breath I was holding, slowly unlacing my hand from his and start to stand. He balls his hand into a fist before standing as well.

Our bodies stay close, neither one of us backing away. I feel a shift is happening. For the first time, I'm not just noticing how my body is reacting being this close to him, but I'm seeing the changes in his as well. The usual steadiness of his breath is a little more ragged, his lips are slightly open, his tongue quickly darting out, licking his lips, wetting them. I see him bury both his fists into his pant pockets once more.

"I should go." I grab my purse from the chair across from where we were just sitting. "I've interrupted your day long enough."

I walk to his office door, my hand resting on the doorknob. I start to turn around to say goodbye when Jax's hand comes into view in front of me, keeping the door closed.

My eyes drift from his open-palmed hand to his wrist that has a classic leather strapped watch around it and then to his face as I pivot around to him.

"Thank you again for the flowers. They're perfect," he says, his eyes moving across my face.

"Wish your mom a happy birthday for me."

"I will."

I nod and turn to leave again.

"Are you busy on Friday night?" His voice freezes my hand in place. "Dylan, he finally got a win and wants to celebrate. He wants to go to some club. Vice I think it's called. I hate clubs. Come hate it with me," his voice is soft.

I smile. "He mentioned something about that."

A small flicker of dislike washes over his face. "Really? Well, I'll have to talk to him about that."

"About what?"

He smirks. “Keeping clear of my girl.”

He moves his raised hand, lowering it to cover mine and turns the doorknob. The sounds of office mingling and phones ringing are a rude interruption to the perfect silence that was just between us.

“I’ll send you the details,” he says quietly in my ear.

I nod dumbly and leave his office. I hear Jax change back into business mode, welcoming his next appointment into his office as though nothing happened while I have tunnel vision all the way to the elevator.

It’s only when I reach the outside of the building that my mind clears. I pull out my cell and call Tess.

“So, how did it go?” she answers, curious.

I don’t think I could answer that if I tried.

“Rachel?”

“Don’t make any plans Friday night. We’re going to a club.”

chapter 14

I CAN HEAR the bass pounding from outside the building as we approach the club. Tess and Sophie are ahead of me as we round the corner and see a ridiculous line to get in. Not expecting a wait, I rcmind myself that it's ten o'clock on a Friday night, and this is what people do when they aren't at home alone watching reruns on TV.

"Shit," I hear Sophie mutter as we watch the line not move.

As promised, Jax called me later that night as I was getting ready for bed. He wanted to thank me for the flowers again and let me know how much his mother enjoyed them. He also let me know the details about Friday night.

"I could pick you up," he offered.

"Thanks, but Tess and Sophie are coming. I'll meet you there." Our fourth, Lana, has her own night planned with her favorite bartender.

"Okay, tomorrow then," his voice sounding faintly disappointed.

"Tomorrow."

But now, seeing this line at the door, I'm beginning to think I may not see him at all.

"Fuck this," Tess says, strutting her way to the bouncer.

I watch as she taps him on the shoulder and leans in closer, speaking directly into his ear. The bouncer nods a few times before leaning back, raising his eyebrows in surprise. A smile come across Tess's face, and the bouncer grins then starts to laugh. He shakes his head a little and moves aside to open the door for her. Tess taps the bouncer softly on the chest a few times before looking over at us, beckoning us to follow her inside.

"What did you say to him?" Sophie asks once inside.

Tess smirks. "Nothing I haven't said once before to get what I want."

I shake my head and follow the girls further into the club. Vice is a popular club with private booths offering bottle service on the second level that overlooks the massive dance floor. Behind the bar, a cascading water wall with changing colored lights shining through reaches up to the ceiling. Loud music is blaring from speakers sitting in every corner. A DJ is spinning from a platform perched slightly above the crowd, mixing current hits with backdrops of music from the nineties. Right now, a Selena Gomez song is mixed with Culture Beat's *Mr. Vain.* You wouldn't think it would work but weirdly, it does. In front of us is a massive dance floor full of bodies moving and grinding to the mix.

I look above us to the private booths. Each one is filled and waitresses in tight black dresses are walking by with trays full of bottles, glasses and garnishes. Tess yells over the music, asking if I've spotted Jax yet. I haven't, but I'm not surprised with how many people are here.

I feel a tap on my shoulder and turn to see Dylan, wide eyed and happy. Gone is the suit and tie, and in its place are black pants and a black button up shirt, the top two buttons undone.

"Well look who decided to stop by and join the fun," he

yells over the music.

In each hand is a glass filled with clear liquid. His eyes rake over me and when they come back up to my face, he grins.

"Very nice," he says.

I know it's all very innocent but I'm glad he noticed. I tried on five different dresses before settling on this one. It's a navy and gold sequin tank dress that falls mid-thigh, and I matched it with a pair of gold strappy heels. My hair is coming down in loose wild waves. "Fuck me" hair Tess calls it.

"Is it always this packed in here?" I yell back.

"Yep. That's why we have a booth upstairs." He nods towards the second floor. Right after, he notices Tess and Sophie come up beside me. The friendly grin he reserves for me turns into a sly one when he sees my friends.

"Tess." He nods her way in acknowledgment. His eyes roam the area around her. "I don't see Mr. Law Enforcement. Couldn't keep him around?" he asks, taking a sip from one of his drinks.

"Night shift," Tess answers, grabbing the other glass from him, taking a long sip out of it.

He smirks, turning his attention to Sophie. "Tess, aren't you going to introduce us?"

I guess they never got around to meeting that first night we met Dylan and Jax.

"Sophie, Dylan. Dylan, Sophie," Tess says before turning her attention back to the dance floor.

I watch as Dylan narrows his eyes a bit at Tess before taking a step closer to Sophie.

It's loud in here but I can still hear him try and charm her, just like the first time we met him. "She's just angry that I've been waiting all my life for you," he tells her.

"Come a step closer and I may have to hurt you," Sophie says in a mockingly sweet tone.

"Hurt me, please!" Dylan pretends to beg. I watch as she

tries hard not to crack a smile but it's useless. Her firm, straight lips begin to falter, a smirk creeping up her face. She's fallen prey. I'm actually a little surprised that his tactics worked on her.

"Let's go upstairs, I need a refill. Two actually," he says as Tess gives him back his now empty glass.

"Is Jax here?" I ask, still not having caught a glimpse of him.

Dylan nods. "Somewhere. We'll be able to find him better from up there."

He winks at Sophie and cocks his head, telling us to follow. We move up the stairs, making our way to his booth.

Dylan definitely knows how to celebrate because it's the biggest one in the club. It can easily fit twenty people. Bench seating outlines the booth, making it square in shape. Small tables are in every corner, each has a bottle of Grey Goose and Bombay Sapphire. Pitchers of juice, fancy bottles of Italian soda and small bowls of cut fruit also fill the tables. I look around the booth and have counted ten people—none of them Jax.

Dylan quickly does introductions and from what I can hear over the music, many of these people are also from his firm. Quick hellos are said with offers to mix us drinks. Before I know it, I have a vodka cranberry in one hand and am sitting in the middle of the booth. Tess comes and sits down beside me.

"So where is lover boy?" she asks, glancing around the booth.

"Good question."

We turn to look over the safety wall and gaze over to the lower level of the club. Our eyes scan the packed bodies at the bar, eagerly waiting to place their order. I take a sip of my drink, happy we don't have to be in that line. My eyes make their way to the end of the bar where I spot Jax sipping from his glass. I know Tess has also found him with the next words out of her mouth.

"Who's the skank?"

The skank she's referring to is Jessica from his office. Logically it makes sense she'd be here, considering this is kind of a work related function. But logic is not processing right now.

Instead, ugly jealousy is taking form in the pit of my stomach, wrapping its way around my back, causing me to sit up straighter. A little of my drink sloshes out of my glass on to the bench with my sudden movement, but I don't pay it any attention.

"Her name's Jessica. She works with him," I answer.

"You mean working him. Or trying to at least. Doesn't seem to be happening though," she states, her eyes squinting, glaring. She's right. Jessica is standing beside him, leaning close enough to talk directly into his ear, but his body is facing away from her, turned towards the bar.

"You need to go mark your territory."

"He's not my territory."

She twists around and looks at me like I'm crazy. Tess swings her body fully facing me, her hand now gripping my face, forcing me to look at her. "Mark. Your. Territory."

Dylan comes and sits between us, breaking our connection, and looks over at Tess. "Sophie wants to hit up the can. Most likely to discuss me. Be nice."

Tess snidely smirks at him before walking out of the booth with Sophie, leaving me with Dylan. I try but fail to keep my gaze from falling back to Jax and Jessica. Dylan follows my stare.

"Ah, you found him." He swings his body around, overlooking the bar below where both Jax and Jessica still stand. "Guys like him throw the bell curve off for the rest of us. If he wasn't a friend, I'd punch him."

I feel a nudge, Dylan's elbow hitting my arm. I shift my eyes from below to Dylan who nods in Jax's direction. "You don't need to worry about her. She's been trying, but it's gotten her nowhere."

Insecure at how obvious I'm being, I tear my eyes away from Dylan and look back at Jax. This time, his find mine as well. I see him say something to Jessica, his eyes still locked with mine as he walks away from her.

"Told you." Dylan nudges me once more.

He gets up and pours himself another drink while I watch Jax make his way to the stairs, heads turning as he walks by. For a moment, I lose him in the crowd. I take a huge gulp of my drink, hoping it will calm my legs from their unstoppable bouncing.

A minute later, he enters the booth. Dressed in dark grey pants and a black button shirt, he smiles as he takes a seat beside me.

"Hey." He leans into me, talking into my ear.

"Hi." I stir my now empty drink.

"When did you get here?"

"A little while ago. Dylan found us and brought us up. Nice booth," I say, nodding at our space.

He nods in agreement. "Yeah, Dylan's running on a high right now."

Our bodies are very close to one another, and I see him take in my dress.

"You look...wow," he says.

I smile. "Thanks."

It takes everything in me not to jump up and down in glee at his reaction, but I stay calm and continue to stir the ice cubes that are left in my glass. I look back down over the wall, watching bodies move against each other on the dance floor. I spot Jessica still standing by the bar, sipping from a glass of wine and brushing off any attention she's receiving from other men. And there have been a few.

"I went down there to wait for you. Bring you up myself. I was cornered into a conversation. Sorry about that," he says.

I can feel his breath as he speaks, soft heat hitting my neck just below my ear. I can smell the faintest hint of alcohol mixed with mint, and a chill runs down my spine.

I shrug and shake my head. His head shifts and follows my stare.

"Just so you know—" he begins but is interrupted when Tess and Sophie come back into the booth giggling.

"Jackson, so nice of you to pull yourself away and join us," Tess yells, her eyes glaring, her smile calculated.

Oh God.

I'm about to insert myself between them, hoping I can get Tess to stop with my own glare. But it doesn't look like Jax needs my help. He simply smiles back at her, an understanding occurring between the two of them.

"I was just apologizing to Rachel for that exact same thing. Believe me when I say it won't happen again."

His hand falls to my knee, staying there, squeezing it lightly. Such a small gesture but one that screams so much. Both mine and Tess's eyes fall to his hand. While it seems to reassure Tess, her body becoming more relaxed, it does the opposite to me. His hand may only be on my knee but I feel it everywhere. The quick strums of his fingers against my skin matches the pace of my erratic heartbeat.

"Good." Tess smiles before taking a seat next to Sophie.

Dylan walks around with the vodka bottle topping off everyone's drink when Jessica comes into the booth. Her eyes immediately land on Jax and not a second later, to his hand. Quickly looking away, she takes a seat next to one of guys from the firm.

A waitress comes in, asking if there is anything she can get us. Tess raises her half empty glass.

"I could really go for a red-headed slut. Two actually, one for my friend over there," she says, nodding to me.

The waitress nods and leaves. Tess turns to Jessica and sends her a sly smile, keeping her glass raised in front of her.

Jessica eyes Tess for a moment before bringing her attention back to the conversation around her.

I shoot daggers at Tess, hoping they'll get her to stop humiliating me by coming to a defense I don't need. She feels my glare, turning towards me, smiling sweetly and shrugging her shoulders as if to say *what*.

Jax's hand starts to shake in rhythm with his laughter. "She's not very…subtle, is she?"

I shake my head, his amused smile easing my embarrassment. "No, not really."

He leans in closer, his lips to my ear. "She's protective. I get it. Seems to be a reoccurring theme with you. But I think you can hold your own." His lips brush lightly against my ear just before he moves away. My breath stills at the touch, and I know he's noticed.

"Okay." Tess stands and comes to hover directly in front of me. "It's girl time on the dance floor." Her attention moves to Jax. "Next time, don't keep her waiting!"

"What about your drinks? The red-headed slut, I believe?" Jax asks, challenging Tess.

"Who cares," Tess shrugs her shoulders, reaching out for me.

Before I know it, I'm being pulled from the booth by both Tess and Sophie. I turn my head back to mouth an apology but the way his eyes look me up and down stop my mouth from working. He is unashamedly checking me out for everyone to see. In Tess's words, he just marked his territory. And…I loved it.

We pass Dylan on the way out, raising his arms in question.

"Dancing!" Sophie yells out.

We slowly make our way to the dance floor, having to maneuver past one body after the next. Tess stops a woman walking around selling shots.

"Three!" Tess tells her. She points overhead. "And charge it to that booth."

We are given our shots, lifting them up in cheers before we drink them. It's been a while since I've had hard liquor, my body already feeling warm after only one drink and now this shot.

Tess leads us near the center of the dance floor where we make a small circle. We're surrounded by bodies bumping into us as they grind against each other. Slowly, I'm able to find my rhythm as the song begins to pick up a faster tempo. I look over at Tess and Sophie, happily dancing to the music, lifting their arms in the air and shaking their hips back and forth. Tess grabs my arm and spins me under hers.

I can't remember the last time I danced at a club. I used to love it. Being here on the dance floor I'm reminded of just how much. I feel myself smiling. I hear myself laughing.

I'm having fun. And it feels so good.

We stay on the dance floor for a couple more songs, circling each other, letting our bodies loosen up. I'm dancing in ways I haven't in years. It's liberating and feels good to let go and get lost in nothing but beats and sounds.

Tess leans into me, yelling over the music, "Don't look, but you're being watched!"

What?

Where?

And how on earth am I expected not look when told something like that?

I raise my head and my eyes meet Jax's. He's bent down against the safety wall, resting on his arms. Following suit, Dylan is leaning into him saying something. Jax nods, but his focus is on me.

I listen as the song changes, a new beat coming over the speakers. I watch Jax stand up, clap Dylan on the shoulder and disappear from view. Trying not to wonder where he's gone, I continue dancing, only to be surprised when I feel hands grip my hips.

I turn and Jax is standing in front of me, so close that I need to tip my head back so I can look at him. He cocks his head to the side, pointing over to the doors leading to an outdoor patio. I nod as he takes my hand and leads me off the dance floor.

Once outside, I immediately feel the cool night breeze against my overheated skin. Jax steers us to the least busy area, a secluded spot in the corner. I lean against the brick wall, his arm coming up, resting next to my head. It's still loud and there are people around us but it's quiet enough that we don't have to yell at each other. He leans his head in, his lips close to my ear. He speaks just loud enough for me to hear.

"I hate clubs. I hate dancing. But watching you dance out there, I'd come here every night to see it," he says smoothly.

Maybe it's the alcohol or maybe it's the racy atmosphere, either way, he's now crossing the line we've both been treading. Stepping into new territory. Just friends to…something more than friends.

"Looked like you were doing just fine before I got here," I answer back. The alcohol is obviously giving me courage, but even so, I'm surprised at myself for saying that. I hope it came out sounding teasing, but I don't think it did.

A look of surprise washes over his face before changing to one of amusement. He bends down slightly, bringing his head a little closer. "That sounded vaguely like jealousy. Were you jealous, Rachel?"

His grin indicates that he's enjoying this, but it just eggs me on.

"I think she has a thing for you."

He shrugs. "So?"

"So?"

He blows out a puff of air with a small laugh. "Maybe you should think more about who *I* might have a thing for."

His words leave me feeling light headed. Goose bumps rise up along my arms—and not from the coolness of the night air.

"Who do you have a thing for?" I ask, knowing the answer but wanting to hear it.

"I think you know. I think you've known for a while."

Me.

I swallow thickly. Even though I wanted to hear it, it doesn't change my sudden nerves at it being said aloud.

"You make me nervous," I whisper.

"Good."

I blink. "Most people would ask how they could fix that."

He leans further into me, whispering in my ear. "Maybe I don't want to be most people to you."

He leans back to watch my reaction. I bite down on my lower lip, a little terrified to answer back. Nervous as to what I might say. What it could mean.

"Go out with me tomorrow night. A date. A real one."

I cock my head to the side, confused. "A real one?"

"Not for a run. No last minute plans. Dinner. Wine. I pick you up. In a car." He grins. "A real date."

"Do you even have a car?" I ask surprised, completely ignoring his actual question.

He chuckles. "Yeah, I have a car."

"And what we've been doing so far..." I trail off, going back to his original question.

"A warm-up."

This makes me laugh nervously, but I watch his eyes light up at the sound.

"Okay," I say, nodding. *What am I doing?*

"Good," he agrees. "Now, let's go back in. I like watching you dance."

He takes my hand and softly presses his lips to my knuckles before leading us back inside—a gesture that has my body flushing before we enter the heated club.

We find Tess and Sophie still dancing with drinks in hand. Dylan is pressed against Sophie's back, grinding against her. Jax leans over and says something to Dylan, then cocks his head towards the booth. Dylan nods, says something in Sophie's ear and then follows Jax off the floor.

As he walks by me, Jax takes my hand and pulls me over towards him, bringing my ear close to his lips.

"Put on a good show."

Stunned by his words, I watch until he's lost in the crowd, taking pride in the fact it's *me* he wants to watch.

"You look like you need it!" Tess smirks, shoving a drink in my hand.

I down it in three quick swallows, juice and the sting of vodka making their way down my suddenly dry throat.

Encouraged by the alcohol, I start to move to the sounds of the music, following Tess and Sophie's lead. I close my eyes, knowing Jax is back up in the booth watching me.

A strange sensation comes over me. I feel anxious but excited. I want to hide among the crowd but at the same time I hope a spotlight shines above so he sees nothing but me.

Curiously, I look up towards the booth and see Jax, back in the same position as earlier, arms resting against the wall, leaning down and just like he said, watching me.

My heart rate rises, and for the first time in a long time, I'm turned on. I haven't felt a want like this since Ben.

It's with that thought I realize what's happening. What I'm doing.

An affair.

I'm having an affair. But it's who I'm cheating on I can't figure out.

chapter 15

THE SOFT KNOCK at the door surprises me. I've become so accustomed to hearing the roar of Jax's motorcycle that it takes me a second to remember he's picking me up in a car tonight.

Because this is a date.

A real one.

I take one last look in the mirror, quickly putting on one more coat of lip gloss before making my way to the door, shoving shoes and a few jackets into the entryway closet. Standing in my doorway dressed in dark pants, a fitted denim like shirt and skinny navy tie, is a man too handsome to be real. He looks so good it's hard to look past anything beyond what's underneath his tailored clothes.

"Hello," he says, one hand in his pocket. In the other, he's holding a large white box with a red bow.

I smile, trying to compose myself, opening the door wider, allowing him to enter.

"Hi," I say, sounding more breathless than I'd hoped.

As he walks past me, a whiff of his cologne floats in the air around me. His smell is becoming addictive, so much so that half of me wants to follow him around the room just to keep breathing him in. I watch him as he takes in his surroundings, never having been past the front door of my house. His eyes roam, lingering on pictures frames scattered around the room. Most are of me and Tess or with my family. There are none of Ben in here.

When he turns and looks at me, it's his chance to take me in. His eyes move slowly over my face then further downwards. I know only seconds have passed, but the way he stares makes me feel like I've been on display for hours.

"You look beautiful," he says appreciatively.

I smile, my eyes moving about the room to distract myself from his stare. I spot the white flower box resting on the side table, too distracted earlier to pay any attention to him setting it down. He follows my stare to the box and walks over to it, picking it up and offering it to me.

"For you," he says smiling.

I take the box, thanking him. "Let me find a vase to put them in before we go."

"No need." He shakes his head once.

I look from the flower box to his face, confused. His eyes light up with amusement. "Open it first."

He holds the box so that I am able to untie the bow and lift the cover. I push aside the tissue paper and begin to laugh. When I look back up at him, an animated smile has spread across his face.

"You didn't expect me to bring a florist flowers, did you?" he asks.

Inside the box are six plastic rose stems, and attached at the head are a variety of delicious looking brownies. Each one different and looking equally delightful.

"You know me well." I break off a corner piece of one of the brownies and pop it into my mouth.

"Not yet, but I'm working on it."

I can't tell if it's the decadent chocolate that's melting in my mouth or the words he said that are causing me to feel a little lightheaded.

"Shall we?" he asks.

I nod, incapable of any other response.

He waits for me to grab my purse and house keys while he opens the door, letting me walk out first. We walk in silence to his car. A black Range Rover with lightly tinted windows and a sports rack on the roof. Before I even reach for the handle, he's there opening the door for me. It's kept very clean on the inside, only an empty water bottle in the cup holder. I watch Jax circle the front of the car and make his way to the driver's side. When he turns on the car, the stereo has Thirty Seconds to Mars coming through the speakers. I quietly laugh at the odds that our music choices are that similar. Jax moves to adjust the stereo, but I stop his hand.

"Don't. I like this song," I say.

He nods and puts his hand on the wheel, leaving the song playing. He pulls out of the driveway, heading downtown.

"How was your day?" he asks, stopping at a red light.

"Good. Two meetings with potential brides. One hopes to put Kim and Kanye's wedding to shame, so I'm sure it will be a very busy project. The day flew after that."

"Kim and Kanye?"

I look at him, unsure if he's serious or not.

"You're kidding, right? Kardashians?"

He opens his mouth slightly. "Kanye married a Kardashian?"

"Oh my god, where have you been?" I ask, astounded that there was anyone left on this planet that didn't know this.

He laughs. "I don't know. I guess it's a good thing I have you now. You can fill me in on the news of the world."

"I wouldn't even know where to start," I say, dumbfounded.

He smiles. "How about we start with the basics. I wouldn't want my head to explode before dinner."

I laugh, knowing he's teasing. "Yes, we better start slow." My eyes once again take in the interior of the car. "This is different," I say glancing around.

"What is?"

"The car. Not our usual mode of transportation. I have to say I kind of miss the bike."

"Next time," he promises, cocking his head towards me. "But I think I like this better. I can actually see that smile when I drive."

I'm not going to lie, being able to see his lips move as he smiles, laughs, and talks is a perk for me as well.

It isn't too much longer before he's pulling into valet parking at Notte, an Italian restaurant that is known for their amazing cuisine as well as their ridiculous wait list. Knowing that Jax has only been back for a few months, I'm a little worried that he's unaware that the wait list is at least a few weeks long. I know this because Tess has complained to me about it many times. I'm about to share my worry as we are unbuckling our safety belts when Jax turns to me.

"Stay here."

I watch as he gets out of the car, stopping the valet boy in his place and coming around to my side. Opening the door, he extends his hand to help me out.

"You're really working the perfect gentleman approach," I say as I place my hand in his.

"I do what I can," he says, guiding me out of the car.

He closes the door behind me, gives the keys to the valet and leads us into the restaurant. We walk in, our hands still together, fingers perfectly intertwined. I smile when I feel him give my hand a squeeze as we move towards the host desk.

"Umm…this place is hard to get into," I murmur quietly, seeing several groups of people waiting by the host desk.

Jax looks around at the people. "I think we'll be okay."

He walks us up to the host desk and the young woman immediately smiles. I want to roll my eyes but think better of it considering the lineup I'm seeing.

"Welcome to Notte," the perky hostess says. "Do you have a reservation?"

Worry overshadows my want to look around, concerned we'll be turned away.

"Yes. Perry," Jax says smoothly.

I whip my head towards him, the hostess looking down at her computer screen. "Perry for two. Please follow me."

I feel Jax give me a little push, urging me to follow her. I'm confused as to how he got a reservation with such little notice. And not only do we have a reservation, but we are being sat at a table in the corner of the room by a window away from everyone else. At my side, Jax pulls out my chair before moving to his own. I'm finally able to look around the restaurant, admiring how beautiful it is. Hushed voices mixed with the aroma of garlic and spices fill the air.

Menus are placed in front of us while the hostess lets us know our server will be with us shortly. Jax smiles and nods, thanking her. She stays longer than necessary before leaving us.

Once alone, I raise my eyebrows, not able to keep my curiosity to myself any longer. "How did you get us in here?" I whisper.

He squints his eyes, looking up from his menu. "Through the door," he whispers back.

I sit back, trying not to seem amused but fail. He grins, and it's so infectious I can't help but return it.

"You do know that there is a wait list a mile long for this place. Tess is number forty-seven on it or something," I say.

He looks surprised. "Really? I had no idea."

"So you aren't going to tell me how you got this reservation? With one day's notice and…" I look around the restaurant once more, "probably the best table in the entire place?"

"Does it matter?" he responds.

I watch him, both amused and annoyed at his secrecy. "No. I guess it doesn't."

It's at this point our waiter arrives, introducing himself and offering us something to drink from the wine list. Jax asks if I would prefer red or white.

"Red. Always red," I answer.

He orders us a bottle of something I've never heard of, only hearing that it's from Argentina. We take some time to look at the menu—all the choices seem so mouthwatering that I can't decide. When the waiter comes back with the wine, I'm still undecided between two dishes.

Jax looks to the waiter. "She'll have both the ravioli and chicken Tuscany and I'll have the lamb." The waiter gives me a strange look before leaving. "If we waited any longer for you to decide, we'd both be leaving here hungry."

"I can only imagine what he must think of my eating habits," I say, a little self-conscious.

"I wouldn't worry. It can't be anything bad. Not with the way you look in that dress," he says, lifting his wine glass to his lips, hiding his grin.

Jax has an uncanny gift of being able to switch from a complete gentleman to a complete smooth talker in a matter of seconds. Both sides of him easily leave me flustered.

Taking a sip of my wine, I lean back in my chair. "You've heard about my day, now it's your turn."

He leans into the table, both arms resting in front of him. "I actually had to go into the office for a few hours. I'm working on a deal and needed to have some last minute details sorted before I leave on a business trip."

I cock my head to the side. "Business trip?"

He nods a few times. "I have to fly to London next week for a few days."

"Oh." I hear the disappointment in my voice, and I know he can too.

"Sounds like someone might miss me." The corner of his mouth hitches upwards.

I don't answer. I simply take another sip of wine.

He chuckles. "Don't worry, I'll be back before you know it. Maybe I'll even bring you back something English."

I'm surprised at how much the thought of him leaving saddens me, even if it is only for a few days. Then, another thought enters my mind.

"Are you going alone?" I drop my gaze, playing with the napkin in my lap. I'm not sure how I'll react if I hear that Jessica will be going with him.

When he doesn't answer right away, I look up and see his expression. He is absolutely loving this right now and doing a terrible job at hiding it. "You know, your right eyebrow raises just the slightest when you're jealous."

I look up, immediately righting my brow.

After watching me for a few seconds, he smiles but relents. "Yes, I'll be going alone."

I release the breath I've been holding.

Jax leans in closer. "I meant what I said yesterday. My attention," his eyes scan over me, "is singularly focused."

My throat becomes dry and I lift my glass, hoping the wine will help. Before I take a sip, he raises his own, gently tapping it against mine.

He quickly changes the subject, going onto tell me more about his upcoming trip and the investment he's presenting. Some of it goes way above my head, but I'm fascinated and find myself wanting to hear more. Mostly because he seems so excited about it and watching him as he talks so passionately about something is euphoric. It reminds me of the way I am at the beginning of a brainstorming session.

"Have you always been so interested in all this… stuff?"

"Investment banking?"

I nod.

"I've always liked working with numbers. In school, math always made the most sense to me. More than any other class. Ask me about prime numbers and I can go on and on. Ask me about Shakespeare or poetry, I'm lost."

I smile shyly. "I don't know about that. You seem to have a small grasp on the notion of romance," I say, looking around the intimate setting we're in.

His eyes darken slightly. "This isn't romance," he says, correcting me. "This is a restaurant with good food and wine. Romance is what happens in between. Moments I haven't had a chance to show you yet."

He watches me, his expression promising that if I let him, he'll show me exactly what he means.

"Okay," I say, my voice shaking.

Our entrées arrive and after the first bite, I understand the wait list for this restaurant. Everything melts on my tongue in the most amazing way.

"It will be nice to go back to Europe, even if it is for a short visit."

It's silly, but sometimes I forget that Jax just finished spending the last few years of his life in a completely different country. We've talked about it, he's told me stories, but when we're together, it doesn't feel like we've only known each other for a few months. When I'm with him, it's easy to forget the sadness there was before him and be consumed in the happiness of the now.

"Do you miss it?" I ask. Worry that maybe he'll want to go back some day lingering in my mind.

"Miss it?" he asks while cutting into his lamb.

"Europe? Living there? The life you had?"

He thinks about it for a minute and then nods. "Parts of it maybe—the culture, the scenery, the food," he says, pointing down to his plate. "It was a great place to live for where I was at that point in my life. But sometimes, things happen, and you need an adjustment. A change."

His word choice sounds like he's skimming over something. Perhaps the real reason he chose to leave Switzerland. Weeks ago, I remember asking about whether he had a girlfriend there.

Nothing serious, he had said.

But it was his tone that left me questioning. A question I can't seem to keep from asking now.

"You mentioned a girlfriend back there," I say, rewording our previous conversation.

He looks up from his plate, perplexed at my words.

"No, I don't think I did."

Shit.

"Oh…my mistake," I say awkwardly.

God this is awful. Why did I say anything?

He looks at me with a questioning stare.

"Was it? A mistake?" he questions, curiosity laced through his voice.

"I'm sorry. It's none of my business. I don't know why I brought it up." I look back down at my food, using my fork to move my ravioli around the plate, avoiding his gaze.

"Rachel?" His tone of voice asking me to look up. "You can ask me anything. It's just… not exactly the conversation I thought we'd have on a first date," he says.

I nod, agreeing. "You're right."

But now there is a silence between us. One I put there with my own stupid need to know about his past, about any women who may have been a part of it. *Why couldn't I have just kept my mouth shut?*

I raise my glass, taking a large gulp, nearly emptying it of all the wine. When I rest it back on the table, I see Jax grab the bottle and refill my glass. He watches me as he refills it, barely giving it a glance. Once finished, he takes a sip from his own glass before speaking.

"Her name was Ingrid. We worked together. I knew she had a crush on me. I never intended for it to go much past flirtation, but then one night after work, I let us cross a boundary we shouldn't have. I knew I didn't reciprocate her feelings, but I let it continue longer than it should have. It became an issue for me at work, and when I ended it, she didn't handle it well. I took full responsibility. I should have known better. She left the company, and I felt terrible about it."

"Oh," I say in response.

I'm not sure what to say. I think I'm in a bit of shock at realizing that Jax is just like everyone else—flawed. He's not the perfectly faultless man I made him out to be. He too has made mistakes and bad decisions. One he just bared to me. And instead of cringing or pulling away after hearing about his past transgression, I want to move closer, hold on to him tighter. Not because he needs affirmation that he's still a good man, but because his flaws make him only more perfectly real.

"Like I said, not exactly something I thought we'd be talking about tonight," he says, taking another sip from his wine glass.

"No, but I'm glad we did," I admit. "I was beginning to think you were too perfect to be real."

The intensity of his gaze at my words suddenly makes *me* feel like the vulnerable one, like *I'm* the one who just shared hidden truths about themselves. For the first time, a small part of me wants to reveal my truth, let Jax see my flaws.

But I don't.

Instead I ask him to bare more of his.

"You didn't think you could love her back?" I know he never used the word "love" to describe Ingrid's feelings for him, but he didn't have to.

He looks at me, surprised by my question. After a long minute, he looks straight at me. No, he looks directly through me, to the whirl of desperation at hearing his answer.

"I knew I wouldn't." He blinks a few times. "That feeling when your heart beats faster, your lungs can't seem to get enough air, your eyes can't look away," he stops, letting everything he said sink in. "I didn't feel that then. I've been . . . waiting."

I swallow.

When I don't say anything, he continues to speak. "After my mom had her health scare, I wanted to be closer. I also started thinking about things. Things that I wanted in life, the *kind* of life I wanted. Things I still hadn't found."

I can understand the yearning for a life you didn't have. I had mine all planned out. Married and making babies by now. It's amazing how quickly everything can change and then become so unlikely.

When our eyes meet, for the first time in a long time, I let someone see my desire for that kind of life too.

Jax lets out a deep breath and then a small nervous laugh. "Well, this was a little deeper than I was expecting."

I smile back. "Leave it to me to make things awkward," I tell him.

"You didn't make anything awkward," he assures me. "You make them feel…very real."

Jax then switches topics to dessert. It happens so fast but I'm grateful for it too. He insists we order it, stating it's the whole point of the meal. We order tiramisu to share and when the bill comes, he doesn't even let me see it. He simply slides his credit card in the billfold and lets the waiter take it away. Once ready to leave, Jax is behind me again, helping me out of my seat. I don't think I've ever met anyone as chivalrous as he is.

The valet brings the car around and we head back to my house. I turn to him, watching him drive, his eyes focused on the road ahead of us.

"Thank you for tonight. I had a really great time."

He glances over, his expression one of gratitude over the compliment. "Me too. Definitely one of the most interesting dates I've had," he says, teasing.

I laugh. "Yes, one of."

He looks over and smiles.

The rest of the drive back we talk about our week ahead, events I have scheduled and preparations he has to make for his trip. Our conversation casually moves to Dylan and the new fondness he seems to have found for Sophie. We laugh, wondering how much of a disaster it could end in.

The conversation between us is so easy I barely notice that he's pulled up into my driveway. Getting out first, again he tells me to stay put. I watch him come around, sad the night is over. When he helps me out of the car, a new feeling arises.

Anxiousness.

This was technically our first date. Dates usually end in a kiss. *Am I ready for that? What if he leans in and I pull away? What if I am ready? What if he leans forward and I want it more than I've wanted anything in a long time?*

When we reach the door, I turn back around slowly to face him.

"Helping me out of the car, walking me to my door—I think you've checked every single item off the gentleman's list tonight," I say.

"As long as you think so, that's all that matters."

We stand there, watching each other, neither of us moving. Finally, he takes a step closer, and a small smile playing at his lips.

As he leans forward, I close my eyes, knowing right then and there that I want this. I lick my lips in anticipation, but it's not my lips that are met with his. His lips rest on my forehead for a few seconds before taking a step back.

"Good night, Rachel," he whispers before turning to make his way back to his car.

I'm a little stunned—and not in a good way. *The forehead? The freaking forehead? Is he serious?*

"What was that?" I blurt out.

He stops and he turns around, his eyebrows drawn together. "Sorry?"

"The forehead?" I point my finger to the area in question. I think I'm both confused and insulted, and my tone shows it. "Who kisses on the forehead?"

I realize I should probably be embarrassed. I'm practically throwing a tantrum over not being kissed. But my disappointment and sudden anger is suppressing any other feelings.

He looks at me for a moment before he takes a step forward. Then another. And another. His steps are almost forceful, dominant. When he reaches me, his final step has him towering over me. His eyes are determined, preparing me for what he's about to do before he even moves again.

"After our little talk, I thought I'd give you some time to digest it all before I kiss you. Because believe me when I say not kissing you right then was the hardest thing I've had to do in a very long time," he says seriously, gazing into my eyes. "If you want this even a fraction of how much I want it, tell me."

His hands come up, spreading across the sides of my face, the tips of his fingers now lost in my hair.

"Are you telling me, Rachel?" he whispers, almost pleading with me to say yes.

I barely have time to nod before he brings his mouth down to mine.

As soon as our lips touch, I'm glad he's holding me because my knees go weak. My right hand rests against his chest while my left curls around his bicep. A soft, quiet moan leaves my throat, giving him the encouragement he was looking for because I feel his tongue softly lick my bottom lip. I open my mouth, hoping to give him more encouragement to continue exploring inside.

He does.

Softly at first, then with authority, his tongue strokes mine, setting a speed and rhythm for me to follow. I easily comply, my eyes rolling to the back of my head when he nips at my bottom lip.

When he starts to pull away, he gives my lips two small final kisses before removing his hands from my hair, gently brushing it back in place.

It takes a moment for me to open my eyes, and when I do, he's still close enough that I can feel his breath when he speaks.

"I lied earlier. Stopping right then was the hardest thing I've ever had to do," he says, his voice a little rough.

I nod, my lips still slightly parted, silently begging for him to touch them again.

Instead, he turns and walks to his car. "Lock the door as soon as you're inside."

As soon as he's gone, I do as he said. Resting my body against the door, I bring my fingers to my lips. They're still wet.

I push off the door and make my way to the kitchen, taking the box of flower brownies with me. Even though I'm still full from our dinner, after that kiss, I have an overwhelming need to do something to keep my mouth busy. The tingling of my lips, the taste he left on my tongue is enough to drive me mad. I need to do something and quick.

I march into the kitchen and rip open the brownie box shoving an entire piece into my mouth. Too large, crumbs are falling out as I chew, landing on the table but I don't care. It's not the fulfillment I craved, but for now, it will have to do.

chapter 16

I FEEL THE gentle rocking of the water swaying me from left to right as I sit in the tiny row boat, the sounds of the waves soothingly hitting the wooden sides, the soft breeze blowing through my hair. The crispness in the air tells me it's fall, but I'm not cold. I open my eyes and know exactly where I am. No other row boats are floating near me, no one is walking along the path near the shore, there are no ducks paddling around.

I could never forget this day. I remember Ben bringing us out here on a slightly warmer than usual day in November. Walking up to the small rented rowboat tied to a metal pole sticking out of the ground, I thought he was crazy. We were on the cusp of winter and he wanted us to get in the boat and float along the frigid water. He insisted we were dressed sufficiently, my UGG boots and jacket warm enough to protect me from the cold breeze.

I told him it would take less than a minute for the weight to pull me down to the bottom of the lake should I fall in, but he was relentless.

I promised him we could come back in the spring.

He told me to live a little.

Lifting me and placing me in the boat, Ben pushed us off the shore, taking the oars and rowing us out into the open water. It really was a beautiful day. The sun was shining and its rays fought to warm my face. Looking around, I noticed we were the only ones out on the water, which really shouldn't have surprised me considering the time of year. All boats had been docked and put away until next season. I didn't even think about why there was still this one lone boat attached to the marina. I should have seen the signs, but I didn't. I thought nothing of the fact that Ben seemed to know exactly where he was going. He wasn't just rowing along with the current. He was heading somewhere—with purpose.

He rowed us towards a small creek that broke off from the lake. After a few minutes, the creek cleared into a little pond where water lilies, un-plagued by the frost, still floated around. The harsh cold nights had yet to kill them. Did he know this was here? He simply shrugged when I asked and gave me a crooked smile.

"It's like a scene out of The Notebook," I told him, a movie I had made him watch many times. He knew it just as well as I did. He looked at me and gave a shy smile.

It was that smile, that look he gave me, that told me everything. Told me exactly what was about to happen. An expression of love and nervousness overtook his face. My life was about to change.

I wish I could remember the exact words he said. Words describing how he felt the minute he first watched me cross the street. Ones expressing how he knew I was special after our first date. Words about the moment he knew he was in love with me, promises that he would love me every day for the rest of his life. But there were only four words I truly remember him saying.

"Will you marry me?"

I lift my face to the sky and feel rays of warmth hitting my cheeks. I smile, sensing I'm no longer alone. Bringing my face back down, I look straight ahead.

"This was a good day," I tell Ben, looking into his eyes.

His smile mimics mine. He's also thinking back to this moment, to the life we planned together that day.

"Yes, it was," he agrees.

Ben takes the oars and starts to softly and slowly row us around the pond. His smile gradually starts to disappear, a look of longing creeping up with every row. Something doesn't feel right. A darkness has set in over us, dark clouds now hiding the sun.

I look over at Ben, his expression void of any of the happiness we felt that day. I want desperately for that smile to come back, for that look of pure affection he reserves only for me to show up on his face.

Ben exhales, releasing the oars and leaves us adrift. "Sometimes plans don't work out how we want."

A lump forms in my throat, making it hard to swallow. I try taking a few calming breaths to ease my anxiousness, but they're too broken to help.

"It's not fair," I whisper.

Ben's eyes fill with sadness. He reaches over, taking my hands in his and bringing them up to his lips. He blows hot air into them, warming them even though they're not cold.

"No, it's not," he answers, looking up at me. He kisses the top of each hand before releasing them and starts to row again.

Usually our meetings are full of hugs, kisses and laughter. This dream has a different feeling to it completely. One I'm not comfortable with. Perhaps it has to do with being in a place that reminds us so much of a future that was stolen from us. A realization that we will never have the happily ever after that he promised me years ago.

A small fear wakes up inside of me, wondering if it has to do with something entirely different. Someone entirely different.

"This was the best day of my life," I tell him, hoping that if we concentrate on this day and this day alone, the reality of what was happening beyond us won't surface.

Ben's eyes momentarily light up. "That's quite the compliment."

"I mean it. It was perfect. From the location to the words, even though I can't remember them all, my heart does. And I'd be happy to relive this moment with you over and over again," I tell him.

He looks proud to hear this, as though he just got confirmation that everything he did that day was everything I could have ever hoped for.

"Well, I couldn't have done it without you," he says, winking.

Shaking my head, I laugh. "You're right! You should actually be thanking me!"

"Don't pat your back too hard," he says, raising his hands as if to calm me down. "You already said I was perfect. No need to say anymore."

"Just as long as your head doesn't explode from ego or anything," I joke.

"Mine? No way!" He smiles.

After a few seconds, his demeanor changes once again. Gone is the cocky grin. In its place is a look of hope. His focus turns to me and I can see he's putting all joking aside.

"Maybe you could tell me about another great moment you've had," he says.

I squint, pulling my head back in confusion. "What do you mean? Another time you were perfect? Wow, you're really fishing for compliments," I say, poking fun, attempting to bring back his smile even though I know it won't work.

He looks down for a moment, brushing his hands against

his jean-clad legs. When he looks back up, his face is serious. "No. I mean a good moment since I've been gone."

His request surprises me, and it must be evident on my face because his expression switches again to worry, like he's afraid he's offended me. The thought of discussing what life has been like without him unsettles me. These are not the kind of things we talk about. We do not discuss him being gone. We do not discuss happy times, if any, since he's been gone. We do not discuss life outside this little bubble. When we're here, we ignore everything else and simply exist together.

"There haven't been any," I reply, almost rudely.

"That can't be true," he says, almost sounding disappointed.

"Well, it is," I snap.

I'm angry he's asking. Because I know he's right. I can feel myself getting defensive and it fuels my insecurities, my guilt. I have had great moments. Several, actually. And having them pointed out to me like this makes them feel like betrayal.

His shoulders slump and he looks off to the side. I feel bad for snapping at him, but guilt has an ugly way of showing itself. But really, what does he expect? What is he wanting to hear? Is he looking for me to admit to something? Is he asking if I've found someone to replace him already? Is he angry? Hurt? Upset? These questions come rushing through my mind and all I can come up with is that this *is not what we talk about when we meet.*

"What are you doing?" I accuse him softly.

He looks back over at me, the same accusatory tone in his voice. "What are you *doing?"*

"I'm trying to have a nice conversation. To reminisce and feel close to you. To remember our life together. That's what I'm *trying to do." I close my eyes and take a deep breath. "I don't want to argue with you. I want to enjoy our time together before I wake up."*

Ben leans in closer to me and cups his hands on either side of my face. His eyes roam over me before he presses his mouth to mine. His lips are soft but his kiss is forceful. It only lasts a few seconds before he pulls away.

"Exactly," he says. He's still close. Close enough that I can feel his breath against my face when he speaks. "This is all a dream. I won't be there when you wake up. I won't be there when you fall asleep. I won't be there for any more of your perfect moments."

Every syllable that just came out of his mouth feels like a punch to the chest. My heart breaks with every word. I push away from him, breaking our contact. His hands are still hanging in the air, elbows resting on his thighs.

"Stop!" I plead, raising my hand in warning. "Stop what you're doing."

"Maybe you need to stop. It's okay, Rach. I want you to have great moments. More than that, I want you to have great days! These dreams? They're just getting in the way of—"

"Don't say it! Don't you dare say it!" I nearly yell, interrupting him. I hate how immature I sound right now, but I have no clue how to stop this conversation from going somewhere I'm not ready for it to go. "I won't listen to this!"

"Rachel, we need to talk about this."

"No! No, we don't!" I argue. "I won't listen to you try and break up with me!"

"Break up with you?" he repeats, dismayed.

I try to keep my voice steady, but my breathing has become harsh and fast. I'm panicking. My eyes jump around from tree to tree, from water lily to water lily. I'm looking for a way out, an escape.

I look back at Ben, his face pleading with me to talk to him. But I can't. Not right now. I shut my eyes tight. I'm not ready for this confrontation. I'm not ready to face my confessions. I'm not ready for whatever it is Ben is looking for us to have.

"Wake up, Rachel!" I hiss at myself.

"Rach, don't do this," Ben pleads, his voice begging me to stay. I try to ignore him as much as I can.

"Wake up! Wake up, wake up, wake up!" I repeat over and over.

"We are *going to have to talk about this," he tries once again, but his voice is beginning to fade.*

I take one long deep breath before I open my eyes and look Ben straight in the eye. I open my mouth and say as fiercely yet as calmly as I can. "Wake. Up. Rachel."

chapter 17

"THERE'S A RULE written somewhere that forbids visitors from showing up at someone's door at seven thirty on a Sunday morning."

Tess's hair is a mess, and the silk robe she's haphazardly tying looks like it's the only thing she has on. I know it's early, but I've been up since five, unable to fall back asleep.

I offer her the cup of coffee I brought, bribing her to let me in. Taking a seat on her couch, I take off my sunglasses. Tess pulls the coffee cup away from her face, immediately concerned.

"What happened?"

My red and puffy eyes must not have cleared on the way over.

I woke up from my dream, my pillow darkened with tear spots. Before last night, I can't even remember the last time Ben and I argued. It was most likely over something stupid like me needing to pick up my clothes from the floor. But never once did one of our arguments leave me feeling like this, leave my heart feeling battered and bruised. The worst part, I have no idea when

I'll be able to fix it.

Keeping secrets from Ben has never been a part of our relationship. I always told him everything. Now it feels like that's all I'm doing. Keeping secrets from Ben. From Jax. I'm keeping parts of my life hidden from everyone around me. Truths I'm barely able to admit to myself.

"I had a bad night," I tell her, taking a long sip from my own coffee cup.

Tess looks me over before raising her hand and lifting a finger, asking me to give her a minute. She heads back into her bedroom where I hear voices.

Shit.

She's not alone.

Before I can get up to leave, feeling awful for just barging in like this, hurried footsteps are making their way down the hall. First I see Paul, followed by Tess who seems to be pushing him to move faster.

"All right, I'm going!"

Paul is fastening the belt of his pants and his shirt is slung over his shoulder. He sees me sitting on the couch and stops abruptly.

"What the fuck? What happened?" He starts to come around the couch when Tess grabs him by the arm and veers him back towards the door.

"Oh no! You need to go. We obviously need some girl time."

Paul's eyes dart from me to Tess several times before he points his finger at me. "If he did something to hurt you—"

Oh no!

I'm up off the couch in less than a second. "No! It's not like that! Really. Tess is right. I just needed a little girl time."

He looks at me with skepticism. The idea that anyone would think Jax has been anything but a gentleman crushes me.

"Really," I reiterate.

Paul watches me for a few more seconds, debating on whether he believes me before he finally nods once. He slips his t-shirt over his head and moves to the door, shoving his feet into his shoes.

"Call if you need me." He looks over at me before Tess gives him a kiss on the cheek and a final push out the door.

When she comes back over to the couch, she grabs the coffee cup from the side table and sits down beside me. "Okay, he's gone. What happened?"

"I'm am so sorry! I don't know why I thought it would be okay to just show up here like that. I should have called or at least waited until the sun was fully up. I've totally ruined your night. And morning."

Tess brushes the apology off, not at all interested in hearing it. "I'm not worried about that. I'm worried that your eyes look like they've been stung by a couple of hornets. What happened? Was it awful?"

I shake my head slowly. I can feel tears starting to pool in my eyes again. "No," I say, taking a deep breath. "It was amazing."

Tess looks confused. "Okay?"

"He was a perfect gentleman. I had a great night and I didn't want it to end. He took me to Notte." I hear the slightest gasp come from Tess, her eyes opening wide with envy. "We talked about a lot of things." I don't feel right divulging Jax's personal business, so I skip ahead a bit. "He made me laugh. I felt special." And I did. He made me feel like I was the only girl in that restaurant. "He kissed me," I add. "Like, *really* kissed me. And I *really* liked it."

Tess is waiting for more, to understand the reason for my tears. Her head shifts to the side, impatient. "I think I'm going to need a little more info here."

"When he kissed me, I thought, *finally,*" I say softly. "When he got in his car to leave, I was counting down until I could see him again."

"So far this is sounding pretty fucking good," Tess says.

I take a minute to gather my thoughts. I can't tell Tess about my dreams of Ben. I can't tell anyone about that. They'll just tell me my conversations with him aren't real, that it's just my subconscious helping me deal with his death. They can't possibly understand how real they feel, how they keep Ben alive.

"I still wear his t-shirts to bed," I tell her. It's not to the extent of admitting how far my connection with Ben still goes, but it's something. "I wrap myself up in what I have left of him, because I can't let him go. I don't *want* to let him go. How can I feel like that then turn around and want to kiss another man?" I feel more tears fall down my face.

"And the worst part," I cry, "is I keep waiting for it to feel more wrong than it does. When I'm with Jax, it's like nothing else matters. It's just me and him. What should have been doesn't exist anymore." I look at Tess, realizing what my true fear is. "What if one day Ben won't exist anymore?"

"That will never happen," she insists. "He will always exist to you, to me, to anyone who knew him. That will never change."

"It feels like I'm cheating," I confess.

I watch Tess put her coffee down on the table and turn back to me. "Have you talked to Dr. Embry about this?"

I look at her and nearly roll my eyes.

"Okay, what about Jax?"

I bark out a small laugh. "Yes, because I'm sure that's what every guy wants to hear. The devotion and love I have for another man."

Tess doesn't seem to agree. "You might be surprised. Maybe you're feeling this way because you're not talking about it at all. You don't have to keep Ben a secret from Jax. You *shouldn't* have to."

I wouldn't even know where to begin telling Jax about Ben.

How do you tell a man that although you think about him all day, you dream of another at night?

"Is it too soon?" I ask, hoping she has the answer. "Too soon to feel like this again?"

Tess takes one of my hands in hers, squeezing it gently. "Rach, it isn't that soon. Ben's been gone for a while now."

I shake my head, disagreeing. "It doesn't feel that way." I take two long staggering breaths before I continue. "Sometimes it feels like I was just with him," I say quietly.

And I was. One minute we're together in a boat, the next, I'm waking up in my bed. Alone. I hate to admit it, but having my realities switch on me so often is beginning to weigh me down.

"Sometimes it feels like this isn't my life. That this is all some weird experiment to see if I go crazy. Am I going crazy?" I ask, half of me joking, the other seriously wondering the possibility.

Is it crazy to chase after a ghost while being caught up by someone very real?

"No, you aren't going crazy. Crazy would be showing up at six thirty in the morning to unleash all your emotional drama." She smiles, wiping the trail of tears off my face with the sleeve of her robe.

I laugh a good, much needed laugh. "I guess I'm safe then. Thank you," I say between breaths.

"Anytime." She picks up her coffee cup and looks around. "Eight in the morning and you didn't even bring donuts?"

THE CAR RIDE home is spent going over my conversation with Tess. I know I haven't been very forthcoming about my past to Jax, but he hasn't actually asked about it either. After last night and hearing him be so open about his past, keeping mine quiet seems...wrong. I go back and forth wondering if I should broach the subject. What *would* I say? What *should* I say? What *shouldn't* I say?

Most people don't begin a relationship as a threesome. How could anyone be okay with that? How could I expect Jax to be okay with that?

The sound of my phone ringing as I pull into my driveway tears me away from my thoughts. It's early for anyone to be calling. I search my bag, trying to find my phone before voicemail picks up. Finally getting hold of it, I slide my finger across the screen, seeing the name that has taken up half of my thoughts this morning.

"Hi," I answer, determined to sound normal.

"Morning." His voice is ridiculously smooth, not at all like mine. "I didn't wake you, did I?"

"No, not at all."

There is no way I'm letting him know how long I've been awake thinking about him. I take a quick glance down at the time and see it is only eight thirty. "Someone's an early riser."

I hear him chuckle on the other end. "Sometimes. And only if I have something important to do."

"Oh?" I grab my purse and make my way to my front door, careful not to make too much noise. "And is there something important you need to do?"

"Very," he says, his voice switching to playful.

I make my way inside, depositing my purse on the inside table, and sit on the couch. "And what would that be?"

"I had a very important call to make, and it couldn't wait any longer. There's this woman and I need to see her again. As soon as possible. For breakfast. It's very important," he reiterates.

"I see. And to be clear, we're talking about me right?" I ask.

I hear him laugh and already I know it's the best thing I'll hear all day. "Yes, I'm talking about you."

"Another date not even twelve hours later? You know

you're failing at the three days rule."

"I like to keep you on your toes," he says. "But I do have an ulterior motive."

"Oh?"

"Yes. I found out late last night my trip had to be bumped up. I'm leaving tomorrow morning, and I'd like to see you before then."

I had almost forgotten about his business trip and now hearing that he's leaving tomorrow twists my stomach in knots. "Well, that…sucks."

"It would really suck if I couldn't see you today. So, how about it? You, me, some coffee?"

Simply knowing I won't be able to see him for a week is enough of a reason. "I do love coffee," I say, agreeing to meet.

We make quick plans to meet in the park, I'd bring the coffee and he'd bring the bagels. I quickly jump in the shower and spend more time than I'm willing to admit trying to look casual for a coffee date in the park.

I EASILY SPOT Jax sitting on a bench, a paper bag beside him. He's dressed in jeans, white street shoes and a hooded sweatshirt. It looks as though he hasn't shaved because he has the perfect amount of stubble growing across his face. When he sees me walking up, he smiles, standing as I approach.

"Good morning."

He presses a soft kiss on my cheek, his overgrown facial hair lightly scratching me. I want him to do it again on the other side.

He takes one of the coffee cups from my hands, leading me to a spot on the bench. Taking a seat beside me, he opens the paper bag, handing me a toasted bagel with cream cheese.

"I'm glad we could do this," he says, taking a sip of his coffee.

"I'm glad you didn't wait the three days," I smile.

Cocking his head, he winks. "No chance. That's a ridiculous rule followed by idiots who haven't yet realized that being around a beautiful woman is much better than not." The corner of his lip lifts, almost unnoticeably. "I'd much rather spend every minute with you."

My head spins. "You make me dizzy," I admit, immediately embarrassed.

His eyes move slowly over my face, my breath catching with every slow blink. "I hope I make you feel a lot of things."

I nod slowly, letting him know he does. His turned up lip stretches into a gratified smile before shifting his attention to the morning joggers running by.

"How long will you be gone again?" I ask, missing him already.

"About a week, hopefully not longer than that."

I nod a few times and look away, mentally circling what day he'd be flying back. I feel his hand brush against mine before completely encircling it with his. He stands, pulling me up with him.

"Let's walk."

We start along the path, the petals from the magnolia flowers covering the cemented ground beneath us. Another season of their bloom now passed. A reminder that time refuses to slow down or even stop—no matter how much you may want it to.

We continue along the path, thoughts about how I had once envisioned my life and how different it's turned out. I worry about how comfortable I'm becoming with it. How painless Jax can make it. How easy it is for me to forget.

"I was supposed I'd be married by now," I blurt out. Not exactly subtle, but then again, I've never been good at thinking before I speak.

"Maybe with a baby," I continue. "I always pictured myself with children. A few years ago, I thought I knew exactly what my future looked like." I stop walking and look at him. "It didn't look like this."

A cautious look creeps up along his face. When I don't say more, he squeezes my hand and keeps us moving forward along the path. Slowly, he lifts our joined hands and my knuckles are swept against his lips. I can feel his lips move against my skin as he quietly speaks.

"A few years ago, I had a really hard time picturing what my future would look like. I knew what I wanted, what I needed to start looking for, but the images were blurry." He looks up from my hands, his thumb brushing over where his lips just left their mark. "They don't seem so blurry anymore."

With every word, every careful mention of a hopeful future, I feel it happen. Like a force pushing us closer together, I understand it now. I'm falling for him and he's falling for me. I should be terrified. A part of me is, I think. But not because I'm falling for him. I'm terrified he'll stop once he knows about Ben.

"Why haven't you asked about my past?" I ask. His face tilts to the side, surprised at my question. "We've talked about yours. You've never asked me about mine."

He opens his mouth, about to answer, then closes it again. I watch his face as he doesn't think of what to say, but how to say it. After a minute, he finally answers.

"I've been waiting for you to be ready, for you to want to talk about it."

I hear the sympathy in his voice, the pitying look I've become accustomed to receiving. I realize then he already knows.

"Who told you?" I ask him quietly, looking down at the ground.

He takes a deep breath. I see his chest move up and down out of the corner of my eye. He takes both our empty coffee cups and deposits them in the waste bin, evading answering as long as possible. When he walks back to me, he looks more prepared to answer.

"The night we met at the bar, after you went home, Tess came back around looking for you. I told her you left, but I asked her about you. I was interested. She mentioned something about not having gone out in a while. I inquired."

Heat rushes to my face. I'm not embarrassed that he knows about my past. It's the pitying look he's giving me, the slight change of tone in his voice—everything I hoped never to see and hear from him. Everything I did my best to avoid.

And I'm angry. I'm angry that Tess never thought to tell me that Jax knew. Never thought to mention her little conversation with him. No wonder she thought talking to him would help. She had already laid the groundwork for me.

"I don't know what to say," I whisper, unsure of how I should react.

I feel Jax's fingers grab my chin, lightly lifting my face to his. "You don't need to say anything. Not now. Not if you aren't ready." He takes another deep breath. "I don't want you to feel pressured to tell me things you aren't ready to tell. We can go at your speed."

His eyes are considerate, his tone cautious.

"I don't know if that's fair."

"Why don't you let me be the judge of that?"

It seems so unfair to let him base his decision off a half truth. Yes, he may know about Ben. He may know Ben died. But he has no idea how alive Ben still is to me. I should tell him the truth. Let him know how crazy it is to fall for me. But I say nothing. The words don't form, the sounds don't leave my mouth. All because I'm selfish. I want Jax too much. My feelings for him have grown so strong that losing him would devastate me. I should have stopped this months ago, but I didn't. I couldn't. I was powerless against him then, even more so now. We are so close, our bodies having moved together without me even noticing. I raise one hand and rest it on his chest. I lift up on my toes and wait for him to bring his lips to mine.

When he does, I open my mouth, inviting him in. Pulling him into my mess, my confusion, my heart. I feel his tongue sweep across my lower lip before it meets mine. His hands come around me, resting on my hips, pulling me even closer. I feel the hardness of his chest as it crushes against my breasts. His grip on my hips gets tighter while my hand bunches the material of his sweater, pulling him closer still. He lightly nips at me and I let out a little moan. The sound must be encouraging because he does it again.

I sense nothing else around me but the feeling of his hands, his lips and the sounds of his breath. All my previous worry leaves me, that quickly, with just a simple kiss. It scares me how easily he can do that. It worries me that I still haven't been able to be completely truthful with him.

When he pulls away, I'm nervous to open my eyes. Nervous he'll see how exposed I am, the secrets I still keep.

"I'm scared I don't have enough left to give you," I confess.

He presses his lips to my forehead. This time it feels much more intimate than it did after our date.

"Don't be," he whispers against my skin. "I just felt you give me everything."

I open my eyes and look up at him, our breathing synchronized. His hands have found their way under my shirt, his fingers leaving their mark on my skin, just above my hips. I am completely lost in him.

"You are so beautiful," he says.

Then his lips are back on mine. Softer this time, without really moving. Our lips just stay folded into one another. We stay wrapped together for a few more heartbeats before we hear the sounds of young laughter. Breaking apart, we both turn our heads towards the noise.

Two young girls—sisters, I assume—are giggling and covering their eyes.

Both Jax and I start to laugh.

"Looks like we gathered an audience," he says.

He removes his hands from my hips, taking one of mine and leads us along the path once again.

As we pass the two little girls, Jax bows his head and smiles. "Ladies."

The girls start to giggle again and it makes us both laugh.

"I'll miss you while you're gone," I tell him.

He looks down at me and smiles. "I know."

"SOUNDS LIKE YOU'VE progressed in your relationship," Dr. Embry states. "How do you feel about that?"

How do I feel about that?

I think about it, running it over in my head several times.

How do I feel *about that?*

How do I feel *about that?*

Truth is: I feel everything—the good, the bad, everything in between.

Jax has been in London for three days. Three days since I've heard his voice. Three days since I've seen his smile, felt his kiss. Three days of missing someone more than I anticipated.

Truthfully, it hasn't been complete silence between us. He's sent me a few texts—one not long after he landed. It was a picture of a welcome sign from the airport. I hadn't realized how much I was waiting to hear from him until I woke up the morning after he left with my phone still in hand, having fallen asleep with it the night before.

He has no idea how much I look forward to his texts. They're little reminders that he's been thinking of me too. My favorite so far is a picture he sent from Buckingham Palace. He's standing beside the Queen's Guard, mimicking his stance. He must have been coming from a business meeting because he's dressed in a suit. I couldn't stop laughing at the caption he sent with it.

Didn't even blink. Bloody brilliant.

I've never hated time zones more than over the last seventy-two hours. They make communicating with him extremely hard. Between the time change and his busy schedule, those short messages back and forth are all we've had.

So when Dr. Embry asks how I feel about my relationship with Jax progressing, my answer is as confusing as my feelings.

"Sadly, happy."

Her eyes narrow. "Care to expand?"

I take a breath and look out one of her office windows. It's a beautiful day outside. The sun is shining, there are no clouds in the sky. It's the perfect beginning of a summer day. And as they do so often, my thoughts instinctively drift to London, wondering what the weather is like there.

"I didn't think I would miss him this much," I say.

"Starting a new relationship can be equally exciting as it can be scary. You've been through a lot in the last two years. More than most. It's expected and natural to feel confused."

"I think a part of me was hoping I wouldn't. That it would make things easier."

"Easier how?"

I shrug. "If I didn't miss him, I'd know the feelings I was having weren't as real as I believed. A small trick my mind was playing on me. A deflection. Assurance that no one was taking Ben's place."

"And now? Knowing that your feelings are real?"

"Every thought I have about Jax, it's one less I have about

Ben." I look down at my hands, ashamed. Ashamed of the truth, at the relief of not having to think about Ben all the time. "The guilt is…overwhelming."

"Why should you feel guilty about that?" she asks. "Life has to move on for everyone—including you."

I snort. "Then why do I look for things around the house that purposely remind me of Ben? I'll pull an old t-shirt out or open my jewelry box and stare at my engagement ring for an hour. Why do I tell myself there will never be another like him?"

I haven't had another dream since willing myself to wake up from the last one. That in itself scares me—that I could purposely choose to leave Ben. What if my dreams don't come back? What if that was the last one? What if I can never tell him I'm sorry and promise that no one will ever replace him?

"There won't be. Yours and Ben's story is unique. You shouldn't look to replace it," she starts. "But it sounds like you are trying to live two separate lives instead of finding a way to balance one. Grieving is a difficult process and is different for everyone. Letting go is always the hardest part, but it doesn't mean you forget Ben or the memories and love you both shared. The goal you should look to achieve, Rachel, is for your loss to be part of your life—not the center of it. Keeping Ben's memory somewhere safe and protected in your heart but leaving enough room for something more to come. It's up to you to let that happen. Otherwise, you'll be in a constant battle. You have to choose how you want to live the rest of your life."

How can I possibly choose? It's an impossible choice. How can I let go of someone I've been trying so hard to keep? How can I keep him if it could cost me everything I've just found? How am I supposed to leave one behind?

"I KNOW YOU'RE ignoring me. Explain."

I look up from my laptop to see Tess standing in the doorway of my office, arms crossed and apparently angry. I find this amusing considering I think I reserve that right. Going behind my back and telling Jax my private business two minutes after meeting him seems good enough reason to be less than thrilled with her.

I watch her make her way over to the chair, sit and stare at me. She crosses one leg over the other and resumes folding her arms over her chest. She raises her eyebrows, waiting for an explanation.

"You told Jax about Ben." No point in beating around the bush.

Her eyebrows drop and her eyes narrow into small slits. After a moment, she nods once. "Yes, I did."

I'm waiting for an apology to follow, but it doesn't come.

"That wasn't your place, Tess."

I stay calm because I know deep down that she would never intentionally go behind my back to hurt me. But still, it was my story to tell and tell it when I was ready.

She re-crosses her legs and straightens her posture.

"I didn't give any details. After you left, he asked me about you. He assumed you were coming off a breakup and that's why you hadn't been out in a while. I corrected him. Let him know you lost someone. I thought I was protecting you. When Sophie told me you went home, I thought maybe I put you in a position you weren't ready for. I felt terrible for it. So I figured I was doing you a favor. He didn't push to hear more. Didn't ask for details. All he said was 'I hope she had fun tonight' and then left with Dylan. Whatever has happened between the two of you since has nothing to do with me or anything I said and everything to do with you."

She sits there glaring, daring me to argue.

Pinpricks of reality come across my arms like a physical reminder that what she said is true. What's happened between Jax and me has been my own doing. I agreed to his offer of us becoming friends. I agreed to that first motorcycle ride. I didn't pull away the first time he really took my hand. I fell for him all on my own. I blink several times before I look back down at my laptop.

"You still shouldn't have said anything," I mumble.

In my peripheral vision, I see Tess stand and come around to my side, wrapping her arms around my shoulders.

"Don't be mad. Besides, we both know you can't stay angry with me."

I look up at her, knowing she's right.

She simply smiles before moving back to her chair. My phone vibrates beside me on my desk, and I immediately pick it up. It's an email notification that my flower order has been processed. My disappointment must be evident because I hear Tess begin to laugh.

"How many times do you do that a day?"

I put my phone down. "More than I care to admit."

"Has he messaged you since he's been away?"

I nod, finding the picture of him with the Queens Guard, showing Tess.

She shakes her head. "God, he's gorgeous."

I take the phone back, afraid she'll lick the screen.

"I know," I say, a little defeated.

"When does he come back?"

"Friday night."

I put my phone away, trying to succumb to the out of sight out of mind mentality. It hasn't worked yet.

"Let's talk about something else. I need the distraction. Talk to me about you and Paul? Still pushing him out the door at seven a.m.?"

Her face changes. Her eyes light up at the mention of Paul.

"Is someone *in love*?" I tease.

She rolls her eyes. "Don't be gross," she snarls. "Something…weird happened the other day."

I raise my eyebrows. "Weird? If this is a sex thing, I'm not sure I want to hear it."

She leans back in her chair.

"A few days ago, we made plans to go for dinner. I was stuck in a meeting so he offered to meet me at work. He waited while I got a few things sorted. Anyways," she waves her hands, "remember Caleb?"

I shake my head.

"Caleb! You know, Cunny Caleb—the model with the name to match?"

Oh, yes. Cunny Caleb. Now I remember. He worked on a few segments for the station modeling menswear. He and Tess had a fling. A few flings, I think.

"Well, he was at the station and came over to say hi. He started flirting a bit, and I stopped him right away, but I think Paul kind of got pissed. I was honest, let him know that Caleb was someone I used to see, but that's all. He stayed pretty quiet most of the night and later when we fucked, it was hard. Don't get me wrong, I liked it," she grins, "but it kind of felt like he was anger fucking me."

Even though Paul and I are pretty close, I don't have much knowledge about his past relationships. I only ever heard what Ben would tell me and rarely did he ever mention anyone specific. I figured he was never looking for anything serious.

"I'm sure it's nothing. Like you've said before, men get possessive. I bet that's all it was."

"Maybe. I hope so. Because you're right. About what you said before." Her voice trails, and I watch her squirm uncomfortably in her seat, embarrassed.

My cheeks hurt from my wide grin. "You're in love!"

Acting unimpressed, she sinks into her chair. "Let's just calm down a little, okay? It's not a big deal."

"Of course it is!" Now it's my turn to come around and give her a hug. "It's a huge deal."

"Yeah, yeah," she scoffs. "It's not like we said it to one another or anything."

I know she's acting aloof about this on the outside but on the inside, I know she's probably panicking. This is all very new to her.

"Let's go for a drink. Right now. I'll finish up here and you can tell me all about it. The moment you knew, how you felt…"

Tess laughs. "That sounds more like *you*."

But I know she wants to when she stands and gathers her belongings. We head out as soon as I close up, because it's not just when you're sad that you drink and eat chocolate. You also do it when your best friend realizes they're in love for the first time.

IT'S AFTER ELEVEN by the time I get home. One drink turned into three, and one dessert turned into a tasting table of multiple dishes. Feeling a little tipsy, all I want is to put on my pj's and get some sleep. After washing my face and brushing my teeth, I fall into bed, closing my eyes, exhausted.

The instant I hear my cell start to ring, my eyes fly open and I'm stumbling to find my phone. I see an international number flash across my screen.

"Hi." I smile into the phone.

"I'm hoping by the way you sound, you knew it was me," Jax says, his tone playful.

"Well, it was either you or Prince Harry. I would have been happy either way."

The earlier drinks must have had a bigger effect than I originally thought. The only other time I can remember openly flirting with Jax was at Vice—after several cocktails.

I hear Jax laugh on the other end. "I'm glad to hear it. I didn't wake you, did I?"

"No, I just got in."

"I go out of town and party Rachel comes out to play?" he teases.

I snuggle deeper into my bed, smiling at his banter.

"Yes. Party Rachel was out stuffing her face in desserts and martini's with Tess. I think I may be a little drunk." I bring my duvet up under my chin and turn on my side, hugging the phone between my ear and pillow.

"Drunk Rachel is my favorite," he says, taunting me. He sounds so sexy.

"How's the trip so far?" I ask, calming my breaths.

"Successful but not nearly as much fun as you seem to be having." I hear him laugh then try to stifle a yawn. I imagine him lying in his hotel bed. I wonder briefly what he's wearing, if he sleeps in his underwear or…nothing at all. The thought sends a wave of pleasure down below my belly button. The sensation surprises me a bit.

"How can that be? You're in London!" I say a little breathless, readjusting myself on the bed.

"Yes but I'm in meetings all day. Even my evenings are all full of business. Today is the first day I have a few hours to myself. Maybe I'll be able to find that English souvenir I promised."

"Harry?" I ask, giggling.

I hear Jax tsk. "Not a chance. I'd much rather you be waiting for me to come home than that ginger."

I stop giggling and smile shyly into the phone. "I'm waiting," I say softly.

"Good," his voice husky. "You sound tired."

I glance down at the phone in my hand and see it's nearing midnight. "What time is it there?"

"Almost six."

"Do you have an early meeting?"

"Yes. A conference call with a brunette. This is the only time I could catch her."

I feel a rush at the realization that Jax woke up early so that he could call me.

"You caught me," I say quietly.

He's silent for a moment, both of us hearing the double meaning in what I've said. I let my words linger between us, images of him in bed coming back to my mind. Without realizing, my hands move upwards to my breasts, my nipples having become hard.

"Tell me you aren't busy Saturday night," he asks. There's a sense of need in his voice.

"I'm not busy."

"Come to my house. Let me cook for you."

"You cook?"

"I'll try," he says.

My hand circles to my other breast, the thought of seeing him exciting me. I hate that tomorrow is only Thursday.

"Okay."

"Good," he sounds pleased. "Now get some sleep. Good night, Rachel."

"Good morning, Jackson," I whisper back.

After I hang up, I slump further down in the bed, restless. My mind is hazy from the cocktails, but my body is on high alert. I feel flushed, heat radiating off me. I know there is only one way I'll be able to fall asleep. Only one way my body will relax.

A release.

My hand slips into my pajama bottoms, toying with the hem of my panties. As soon as my fingers fall beyond the thin layer of fabric and make their way underneath, I'm not surprised at what I find—what the sound of Jax's voice has done to me. Wetness covers my fingers and I'm already incredibly sensitive to my own touch.

After living alone for two years, I've gotten myself off often enough. This time is different. This time feels new. This time, when my eyes close and I circle my most sensitive spot, I picture gray-blue eyes, sexy dimples and the voice from the phone whispering my name. I picture him in his bed in London, thinking of me, maybe doing the same thing.

And I come hard, keeping my eyes closed so I can keep that image in my mind just a little longer.

As soon as my body starts to come down and relax, my arms come up and rest above my head on my pillow. My breathing is slowing and my legs begin to feel heavy. The earlier exhaustion I felt is slowly creeping back upon me. I fall asleep easily after that and don't wake until morning.

chapter 19

WALKING THROUGH THE lobby of Jax's condo building, I notice the same security guard sitting at the concierge desk as last time. He smiles kindly.

"Good evening, Miss Miller. Mr. Perry is expecting you."

I smile but my focus is quickly brought back to the elevators that will take me to the twenty-seventh floor—and the man who waits for me there.

These last few days have gone by at a snail's pace but now that I'm here, I wish I had a little more time to prepare, because after tonight, I know things will not be the same between us.

Tess's thoughts about what this night would bring only increased my nerves.

"Did you shave?" her voice came through on speaker as I finished applying my mascara.

"What?" I blinked so fast, nearly poking my eye out.

"Did you shave?" she repeated.

I thought back to an hour prior, in the shower, my razor in hand. "I'm wearing a dress. Of course I did."

"I'm not talking about your legs."

I continued to apply my mascara, refusing to answer.

"Yeah, that's what I thought. Explains the nerves."

"You're unbelievable," I said, shaking my head.

Tess laughed. "Tell me it's not true and I'll shut up right now."

I looked at myself in the mirror; makeup done, hair tied back in a messy bun. It took me twenty minutes to make it look like I spent no time on it. On the outside, I look self-assured and confident. It's my insides that are betraying me, my stomach tied in knots, my heart beating like it's trying to burst out of my chest.

Everything Tess said is true. Any argument I had was squashed by the extra fifteen minutes I spent in the shower making sure my body was completely buffed, shaved and ready. Being intimate with a man is not something I had seriously thought a lot about. Not until recently. Not until two nights ago.

It scares the hell out of me. What if there are some new trends that I haven't been made aware of? What if I've forgotten how to work a man? For years, I knew exactly what to do, how to do it and what felt good. I've been out of practice for nearly two years. A lot can change in two years.

"It's like riding a bike," Tess assured me.

Easy for her to say. The tires on her bike never stopped spinning.

As the elevator doors close and the floors light up as it climbs, I take a few deep breaths.

Maybe I'm getting ahead of myself. Maybe taking this relationship to the next level is not even something Jax has thought about. Maybe it's not even on his radar for tonight.

I have just enough time to roll my eyes at the thought before the doors open and I've arrived on his floor.

Knocking on his door, I can hear a small amount of shuffling before the sound of footsteps start making their way closer, getting louder with each step. It's been nearly a week since I've seen him, his flight from London only having arrived this afternoon. My nerves start to dissipate and excitement takes over at finally being able to lay my eyes on him again.

With one arm resting on his hip, the other holding the door open, is the man I've thought about over and over these last few days.

"Christ. It's good to see you," he says smiling. He opens the door wider, pulling me inside. Within seconds, his face is as close to mine as possible without actually touching me.

"Hi," he whispers.

"Hi," I whisper back, even more quietly.

We stand close, our eyes glued on one another. I impatiently wait for him to dip his head that extra inch closer, to place his lips on mine and show me he's missed me like I've missed him.

But he doesn't.

Instead, he winks and takes a step back, walking right past me into the kitchen. I can do nothing but follow him.

"It smells really good in here," I say, inhaling the aromas coming from the stove. I look over at the counter, cheeses and fruit are carefully arranged on a plate, and a bottle of wine sits right next to it.

Jax turns the burners off and rests against the counter, crossing his arms. Raising an eyebrow, he cocks a small grin.

"You say that like you're surprised."

I shake my head. "Not at all. Over the last few weeks, I've come to expect the unexpected from you."

His grin becomes wider, pleased with what he's heard. My eyes can't help but drift downwards, taking him in fully for the first time since walking into his home. Dressed in navy pants and a gray t-shirt, he looks perfectly relaxed.

Pushing away from the counter, he takes two steps towards me, both his arms reaching around me, caging me between the counter and his firm chest. Our bodies lightly brush, my breath catching on contact. I bring my hands in front of me, ready to rest them against his chest, desperate to feel him.

But before I have a chance, he steps back, wine bottle in one hand and plate in the other. He nods his head towards the two empty wine glasses, telling me to grab them as he makes his way into the living room.

That's twice he's done this now—teasing me by coming so close, only to back away within seconds.

Walking into the living room, it still seems pretty bare, but I can see small additions and changes he's made. Curtain panels have been put up by the large windows and a dark wood dining table with four chairs now sits by the fireplace, currently set for two. My eyes automatically move to the painting above the fireplace, still hanging beautifully over the mantel.

We sit on the couch as he pours the wine, handing me a glass. Lifting his, we softly clink them together.

"To you being home," I say.

"I'll drink to that," he says, smiling.

I take a small sip, thankful for something to coat my drying throat. I lean back against his couch, feeling a bit more relaxed.

"Tell me about London," I say, wanting to hear about his trip.

He lets out a small sigh. "Well, it was rainy and gray, and I spent most of the time in meetings. Business wise, it was great. Tourist wise, not so much."

"You've never been before?"

He shakes his head. "Strangely, no. Even during my years in Switzerland, I never made it over to London. I'd like to go back one day—when I'm not stuck in an office the entire time. There's so much to see," he says, strumming the head of his wine glass with his fingers. "I did have one afternoon where I was able to walk around a bit. Speaking of..." He raises a finger, resting his glass on the table.

He stands and walks towards his bedroom. I lean back over

the couch as far as I can and my eyes follow him until he's out of sight.

I hear him yell from his room. "I did say I'd bring you back something English!"

Seconds later, he walks back to where I'm sitting, his hands hidden behind his back. I sit up, shaking my head.

"You shouldn't have gotten me anything," I scorn.

"See what it is first," he teases.

From behind his back appears something large and black. When I realize what it is, I start to laugh.

Jax places the tall bearskin cap on my head and pulls the elastic band under my chin.

"How did this even fit in your suitcase?"

He leans back and examines me. "Not easily."

My arms have to extend all the way up just so I can feel the top of the cap. Doing my best to keep my face expressionless, I speak with what I'm sure is a horrible British accent.

"Do I look posh?"

He eyes my body up and down, slowly, unapologetically. "Very."

I smile shyly. "Thank you. I can honestly say this is unlike any present I've ever gotten before."

Jax smiles before reaching around behind the couch. "Well, I hope you can say the same about this."

He hands me a large shopping bag, the words BURBERRY LONDON neatly printed across.

"What's that?" I ask.

He laughs. "Your real present."

I take the shopping bag and lift out another protective cloth bag. Untying the knot, I pull out a gorgeous black leather handbag. The front and back are hard cased, but the side panels are a beautiful camel color with black hearts.

"I was once told a woman can never have too many handbags. I must admit, the sales lady helped pick it out. Do you like it?"

Do I like it? It's gorgeous! I've never owned a bag like this. I don't even want to think about how much it cost.

"It's beautiful," I say, turning it over in my hands. I probably shouldn't accept this, but my hands won't put the bag down.

"Good. I'm glad."

I look up, his face happy with my reaction.

"Are you sure this is for me? Maybe you meant to give this to someone else? Your mom maybe?" I say, my eyes moving back to admire the bag.

He chuckles and leans forward, taking my chin between his thumb and forefinger. Our eyes lock.

"Most definitely. It's for you."

I look down to his lips, my mind screaming for him to kiss me. He glances down at my mouth, and my heart starts to race with expectation. He sees it too, with the way I lick my lips, keeping them slightly parted.

Just then, the buzzer from the kitchen rings breaking our connection. He releases his hold on me.

"I hope you're hungry," he grins.

I watch him get up and walk to the kitchen. Frustrated, I get up and take our wine and glasses over to the table where a salad is already made and waiting.

"Need some help in there?" I call out to him.

"Sit down and prepare to be amazed," he says from the kitchen.

I take a seat, watching him move about the kitchen. My eyes follow his every step, even as he walks back to the table.

Set in front of us is a remarkable offering of roast chicken and summer vegetables.

Impressed, I look over at him. "You made all this?"

Amused guilt passes over his face. "It depends on what you mean by 'made.' If you meant 'did I pick this up and follow the reheating instructions' then yes, I made this."

I laugh. "It's the thought that counts."

"I wanted to make a good impression. I'm afraid my culinary skills lie with boxed macaroni and cheese," he says. When he looks back at me, his eyes become intense. "I figured tonight deserved better than that."

"I love macaroni and cheese," I whisper.

He smiles and it's so sexy. "Next time," he promises.

My earlier nerves and anxiousness disappear, only to be replaced by lust and want. I hope he sees that same intensity through my eyes, that they are communicating everything my lips won't say.

Yes, I understand what this evening means.

Yes, I've been thinking about you every minute you were away.

Yes, I want you too.

Without saying a word, Jax takes my hand and presses a kiss on the top of my fingers. "Eat," he says, before reaching for a plate.

We eat and he tells me more about his business meetings in London. We talk about the shop and I let him know about two new events I've been hired for. I go into detail about the flowers and colors I'll be using. I know men sometimes get lost in all the details, but Jax listens intently to everything thing I say. He even asks questions. I laugh at most of them as they all seem to be all along the lines of *what do those look like* or *how many possible shades of pink are there*.

A comfortable intimacy surrounds us. Even when we aren't speaking, there's no awkwardness. I think we are both trying to learn more about each other in silence as much as we are while talking.

With every moment that passes, I crave for another to come. Every smile and laugh Jax gives, I want to hear it again. Every move his body makes, I hope for it to come closer. Every light touch from his hand or brush of his leg under the table, I ache to feel more.

Long after we've finished eating, Jax stands and takes away our empty plates. Walking into the kitchen, he glances back.

"There's still dessert. Thought I'd mix things up this time."

I stand, following him, watching him as he moves about the kitchen. On the counter, I see a dessert box. With his back to me, he opens the lid, removing a perfect looking pie. Reaching for plates, his shoulder muscles roll under his fitted shirt, their movements hypnotizing me for a moment.

I want to see them without the shirt. I want to know what those muscles would feel like under the tips of my fingers. I *need* to know what it would feel like to have his bare skin touch mine.

I slowly walk up behind him, only inches separating us.

"Strawberry rhubarb. It's been my favorite since I was a kid—"

He stops talking the minute I rest my hand between his shoulder blades. I feel those exact muscles shifting slightly when he drops his arms to his sides. Slowly, he turns to face me, my fingers brushing across his arm then his chest as he moves.

Once face to face, Jax looks down at my fingers just barely grazing him before lifting his gaze and meeting my stare, a question in his eyes.

"I think," I begin, moving even closer to him, "dessert can wait."

My eyes drop down to his lips, and I watch his mouth open slightly, silent for a few seconds before he responds.

"For what?" he questions. There is a low growl in his voice which suggests he knows exactly why strawberry rhubarb can wait.

But for whatever reason, I can't verbalize an answer. I turn mute, my earlier confidence beginning to dwindle. I'm hesitant, over thinking every move I make, unsure of what I should do. With every second that passes, his eyes darken, waiting for me to do something, say anything.

He lowers his head, keeping it just inches away from mine. I lick my lips, his eyes following the movement of my tongue. Finally, he speaks.

"Kiss me."

Two simple words. One simple instruction.

It takes me a second but the minute our eyes meet again, I understand what he's doing. He's easing me into this. Starting us off with one small step.

But there is something else I see when I look into his eyes. He wants me to make the first move. There's a part of him that needs me to. He needs to know, to be shown, that I want this just as much as he does. He's telling me how to show him.

I press my hand harder against his chest, inching myself closer to him. I feel his heart beat under the firmness before I raise my hands and cup the sides of his face. Lifting up on my toes, I close my eyes and bring my mouth up to his.

Soft at first, my lips lightly press against his, but when I feel his hands come around and rest at the bottom of my spine, pulling me even closer, something inside of me awakens. With more forcefulness this time, I press my lips harder against his and move my hands up through his hair to the back of his head, trapping him against me, leaving him no room to back away. His fingers spread open on my back, digging into my skin with his fingertips, pressing me closer and harder against him.

My mouth opens wider and when his tongue finds mine, I let out a soft moan. My hands run through his hair once again, encouraging him, begging him to continue. Our lips have yet to separate, and I'm doing everything I can to make sure it stays that way. I run my hands down his body, my nails lightly scraping his chest and moving down to the hem of his shirt. My fingers find their way underneath, touching his hot smooth skin, the little bit of curly hair under his belly button. As soon as I run my nails through his trail, he pulls his lips away from mine.

"Rachel—" he starts, his hands coming up and cupping my

face.

But I don't want him to finish his thought. I don't want him to think of anything except us, right here and now. And more than anything, I don't want this to stop.

"I need this," I interrupt him.

His eyes scan my face, looking for any sign of uncertainty, but he won't find any. I take one of his hands in mine and I rest it over my chest, over my heart so he can feel it beating, pounding hard and fast.

"I *want* this," I insist again, hoping my voice conveys just how much I do.

He swallows and takes a step forward, closing the momentary gap between us. I close my eyes and he's kissing me again, this time taking more control. His fingers get tangled in my hair, balling what little he can in his fists. Mine, on the other hand, can't seem to stay in one place. They're constantly moving from his face to his chest to his waist. I feel him start to lead us out of the kitchen, down the hallway and to his bedroom.

With his hands still lost in my hair, I lift mine to meet his, looking for the elastic so I can let my hair fall free. As soon as my hair hits my shoulders and falls down my back, Jax brushes it aside, kissing his way down my neck, lightly sucking and biting.

I run my fingers once again against his stomach, needing to feel more of him. I take the hem of his shirt and lift it over his head, his lips leaving the crook of my neck just long enough for me to rid him of the material before his lips are back on mine, kissing me fervidly.

I know we've entered his bedroom when he stops walking. The sky is dark, but there is a dim light coming from the corner of his room. He kisses the side of my mouth before taking a step back, his fingers slowly sweeping across the middle of my chest, between my breasts and lower to my stomach. His fingers reach the seam of my panties, toying with the hem through the silk of my dress as he bends down, bringing his lips to my ear.

"Are you sure?" he asks softly.

The sensation of his fingers running along the edge of the lace doesn't allow me to speak. It takes all the concentration I have to simply nod yes.

I feel his mouth form the slightest smile before he slowly drops to his knees in front of me. His hands wrap around one ankle, resting it on his bent thigh as he unties my sandal. My hands fall to his shoulders for balance, and I watch as he takes my other foot and removes that sandal as well.

He doesn't stand afterwards. Instead, he looks up from where he's kneeling, meeting my stare as both his hands disappear under the long skirt of my dress, running his palms up and down the back of my calves. My breaths are short and sharp. Every time his fingers brush the back of my thighs, my legs become weak. I dig my nails into his shoulders each time, hoping it will keep me from falling over.

His hands leave my legs, and I feel my dress being lifted from the bottom. He slowly stands, bringing the dress up with him, and when we are face to face once again, I raise my arms above my head, letting him rid me of it completely. I'm stripped down to a black lace strapless bra and matching panties as he lets my dress fall from his hands, not giving it another thought as soon as his eyes fall back on me.

I thought my first instinct would be to cover myself. But it's not. I feel comfortable, confident. I feel *sexy*.

The only thought that does enter my mind is that I want to give him more. *Show* him more.

I reach behind my back and unclasp the two small hooks. Jax's eyes don't leave mine as I'm doing this but the moment I let the bra fall, his eyes drop to my breasts.

"You have no idea what you are doing to me right now," he says, desire thick in his voice.

I glance down to the crotch of his pants.

"I think I have some idea."

I step closer to him, letting our bodies—our skin—touch. His fingertips run circles along my back as I work on the button fly of his pants. I can feel how hard he is, my hand brushing against him as I go about my task. One hand comes around, cupping my breast, his thumb grazing over my nipple, circling its tip.

His pants fall to the floor and he steps out of them, watching me as I move backwards to his bed. Sitting on the edge, I count the three slow steps it takes him to reach me, admiring every inch of his body.

Slowly, Jax bends down and grips me by the sides, his hands covering my ribs. Gently, he lifts me and sets me down further on the bed while he climbs over top of me, kissing his way up from my belly to the valley between my breasts to my chin and finally, my mouth.

One hand rests on my hip, gripping it hard enough that I can feel the pressure from each fingertip. I raise my leg, wrapping it around his. His fingers bunch at the side of my panties, pulling them away from my hips slightly. The friction it causes between my legs is enough for me to let out a soft moan, pleading for him to do it again.

He kisses me long and soft, and I find myself pressing into his groin, feeling him, rubbing against him.

He pulls away from my mouth just slightly. "You better watch yourself or this could be over quicker than I want," he whispers against my lips.

I rest my hips back down against the mattress, but my hands find the band of his boxer briefs and start to pull down. Smiling against my lips, he lifts his lower half, helping me remove what little is left of his clothing.

Standing on his knees, I can't help but look, needing to see what I've just uncovered. Just like the rest of him, he's trimmed, gorgeous and…well equipped.

"Seems a little unfair. You get to see mine but I can't see

yours." A small cocky grin appears, his fingers play with the hem of my panties, teasing me.

He moves between my bent legs, softly kissing each knee before running his tongue up my thigh. His lips place soft kisses along the band of my panties before his hands start pulling them down, revealing me. Sitting back on his knees, he slips the black lace down my thighs, calves and over my feet. With the panties in one hand, he lifts them, letting them hang from his index finger. His eyes glance appreciatively from them to me before he throws them over his shoulder.

My legs close and when I feel Jax place his hands on my knees, I take a deep breath. Gently pushing my legs apart, I watch as Jax looks at me—all of me.

"You are so gorgeous, it's actually painful right now," he says before falling over me, kissing one breast, taking my nipple inside his mouth, lightly sucking on it.

My eyes fall closed and my hands get lost in his hair, pressing his face further into my chest. The need to have him close takes over, and I wrap my legs around his waist. He moves from one breast to the other, nipping and biting his way to my other nipple. I try hard to stifle the moan that comes out of my mouth, but it's no use.

"I love that sound," he says between each suck and bite.

He kisses the tips of my hardened nipples before making his way slowly down my body. I tense slightly, but it's enough for him to notice. He looks up, his eyes cautious.

"I won't if you're not ready, but I really, *really* want to taste you. See just how sweet you are."

Those words turn me on so much I forget about my initial reaction and rest my head further against his pillow, letting my legs fall apart. When I don't feel anything happen after a few seconds, I raise my head to find him scanning my body. Nervous that something is wrong, I open my mouth to ask if everything is alright when he speaks.

"I'm wild for you," he meets my eyes. "I need you to know that."

I blink a few times before nodding, and then watch him as he lowers his body, his head disappearing between my legs. I press my head back into the pillows when I feel his fingers spread me open. Warm air from his mouth softly hits me, causing me to jump. I hear him let out a quiet laugh.

"I haven't even touched you yet."

"Please," I quietly plead. "*Please* touch me."

And with that plea, I feel the tip of his tongue run over me. I fist the pillows by my head, squeezing hard. His tongue runs small circles, finding where I like it most. I feel like my whole body is on fire.

"You're so sweet," I hear him say. "So wet."

I feel one finger, then another, enter me while he flattens his tongue against me, the heat from his breath almost enough to send me over the edge.

With his fingers moving in and out of me and his tongue tasting everything I have to offer, it's not much longer before I *do* fall over the edge. Squirming, Jax holds me down, his hands gripping my hips, not letting me move while he continues to work me. Looking up, his eyes are intense, his want for me evident. He runs his tongue across his lips, tasting me again, and it's the most erotic thing I've ever seen.

"I know you can give me another," he says.

"Jax," I whimper.

"Shhh. One more." Then his head is back between my legs.

I've never had two orgasms so close together before. I'm not even sure I can. My body is still shaking from the first, but surprisingly, I feel another quickly beginning to build. After another minute of Jax kissing and licking me, I'm exploding with my second.

"Oh God!" I yell, my body convulsing.

Jax sits back up on his knees, my eyes open enough to see

him pump himself a few times before climbing over my body, dropping kisses along the way. Once he reaches my face, I see he's hesitant, unsure if he should kiss me on the lips. I lift myself up, bringing his lips to mine, tasting myself on his tongue.

"I *want* to feel you inside me," I say between kisses.

"I *need* to be inside you," he pants between hot breaths, tugging at my bottom lip with his teeth.

He leans over to his bedside table and opens a drawer. Pulling out a foil wrapper, he sits back on his legs, one hand running over me, teasing me, ensuring I'm ready as he tears open the wrapper with his teeth. I watch unapologetically as he sheaths himself, completely turned on by it, before he falls on top of me. His hands brush the hair off my face as I open my legs, making room for his hips to fit between them. Small nerves start to resurface as I remember that it's been nearly two years since I've had sex.

Will it hurt?

Jax takes my chin between his fingers, bringing my attention to him.

"I'll go slow," he promises like he was reading my mind.

I nod once before he kisses and enters me at the same time. The first thrust is an adjustment, to both his size and because it's been a while. But I'm so wet and wanting that by the third thrust, I'm panting for more.

"Fuck," he whispers as he moves in and out, kissing my neck. "You're so warm. I don't think I'm ever going to want to leave."

"Don't," I breathe in unison with every thrust.

"You feel so good. So good," he says, his voice almost pained.

"Jax…" I moan, raising my hips to match his movements.

His lips find mine again as he lifts one of my legs, resting it over his hip. I can feel his breathing becoming harsher as he continues to move inside me.

"Feel me. Feel *this*," he says bringing his face to mine, kissing me, matching each of his thrusts with his tongue inside my mouth. "Feel how amazing this is."

"I am," I say between labored breaths.

And it does.

He feels amazing.

With every thrust, every kiss, every small bite.

I feel Jax become more rigid in his movements, his stomach tightening, and I recognize that he's close. His back stiffens, small pools of sweat gathering at the base of his spine. I wrap both legs around his waist, the heels of my feet digging into his behind. I hear him let out a shaky breath while he utters my name. He collapses on top of me, my hands gripping his back, our chests damp with sweat, pressed together. After a moment, he lifts his head, watching me.

"You okay?" he asks, scanning my face to be sure I'm all right.

"I'm more than okay."

He smiles and gently pulls himself up and out of me. "Don't move."

I watch him walk to his bathroom, smiling at the view, his ass made for a Calvin Klein underwear ad. I hear him dispose of the condom and turn the faucet on. He walks back to the bed with a damp cloth.

He comes around to the side and smiles down at me. Sitting, he opens my legs and wipes my thighs and folds gently, cleaning me. While he's looking down and focusing on what he's doing, my heart aches watching him. When he's finished, he looks up to find me staring at him.

"What?" He grins.

"No one has ever done that before," I say quietly.

His grin softens.

He throws the cloth back towards the bathroom before climbing into bed, bringing the top sheet over us, covering us only to our hips. He wags his eyebrows mischievously, leaving my breasts uncovered on purpose. He turns towards me, resting on his side, one hand lightly scaling the length of my arm. He takes my hand in his and kisses my open palm. My eyes roam his face, and even though there is little light in his room, I can see the redness of exhaustion around his eyes.

"You must be so jet-lagged right now," I say, hiding my smile in the pillow.

As if on cue, his face breaks into a yawn. "A little. But it's worth it."

He brings one arm up, resting it above my head while the other drapes over my hip. I can see him fighting to keep his eyes open, but it's a losing battle. After a full minute has passed without him reopening his eyes, I kiss the tip of his nose, moving in closer to him.

"Good night, Jackson," I whisper.

I close my eyes and let sleep take over.

The image block contains the chapter heading.

I ROLL OVER slowly, my body feeling content, my mind at peace. My head perfectly melts into the pillow and the blankets cocoon me, keeping me warm. I remember this feeling. I recognize it, although it's been a while since I've felt it.

Happiness.

I relish in it for a few minutes, not wanting to open my eyes, not wanting to feel anything other than what I do in this moment. I stay still with my eyes closed, avoiding the world beyond my lids for just a little while longer.

I stretch my hands out above my head, touching the headboard. The soft suede fabric runs across the tips of my fingers. Usually, this wouldn't cause me to stop and furrow my eyebrows, but something about the feeling of this headboard doesn't feel right. It feels out of place.

I slowly open my eyes and face the ceiling of my bedroom. My head turns to the left and I recognize my nightstand, my lamp with its cream shade and the book I've been reading right next to it. All is in its right place, but I can't shake the feeling that none of this is supposed to be here.

"Good morning," I hear a deep yet soft whisper come from beside me.

I've woken up to this voice too many mornings to count. I turn, facing the man who's dominated my dreams for months.

"Good morning," I smile, burrowing myself further into the pillow and blankets.

"It's been a while," Ben says, brushing some hair behind my ear.

I close my eyes, nodding in agreement. I think back to the last time we spoke. How things ended.

"I don't want to fight," I tell him.

His lips come down to my forehead, giving me a kiss. As soon as his lips touch my skin, I feel relief that he's come back. Relief that I can still talk to him. His lips linger, but they feel different. Rougher. Not as soft as I was expecting. Somewhere in the back of mind, I know why, but it won't come to me.

"Do you remember the day we moved in here?" Ben turns onto his back, looking up at the ceiling. "I remember thinking, 'Finally, something that's mine.' And that I was doing it with you just made it even better."

"That's not exactly how I remember it," I say.

"No? How do you remember it?"

"I remember you yelling at how many boxes still needed to be carried in. I remember us fighting in the driveway about you bringing in your old ripped and stained couch. I remember you storming out of our bathroom annoyed that there was no room for your stuff after I had unpacked mine. Oh, and my personal favorite, the shower you took that night and the shower head falling off the wall. You were so pissed."

That memory always makes me laugh thinking of it.

I look at Ben as he tries to hide his own laughter.

"That's not how I remember it at all," he shakes his head, arguing. "Except for the part about you having too much stuff in

the bathroom. That I do remember!"

I roll my eyes.

But when I think back to all of those moments, all that really sticks out is how happy we were. Those first few weeks of us living here, the fresh paint and new furniture, new plumbing, the WELCOME mat I bought for our front door, all those things made this house our home.

"This was a great home," I say.

Our eyes lock, both of us noticing my use of the past tense. Silence fills the room.

Ben's eyes wander about the room. "Doesn't look much different."

"You thought it would?"

He shrugs. "I don't know. Maybe."

My eyes follow his, scanning the bedroom, looking to see what Ben had anticipated. The only thing I can really see as different is the closet. Most of Ben's clothes are gone. Boxed up and donated a while ago, save for a few particular items I didn't want to part with.

"A lot of your stuff is in the garage," I tell him, suddenly feeling the need to assure him. "Your work bench, old gym equipment. It's all there."

I see him nod, biting the inside of his cheek. For the first time in a long time, I have no idea where his thoughts lie. We used to be able to finish each other's sentences. Now, I'm left clueless.

After another long minute, Ben turns to me, taking my hand in both of his. He rests them between us and kisses our intertwined fingers. "Maybe it's time you started to clear all that out."

I pull my head back in surprise. "Why would you say something like—" I start to say but then remember the last meeting we had. "You're trying to break up with me again," I accuse him.

He squeezes my hand. "Nothing could break us," he states. "Nothing."

His expression turns sad, pained almost. I want the right words to comfort him, but what's more, I want him to have the same for me.

"I had so many dreams for us. I pictured our future. I saw a couple of kids running around in the backyard. I pictured bringing them down to the lake, teaching them how to fish and roast marshmallows by the fire. I imagined what they'd look like and prayed they'd look just like you." He smiles, kissing my fingers again. "I knew from the minute I saw you, you were it for me. I know I've told you that before, but I really need you to hear it. You were IT for me. Anything before you didn't matter and anything after didn't matter because once you walked into my life, my heart beat only for you."

My eyes start to burn, tears threatening to fall. I fear where this is leading.

"Don't say goodbye," I plead.

"I love you, Rachel. With everything that I am, everything I was, I love you."

"I love you too," I profess. "Forever." I try to move closer to him, but he resists. Every inch I move, he takes one moving back.

"I know you do." He furiously nods, but his eyes stay on our joined hands. He won't look at me, and that's when I know that what he's about to say will be painful.

"You can't keep us both."

I stiffen. My mind becomes jumbled with thoughts that are moving too fast. Like a tornado, picking up a few mental images, spinning them in my mind before spitting them out and grabbing another. I don't have time to hold on to one before it's replaced with another. Images of this house are mixed with rooms that have dark hardwood floors. Lived in, worn out furniture is mixed with new dark brown leather.

"You were confused waking up. Being here. Like this isn't where you're supposed to be."

His voice is softly encouraging me, prodding me to follow. Everything he says is true, but I still can't make a clear thought form. Not until he speaks again.

"This isn't where you fell asleep last night, is it?" his voice hushed.

Thoughts of Jax flood my mind. Of our date last night. Him opening the door and the feeling of excitement I had that he was finally home. Being in his home. Dark hardwood floors and leather furniture. The bear cap he brought back for me as a joke.

The dinner he cooked.

The dessert we didn't eat.

Ben's right. I didn't fall asleep in this bed last night. I'm not even there right now.

Clarity hits and it's a slap in the face. I'm asleep in another man's bed after having just made love with him and I'm dreaming of Ben.

"Oh God," I say turning onto to my back, covering my mouth with my hands. I feel hot and sweaty. Disgusted. I feel sick.

"Rach, take some deep breaths," Ben says, concerned.

His hand runs up and down my arm, hoping to comfort me, but there is no way to be comforted after something like this. I shake my head over and over.

"What kind of person am I?" I ask, appalled.

"A good person. Never doubt that," Ben says unequivocally and with so much affection. It only shames me more.

"No. No, I'm not. A good person doesn't lie in bed with one man and dream of another."

Ben caresses my cheek with his hand, a gesture I used to love. Now it only sends revolution through me. I can't tolerate the kindness he's trying to show me, the love.

"A good person doesn't do this to the man she loves," I ar-

gue. Either of them.

"Rachel—"

I turn to face him, stopping him, not letting him continue.

"No! You were right to say those things. This isn't fair." My mind starts to spin. "I have to fix this," I say with determination.

"Rachel, you're not listening—"

"I am! I heard what you said!" My voice cracks, tears now falling freely.

I can't be here in Jax's bed any longer dreaming of Ben. But I dread waking up. The thought of what I need to do once I'm awake pains me in a way that's sadly familiar. The pain of another loss. I want to give myself a few more seconds, but I feel myself stirring, my emotional state waking me from my dream.

chapter 21

THE SHEETS UNDER me are damp from the sweat and tears. I turn my head and see Jax completely still as he continues to sleep. He looks so peaceful, completely unaware of the breakdown I'm having only inches from him. His hair is a mess, both from sleep and from my hands tugging at it earlier in the night. I raise a hand and softly brush a little of it away from his face. He doesn't even stir.

I take these few minutes and watch him sleep. His chest is slowly rising, his lips parted. I know that if I were to lay mine overtop, they'd fit perfectly in that little space.

I get up slowly, unable to stay lying next to him any longer. I gently remove his arm that's resting over the top my hip. When I stand, he simply rolls over onto his back, his arm now above his head. It's nearly impossible to tear my eyes away from him, but the longer I stay here watching him, the harder it will be.

I walk on the tip of my toes to the bathroom, picking up my discarded panties along the way and quietly close the door. I slide them over my legs and move over to the sink, turning the water to a gentle flow. I splash cold water on my face hoping it will help clear my head, help me focus on my next move.

Staring at my reflection, I'm hit with how real this has all become. My eyes are red-rimmed and puffy, proof of how real my dreams feel and how sad my reality truly is.

Ben was right. I can't keep them both. I was stupid to think that I could live one life with two realities. That I was capable of keeping my thoughts, feelings, and two worlds separate.

I knew my relationship with Jax was changing, becoming something more, something other than just friendship. I knew it long before I came here tonight—that we were heading to a point of no return. Tonight, I even initiated it. And now, I'm going to have to leave it behind.

I turn off the water and pat my face dry. I take a quick scan of his bathroom counter. A toothbrush stands alone in its holder, his razor sitting not far beside it. I pick up the bottle of cologne and bring it to my nose, inhaling it several times, committing it to memory.

I ignore any impulse telling me to stop and rethink. I push it all aside because there is one thing I know above all else—Jax deserves better. He deserves someone who doesn't spend the night in his bed dreaming of another. He deserves someone who can give themselves fully and completely.

I *wish* that could be me.

I *know* it can't.

"You can do this," I tell myself.

I walk out of his bathroom, tiptoeing around the bedroom. I take another quick glance at Jax who still hasn't moved. I pick up my clothes and sandals off the floor, making my way out into the living room. It's much cooler now in the condo, my body covered in goose bumps as I start to dress. I don't even bother with the bra, shoving it in my bag instead.

Sitting on the couch to tie my sandals, I feel the British cap against my back. I reach around, laying it in my lap. I run my fingers over its fur, dismayed once again at how things can change in such a short amount of time. Just a few hours ago, this cap brought so much laughter. Now it threatens to bring tears.

A minute in time. That's all it took to throw my world off its axis. Again.

I lay the cap back down on the couch, not wanting to be reminded any longer.

I walk into the kitchen, looking for anything to write on and with. I find an empty envelope and a pen in the first drawer I open. I hastily write the only two words that I can think of.

I'm sorry.

I look down at it.

"Coward," I say to myself in disgust. I leave it on the counter, somewhere I'm sure he'll see, then make my way to the door.

"Rachel?" a sleepy, quiet voice startles me, stopping me in my tracks.

I turn slowly as Jax flips a switch and light bathes the hallway. I see him standing there nearly naked except for the boxer briefs he had on last night. His eyes take a second to adjust to the light and then he sees me, dressed and ready to walk out the door.

"What's going on?" his voice hoarse from sleep, his brows furrowed.

I swallow the lump in my throat, knowing that having to face him will make this so much harder.

I clear my throat. "I remembered I had a lot of work waiting for me tomorrow at the shop. Thought it better that I leave now. Get an early start tomorrow."

I lie because I can't speak the truth.

I watch him run my words over once more in his head. He brings his hand up, massaging the back of his neck.

"You thought it would be better to leave at," he looks to the clock in the kitchen, "four thirty in the morning?"

"I tried not to wake you," I say, my fingers tapping nervously against my bag.

His expression lets me know he couldn't care less if I woke him. "You should have if it was that important." His voice is low, worried. "Let me put some clothes on. Make sure you get home all right."

He turns and starts to walk back towards his room, and I panic.

"NO!" I shout after him.

He turns back around, confusion on his face. In the bathroom, I didn't think I could hate myself more, but right now, I know I've reached a whole new level.

"Please don't. I'll be fine."

My eyes move to the note I left on the counter. I feel his follow mine, and I know he sees it too. I turn back to the door. As soon as my hand is on the knob, I hear him release a shaky breath.

"Rachel, what are you doing?" he asks. His tone is different than I've ever heard. Disbelief. Angry even.

"I told you. Busy day tomorrow." I don't turn around to look at him.

"Yeah, I heard what you said."

I continue to stand there, my back to him. The silence that surrounds us feels like a heavy, stifling blanket. No longer able to take it, I turn and face him. I see the anger I heard earlier in his eyes.

"I'm sorry," I say quietly, my voice breaking slightly.

"Don't be sorry. Just tell me what's going on," he says, his voice steady.

I take a minute and quietly prepare myself to destroy the best thing that's happened to me in two years.

"I can't do this," I say looking him in the eyes. "I think we…I need to take a few steps back."

My heart tears in two as soon as the words leave my mouth.

Jax casts his head downwards, giving a few quick nods. He places his hands on his hips, his fingers tracing the band of his boxers. When he brings his head back up, his lips are pressed together, his face hard.

"I see."

His short curt answer hurts, but it must be nothing compared to what I'm doing to him right now. I need to leave and soon. The longer I wait, the longer I stay, the bigger the chance I'll fall apart.

"I should go," I say, turning back towards the door.

I hear Jax takes several steps closer to me.

"No, I don't think so," he says, his voice authoritative. "You're not going anywhere," he challenges.

"Excuse me?" I turn, questioning.

"I don't believe you."

He takes another step forward.

"I. Don't. Believe. You." He enunciates every word slowly. "I don't believe you can't do this. I don't believe you want to leave right now. I *do* believe you're feeling a lot of things right now, but none of them are about how you *don't* want this." He takes another step forward. "Don't want us."

His voice is so forceful. Because he knows he's right.

Leaving here right now is not what I want but what needs to happen. He doesn't know how unfair I've been, the secrets I've been keeping. He doesn't understand the hold Ben still has on me. Staying here and arguing about it is not going to change anything. It will only make things worse. If I can't tell him the truth, maybe the best thing would be to lie. If he won't let me leave, maybe I need to get him to push me out.

"I don't know what you want me to say." I change my tone, becoming defiant, hostile even.

I hate how I sound but it's the only way.

"Yes. You do," he says adamantly. "Just tell me the truth. Tell me you are having a hard time, and I'll do what I can to help ease us through this. I told you before I'd never pressure you into talking if you weren't ready, but I refuse to let that be the reason we don't talk at all."

He takes another step closer. One more and he'll be right in front of me, within reaching distance. I can't let that happen. I can't let him get that close.

"Stop!" I say, holding up my hand.

He stops mid-stride, his hands coming up in compliance.

"Just talk to me." His voice is softer now. "Tell me how I can help you."

My brows scrunch together. "Help me with what?"

"Anything!" he replies. "Heal. Forget. Let me help you… anything."

"Forget?" I say, angrily. Only this time, my tone is real. "I don't *want* to forget. That's what you're not understanding. That's why I can't do this. I won't forget. *Ever*."

"That's not what I meant," he says. "I would never try and replace—"

"You can't!" I scream.

His face looks shocked at my outburst then turns into something different.

Hurt. Disappointment. Humiliation.

And I put it there.

"You're scared," he whispers. "If you're feeling guilty—"

"Guilty?" The word strikes a strange chord inside me, causing me to stiffen.

He takes a deep breath and looks at me. Pleads with me. "Yes. Guilty. I can't imagine what these last two years have been like for you. I can't imagine losing someone so close to you. I know this can't be easy."

He tentatively takes that last step, closing in on me. His hands come up to my face, holding me carefully. "I know we can do this. I know it because I know we're worth it. You know it too."

I feel a tear fall, getting lost under his fingers. He seems so sure of everything he's just said. So sure of me. It only fuels my decision further.

Because he doesn't know the truth. He doesn't know my inability to let another man go. If he did, he'd know I wasn't worth it.

"You don't know anything," I say, trying to sound as emotionless as possible. Inside, I fall apart at every word.

"Don't do that," he says, shaking his head. "Don't talk about us as if we're inconsequential. Like what we have isn't something good. Something amazing!"

The pain in having to look him in the eye and lie about my feelings for him can only be compared to one other moment in my life. Ironically, it's that same moment that made being here with Jax even possible.

"This was a mistake," I say. I take his hands and remove them from my face.

He shakes his head, running his fingers through his hair, frustrated.

"I don't believe that. This was not a mistake. I know what this is! You know what this is!" There is determination in his eyes when he looks back at me. "This is love, Rachel. We are falling in *love*," he states confidently.

My heart stills at his words. I know he's right. He knows he's right. We've been falling slowly and too quickly all at the same time. I've been both fighting it and longing for it. I've pushed him away as many times as I've pulled him close. It only makes the reality of what I've been doing to him all that much worse.

"Say something," he begs. "Tell me I'm not alone in this."

You're not alone, Jax. I'm right there with you.

But I can't stay. Not if that means I have to push someone else out. I'm not ready to close my heart to someone who has lived there for so many years.

"I'm not in love with you, Jackson. I'm sorry."

Hurt unleashes across his face, and it's too much to bear. I look down at my feet before turning around and walking back to the door.

This time I know I won't stop.

"Rachel…"

But he says no more. What more can he say?

I open the door and force myself out, refusing to look back. I hear the closing click behind me, and thankfully the elevator arrives as soon as I push the call button.

Once the doors close, tears fall down my face and I let out a quiet sob.

I cry as I did the night Ben was killed. I cry, because for the second time in my life, my heart is shattered.

Only this time, I've shattered someone else's along with it.

I CAN HARDLY remember what the first few hours were like for me after Ben's accident. It was as if time stood still, I was too numb to notice anything happen around me.

These last few hours have gone by differently. The only similarity is the slow, snail-paced way time has moved forward. But I felt every minute of it. Every heart-stabbing-can't-catch-my-breath second painfully accounted for. I wished for that numbness to find me again, to help me stifle some of the hurt, even if it was for just a minute.

A tissue hangs in front of me, offered by perfectly manicured fingernails.

"Shit," she says, worry and sympathy evident on her face. "Then what happened?"

"I left. I turned and walked out the door." That moment replays in my mind over and over like a movie. I want so badly for it to stop, yet I'm unable to turn it off.

"Shit," Tess mutters once again, her forehead scrunching.

"Yep," I agree, sniffling into the fresh tissue. A pile of used, tear-wrinkled white squares are already piled high in front of me.

Hurting someone you love is torturous. Realizing how unfairly you've treated them is not an easy pill to swallow. Especially when that pill is half the size of your heart.

"It's better this way," I repeat, hoping the more I say it, the truer it will feel.

"You really believe that?" she questions.

I nod furiously, telling her I do. "I can't give him what he needs. What he deserves." I let more tears run down my cheeks. "He deserves to be loved by someone completely, someone who isn't incomplete like me."

Tess shakes her head. "You aren't incomplete. Sometimes falling in love is scarier than it is wonderful. But it can be worth it," she says, trying to be optimistic.

I look up from my wrangled tissue. "I didn't mean for it to happen," I whisper.

Tess gives me an understanding smile. "I know, sweetie. No one ever does. Some people fall willingly, others trip into it." She pauses. "Either way, when the bottom hits, it hurts like a son of a bitch."

Her words sound…knowing. They give me pause and I look at her—her hair a mess, held back by a single clip, and she's wearing a ratty old t-shirt overtop a pair of leggings. But it's the red-rimmed eyes that really catch my attention. Eyes that tell me she had been crying before she came over today. This entire time we've been talking about my heartbreak and it's only now I'm noticing the same in Tess.

"Are you okay?" I ask.

I berate myself for only now noticing that something is obviously bothering Tess. It seems like I've become selfish in all my relationship drama.

She brushes my question off with a wave of her hand, but I know something has upset her enough to cause tears.

"What's wrong?" This time, I ask with more urgency.

She takes a deep breath and lets it out with a sad laugh. "I think I've hit bottom too."

When she looks back my way, I watch a lone tear escape her eye, slowly falling down the side of her cheek. She doesn't bother wiping it away. I pull a fresh tissue from the box, and this time, it's me offering it to her.

"What happened?" Concern for her now overshadows my own feelings.

"The funny thing is, I don't even know. One minute it's all dirty talk and tearing at each other's clothes. The next he's telling me how we live in different worlds and we don't see things the same way or some bullshit like that. He left this morning saying that maybe we should 'cool it for a bit.' Whatever the hell that means."

I can't believe that Tess and Paul were having a similar fight like Jax and I were. Like some weird twilight zone aimed at causing nothing but grief. I didn't think it would be possible for my heart to hurt any more this morning that it already did, but seeing Tess so sad and confused shows me that a heart can continue to break long past the brink you thought it reached.

"This happened this morning?"

She nods slowly. "Yup. After I got off the phone with you. I didn't tell him anything!" she assures me. "I lied and told him a work emergency happened that only I could fix. Like, who fucking gets mad at something like that? Before I knew it, he was saying all that stuff and walking out the door."

"Tess, I'm so sorry! That doesn't sound like him. Something else must be bugging him. I could talk to him, see what's going on…"

"No!" she nearly shouts.

"Maybe he's—"

"Maybe he's just an asshole!" she interrupts me. She takes a breath and starts again. "Whatever the issue, it's Paul's. And he needs to figure shit out himself."

I relent, nodding slowly. After a few seconds of silence, I hear her start to laugh. It's a sad, pathetic laugh.

"Look at us," she starts. "I can't keep a man and you've got too many."

A small laugh escapes my own lips. "Pretty pathetic, huh?"

She nods in agreement before she drops her head into her arms for just a few seconds before lifting it again.

"I don't want to be one of the ladies who only has cats," she says, her voice sad.

"Me neither," I answer.

She rests her head back against her folded arms, and I mimic her stance. After a few seconds, her face softens.

"Ben would have wanted you to be happy," she tells me.

I sit up, not wanting to hear this.

"Just let me finish," she says. "I've seen you over the last few months. You've been happy. He put a smile back on your face when no one else could."

As much as I know what she's saying is true, it still doesn't change anything.

"I know," I whisper. "But I can't be with someone when I can't let the other one go." My mind wanders from Ben to Jax, back and forth, over and over again. I feel my heart break more and more. "Who would have thought love could be so heartbreaking?"

Tess snorts. "That's how you know it's real."

chapter 22

"DID YOU FIND the relief you were looking for?" Dr. Embry asks, closing her notepad and resting it on her lap. I scrunch my eyebrows together at her choice of words. "Relief" is not what I would have chosen.

"Relief?"

She gives a small nod. "You've made your choice. You ended your relationship with Jackson—" I watch as she mentally counts back in her head.

"Two weeks ago," I offer quietly.

"Yes. Two weeks ago," she repeats. "Did you find the relief you believed your decision would give?"

I look up from where I've been playing with my fingernails. She's watching me, looking for a reaction, an acknowledgment of the truth. A truth she already knows, a truth easy to see.

Each morning, I've woken up with a heavy weight on my chest. A sadness. A burden. It doesn't cease. It doesn't lift. I wake up thinking of the man I lost. I go to sleep thinking of the man I gave up. The wounds over Ben are still very jagged, the fresh cuts from Jax running deep.

I tell myself I made the right decision. That there must be a reason I keep Ben alive in my dreams. A reason we continue to meet and be together. A reason I don't completely understand but that I can't ignore.

I tell myself Jax is better off without me. He deserves better. He'll meet someone new, someone who will give him all those feelings he once told me he was searching for. Someone who will give them back easily, without effort, without hesitation. Every time I tell myself these things, tears fall at the thought of them actually becoming true.

"Rachel?"

"I know what you're doing," I say.

She looks at me perplexed. "What is it that you think I'm doing?"

"You're trying to get me to admit that I made a mistake. That I was wrong. To admit a different truth."

"Is there a different truth?"

I look out her window to the overcast day outside. Gray clouds hover over the city, promising rain. My mind drifts to a memory of Ben and me getting caught in a rainstorm. Neither of us prepared, neither with an umbrella or even hoods to cover our heads.

At first, we both started to run for safety but the rain came down so hard that in seconds, we were soaked. After that, finding shelter seemed pointless. Ben took my hand, slowed us down and casually led us down the street, stopping to look inside store windows as if nothing had happened.

"Do you think it's possible to be in love with two people at the same time?" I ask, hearing the light drops of rain starting to hit the office window.

"I believe life is full of possibilities," she starts. "When it comes to love, sometimes that's where you'll find the largest of them all."

"It doesn't feel…right. It feels disloyal."

"Perhaps you feel that way because you didn't fall out of love."

I look at her, questioning.

"Your relationship with Ben. It didn't end by choice. It didn't end because you fell out of love. It was taken. Unfairly, unjustly. It's not how your story with Ben was supposed to end. You didn't lose the love. You lost the man. Then to fall in love again," she looks at me, and for the first time, I feel like someone else understands, "it must be very hard to balance those feelings. To once again have no control over a situation."

"Sometimes it feels like I can't breathe," I admit. "Like my heart is going to explode. Going back and forth, having to choose between Ben and Jax, it's too much."

"Why do you think you have to choose? Can't there be room for both?"

"I wouldn't even know how I could."

"Rachel, the fact that you can admit now that you did fall in love again, proves you can."

Her words create a lump in my throat, one that's hard to swallow. "He made it so easy," I whisper.

She doesn't even need me to clarify who I'm talking about. "He must be very special then," she answers.

I think of Jax. I think of every single feeling I've felt being with him, feelings that seemed so impossible not that long ago.

"I think there are instances in our lives that help mold us. Shape us. Help us become the people we are meant to be. The lessons we learn, the chances we take. They come into our lives to teach us. Sometimes, the lesson isn't clear until much later."

"You mean Jax?" I ask, my voice quiet, shaking.

"Maybe Jax. Maybe Ben. It's not easy," she says sympathetically. "Moving forward, readjusting." She leans forward, and for the first time in all of our sessions together, she reaches out and covers my hands with one of hers, squeezing gently.

"Letting someone in doesn't mean you're letting another go. It just means your heart is growing. Making more room."

AS AWFUL AS the last two weeks have been, watching Tess go through her own heartbreak was just as hard. She may be much better at hiding her feelings and putting on a brave face, but I could see the sadness in her eyes. She and Paul had yet to really talk since that morning. I know she's reached out to him, tried calling and texting, only receiving short, non-committal responses back. I offered again to speak to him, but I still got the same answer.

"Fuck that! Let him grow a pair and break up with me to my face! Fucking asshole."

I hated seeing her this way. I hated even more not being able to do anything to help. I slowly started fearing losing Paul myself. We shared a connection, a bond. A friendship. I couldn't think of losing another.

And to top it all off, after hearing that Jax and I are no longer 'friends', my mother has been incessantly calling. Wondering what happened, why we are no longer speaking. So many times I've had to stop myself from asking if she's seen Jax's mother, if he's mentioned me to her in any way. Not knowing how he's feeling is just as painful.

I KNOCK ON the door, relieved to hear footsteps. As soon as the door opens, I see a look of surprise on his face.

"Hey, Rach. What's up?"

Paul holds the door open, inviting me in. His home looks just like what one would expect a bachelor's to look like. Plain walls, only a couple of frames hanging. A dartboard in one corner. A small couch and chair sit in front of a flat screen which is currently playing a Sylvester Stallone movie. It reminds me of

Ben's apartment before we moved in together.

My eyes sweep across the room, looking for clues as to how he's been coping over the last few weeks. Other than an empty pizza box and a few beer bottles littered around the room, the place is pretty clean and tidy. Part of me had hoped I'd find it in shambles, evidence of…heartbreak maybe? But looking around, I see no sign of a broken man.

"Have a seat. Want a beer or anything?" he offers, heading into the kitchen. I hear the rattle of the fridge door opening. "Sorry I don't have much else, wasn't expecting anyone," he says.

"I guess we have that in common," I say, remembering only being able to offer him diet soda last time he showed up at my house. "A beer sounds great."

I sit on the couch, setting my purse on the floor. In all the years I've known Paul, I've only been to his apartment a handful of times. Mostly just to the front door, dropping something off or picking something up. He and Ben usually always hung out at our place.

I watch him walk back into the living room, handing me a beer as he passes by, sitting on the other end of the sofa. An explosion from the TV grips our attention, and I watch as Stallone starts running from a group of men just before Paul sets the movie on mute.

"So, this is different. You being here," he says with a smile.

I return the smile, easing back into the sofa. "Yeah, well I hadn't seen you in a little while. Thought I'd stop by for a visit."

He cocks an eyebrow. "Well, that's nice of you," he says, taking a sip from his beer. He sets the bottle on the coffee table and looks up at me. "Sorry I haven't been by lately."

I wave my hand dismissively, letting him know not to worry about it.

"Don't, please," I start. "You've got a life too."

"I know, but still," he says. "And it's not because I think I have to, but because I want to."

I smile, silently thanking him.

"So what's up?" he asks, relaxing a bit.

"I was just about to ask you the same thing," I answer back.

He looks up from the bottle in his hands, understanding sweeping across his face.

"So that's why you stopped by," he says.

I know there is no sense in lying because, yes, that is one of the reasons I stopped by.

"Yes. But not the only reason. I do kind of miss seeing you," I grin.

He leans back against the couch, his bottle resting on his chest between his hands. I sit up and lean forward.

"Tess thinks you're breaking up with her."

His eyebrows raise a little. "She said that?"

I nod.

Paul sits back up.

"Maybe it's for the best," he swallows. I can see he doesn't really mean it, doesn't really want it to be true.

"Okay, what's going on? One minute, you're both happy and doing great, the next…" I know it breaks every rule in the best friend handbook confessing this to him, especially since she told me not to, but if I could help, I need to try. "She's heartbroken. And Tess doesn't get heartbroken."

I watch him spin the bottle around and around in his hands, his jaw tightening.

"We're just too different," he says finally, his shoulders jerking upwards.

"Since when has that been an issue? You've always been polar opposites."

"Since I saw her for what she really is," he takes a breath. Then quietly, he says, "Amazing."

I shake my head, confused. "I don't understand."

"That girl," he says pointedly. "That girl is like no other

I've ever met. Looks like a fucking model, personality of a fire-cracker. Shit, some of the stuff that comes out of her mouth, I haven't even heard in a locker room." He takes a small inhale. "And she's fucking brilliant."

For the first time, I see his feelings for her written all over his face. He's in love with her. Which confuses me even more.

"Now I really don't understand. If she's so perfect, why do you want to break it off?"

He shakes his head. "Because she's meant for better."

"That's not true," I insist.

"It is," he laughs harshly. "A few weeks ago, I picked her up at her work. I watched her be the boss. I watched as people followed her around, looking for her approval. Interns wanting to be her. I overheard a few old guys in suits talking about how she's going places—New York or L.A. When I saw her barking orders at people and watching them do everything she said, I knew they were right." He takes a sip from his beer. "And this is where I'm going to stay—forever. I can't be the reason she doesn't get everything she deserves, everything she's worked for."

Recollection of the conversation Tess and I had about Paul meeting her at the station comes back to my mind. She was under the impression this was all about Cunny Caleb and jealousy. Now I see it had nothing to do with that at all.

"I'm doing her a favor."

I'm a little shocked at hearing all this that it takes me a moment to form a thought. I had no idea Paul felt this strongly about any of it. It just shows how much he cares for Tess, how much he wants what's best for her. I can't believe he doesn't include himself in it.

"Everything you said about Tess is true. She's beautiful and smart, and yeah, sometimes the stuff that comes out of her mouth worries me," I say. "Over the last two years, she's been there for me whenever I needed her. No matter what time or where she had to come from, she was there. And for these last two weeks, she needed me."

Paul tries to interrupt, but I continue on. "I'm not saying this to make you feel bad or guilty or anything like that. I'm telling you this so you understand. Two weeks ago, Tess needed me because she feared losing you. You're wrong, Paul. You're wrong if you think she doesn't need you or that she'd be giving up too much to be with you. She loves you," I tell him. "She's *in* love with you. And you are obviously in love with her. And if you think that she cares more about some high-profile life than being happy, then you don't really know her at all. Those feelings you have for her, they aren't going to go away by ignoring them. And hers aren't going to go anywhere either. No matter how much of an ass you're being."

He looks over at me, insulted.

"They are going to stay and weigh you down until you can't stand anymore." I say sadly. "Trust me when I say you'd be stupid to waste your time over thinking being in love than living in it."

"Isn't that what you're doing?" Paul challenges. "Over thinking being in love with that guy instead of just 'being in it'?"

I shake my head. "My situation is completely different."

Paul laughs. "No, it isn't. It's the exact same thing. Instead of worrying how this relationship will affect your future, you're too worried on how it will affect your past."

I freeze, not knowing how to argue his point. *Is there even an argument?*

He scans my face, his expression becoming serious. "I realize that I may have come off as..." he looks to be thinking of the right word, "disapproving over things with you and..." he waves his hand, looking to me to fill in the gap.

"Jax," I offer, even though I know he knows Jax's name.

"Yeah." He looks over at me again, his cheeks blushing. "I was a dick. That wasn't fair."

I move from my end of the couch and sit near him. I take one of his hands in both of mine, thanking him but knowing that it really doesn't matter anymore.

"You were happy with him," he says. It's not a question.

"Very. Ben made me very happy."

Paul smiles. "I know that, but that's not who I was talking about."

I look up at Paul, surprised. After a moment, I give him the slightest, smallest nod. He squeezes my hand, his lips press together.

"I ended it," I tell him.

He nods slowly.

"Love sucks," I say sadly.

Paul laughs. "I guess," he says, thinking it over.

I hope I've said enough to get him to rethink things. To move past what he *thinks* is right and do what *is* right.

A silence comes over us, both knowing we've said all we can.

"Want another beer?" he asks, standing.

I nod. "Sure."

Paul comes back with two new bottles of beer. He takes the TV off mute and explosions are once again filling the screen.

"Perfect. This is the best part. Rambo's about to kick some serious ass," he says.

And for the next twenty-five minutes, we watch in silence as Rambo does exactly that.

chapter 23

I SHIFT EVERYTHING I'm carrying from one arm to the other, trying to find a comfortable position. The sidewalk is filled with people running errands and heading to lunch. Most are speaking into their phones, not paying any attention to where or who they are about to bump into. Stupidly, I decided to walk from the meeting I had with a new client back to the shop. I failed to take into consideration how awkward it would be to walk the six blocks with a laptop, folders and catalogues in hand.

Shuffling and reshuffling all my presentation items, I come around the corner and am hit in the arm by a man on his phone, causing me to drop some of my folders. My eyes follow the man as he continues to walk away without even looking back.

"Asshole," I say to myself.

I bend down to pick up my fallen folders, numerous pairs of legs hurriedly walking by. As I pile them all together, I lift my head, looking into the large street front windows of a busy downtown restaurant. Every table is occupied. Filled with people talking, laughing and eating. The walls are white, as are the linens and chairs. So when a splash of vibrant red appears on the opposite side of the restaurant, my eyes can't help but be drawn to it. And then, I wish more than anything I hadn't.

I watch Jessica Vasquez strut elegantly between tables. Dressed in a form-fitting red dress with a white blazer, her long red hair tied in a sleek ponytail, exposing her long neck and the delicate necklace that hangs around it. She approaches a table not far from where I'm crouched down, spying.

And then my breath stills, a pain so powerful in my chest it nearly knocks me over. Twenty feet away from me, sitting so close but with so many obstacles between us, dressed in a soft pinstriped suit and a pastel tie, typing on his phone, is half the reason my heart beats and breaks.

I watch as Jessica reaches his table, her hand coming over his shoulder, resting on his chest, looking for his attention. Ugly thoughts run through my mind. His confession about Ingrid and his workplace tryst. *Has it happened again?*

A rush of pure jealousy slams through me as I watch her hand slide down his arm as she takes a seat beside him. I feel sick watching this, but I can't look away. My stomach hardens with bitterness as I watch Jessica squeeze his wrists and lean in closer to him. The unbelievable urge to barge in there and demand to know whether anything has happened between them overcomes me.

The only thing that stops me is Jax's reaction.

Every attempt at closeness from Jessica, he leans further away. He removes his arm from her grasp and reaches over, offering her a menu that's sitting on the table.

The honk of a car horn directly behind me snaps me out of my trance. I blink a few times, ashamed at my behavior.

And as much as it kills me to see Jax with anyone, I need to remember that I'm the one who did this.

I did this to us.

To him.

To me.

I just wasn't prepared for it to hurt as much as it does.

I bring my attention back to the folders in my lap and stand, wanting to be as far away from this place as possible. Just as I'm about to turn the corner, I'm stopped by a hard chest clad in a light blue shirt and purple tie. This time, however, I get an immediate apology followed by something else.

"Well, well, well. Look who it is."

I look up to see Dylan's smiling face peering down at me. I quickly wonder if he saw me watching Jax, and if so, for how long. Whether he knows anything about our breakup. If he knows anything about why Jax and Jessica are having lunch together.

Jax and Jessica. I hate how that sounds.

"Hey, Dylan," I say, straightening. My discomfort at the possibility of being caught has me standing so stiff that I'm once again losing control over everything I'm carrying. I try and rebalance everything when Dylan's hands come out, helping me hold everything together. He readjusts a few of the folders, allowing me to have a better grip.

"Thanks," I say.

"Sure. How have you been? I haven't seen you in a while."

His demeanor is friendly, just as it always has been. It relaxes me enough to smile, but my answers come out clipped and short. "Good. Busy."

He nods. "Good. Glad to hear it."

His eyes quickly scan the inside of the restaurant, and I can tell the moment he locates Jax and Jessica. I can't help but follow his line of sight, glancing inside the restaurant once more. When I turn my head back towards Dylan, I see he's watching me.

"I should get going." My eyes shift down to all the papers in my arms.

I nod as if to say goodbye and start to walk away. After only two steps, Dylan calls out after me. I take an encouraging breath and slowly turn back to face him.

He takes a step closer to me and cocks his head to the side, towards the restaurant. Towards Jax and Jessica. "It's a business meeting. Nothing more."

I shake my head and give a quick smile. "It's really none of my business."

Dylan raises his eyebrows. "Okay," he nods. "Just thought I'd let you be clear on it."

He must know Jax and I are no longer seeing each other, but he doesn't let on whether he knows what actually happened or why things ended. Unsure of how to react to his words, I just nod. I give him another quick smile and turn, this time not stopping for anything.

I practically race down the streets towards the shop, replaying seeing Jax in the restaurant over and over in my mind followed by thoughts of our last night together. How he touched me, tasted me, treated me as though I was the most gentle and precious thing in the world. Hearing his voice, the feel of his body close to mine, his breath softly hitting the surface of my skin before he kissed me. God, I missed him. I hoped that as time went on, it would become easier.

My hurt propels me to run faster, from the crowds, the noise, but mostly, from the man in the pinstripe suit sitting in a restaurant a few blocks away.

AFTER A LONG day, I get home, the need to run is exceptionally strong. I need to clear my mind, focus on something simple. Listen to someone else's voice through my earphones as opposed to my own.

As soon as I'm ready, I take off, jogging along the streets of my neighborhood. I run along the sidewalk, catching glimpses of families through their front windows. Kids jumping up and down, throwing themselves at their parents, laughing and smiling. I pass an elderly couple sitting out on their front porch, holding hands. They smile at me as I pass by.

I make my way to the park, not stopping once. I run my usual route, passing the playground which is now empty and the side banks of the water which are calm and quiet. I check my running watch, noticing that I'm already coming up on three miles.

As I follow the bend in the path, I come up to the magnolia trees. I slow my pace, stopping in the middle of the path. I bend over, resting my hands on my knees, trying to catch my breath.

I allow myself some rest and sit on one of the benches. The sun is nearly set, casting shadows from the now flowerless trees onto the pathway, causing dark shapes to sway and dance across it. They remind me of cartoon ghosts, drawn only as dark shadows floating across the ground.

I know I should start moving again, not lose momentum, but there is something that is not letting me leave yet. A feeling of calmness I'm not ready to let go of. A feeling of belonging I haven't felt in weeks. I sit and try to absorb as much of it as I can, knowing that once I leave here, loneliness will once again take over.

I take a few more minutes before forcing myself to stand. With one foot in front of the other, I take off, a slow jog at first before I start pushing myself into a full run.

As soon as I enter my house, I start to strip my clothes off. By the time I reach the bathroom, all that's left is a pair of panties and sports bra. I turn the water in the shower as hot as I think I can handle and the room starts to fill with steam. I wipe the mirror down with a hand towel and stare at my reflection. I look tired, and I know it's not just from the run. I'm drained and I fear what will continue happening if I keep on like this.

I never thought I would feel more alone than those first few nights after Ben died. Never feel as depressed, never as scared as

I did then. I'd probably still feel that way if he was still the only love I'd lost.

Now, living with double the amount of mourning is nearly unbearable.

I pushed myself as hard as I could tonight so that I could fall asleep easily. If my body was as exhausted as my mind, chances were better I'd get what I've been waiting for, what I've been needing every night over the last few weeks. Assurance. Faith. Understanding. Confidence in the choices I've made.

Closure.

After I shower, I put on a pair of sleeping shorts and a t-shirt. Tying my hair up high on my head, I settle into bed, tossing and turning until I find a comfortable position.

I feel my body start to appreciate the softness of the bed because my legs begin to tingle. It's not too much longer before I feel my eyes getting heavy and my mind start to quiet.

Before I completely lose myself to sleep, I quietly beg for him to come.

SHADES OF GREEN and pink are blowing in the light wind, the rustling of branches the only sound I hear. A breeze comes up from behind me, causing my hair to fly up in front of my face. I look down at my wrist and find a hair elastic, exactly as I need. I tie my hair up in a knot, keeping it pulled back and out of my face.

I sit on a wooden bench, patiently waiting. Usually, it only takes a moment for Ben to appear but this time, the wait is longer than usual. Bits of panic start to creep up my spine, causing my shoulders to feel very heavy. I scan my surroundings, looking, waiting.

Finally in the distance, I see him. Dressed all in black, he runs towards me. I stand from the bench, raising both hands, waving them in the air, letting him know I'm here. He continues running, getting closer and closer but then veers left and runs off in another direction.

"Hey! Where are you going?" I yell after him. He doesn't look back. He just continues to run further and further away. I

try to whistle, putting two fingers in my mouth but hardly any sound comes out. Aggravated, I get ready to yell after him again, but a voice from behind stops me.

"You've never been able to whistle."

I whip my head around to see Ben sitting on the bench, one leg casually draped across the other, his hands held together over his stomach. He's grinning, almost laughing.

My eyes scrunch together, confused. I look back to where I saw him running just a few seconds ago, the area now empty but for the trees and grass. The man in black is gone. I point to the area, looking back at Ben clad in light jeans and a white Chicago Cubs t-shirt.

"How did you do that?" I ask.

"Do what?"

I stand there for a few seconds longer before shaking my head, deciding to forget about it and concentrate on Ben. I move closer, taking a seat right next to him. His arm comes up and around my shoulders, snuggling me in.

"Where have you been?" I ask softly, raising my hand up and intertwining my fingers with his.

"What do you mean?" he shifts his head in my direction.

"I've been waiting for you," I tell him. "For weeks. Why haven't you come?"

His eyebrows raise. "Babe, I told you before, I have no control over this. This is all you."

His answer doesn't offer me any comfort. I wanted to hear that he's been fighting to make his way back to me. That he's been just as impatient. He sees my reaction and squeezes my hand.

"I'm here now," he says.

I nod and try to put the rest out of my mind. He's right. He's here now, and that's all that matters.

We both look out at the scenery around us. There's so much greenery and beauty. The splashes of white and pink from the magnolia petals are soft but stand out fiercely.

"I love it here," I say, closing my eyes and inhaling the warm air.

"It's nice. I don't think I've ever been here before."

My eyes open.

How could he not recognize where we are? This bench, these trees, the flowers. All so familiar. I'm surprised at his words.

"What are you talking about? We've come here before," I tell him. I look at him, waiting for him to recall what this place is.

He scratches his face, his short stubble making a soft hissing sound with every graze of his fingers. He looks from left to right.

"I'm sure I've driven by here lots but never just sat here. It's nice. Peaceful."

I'm even further confused. How could he say that? I look around us. Everything about this place warms my heart. How could he not remember it? I think maybe he might be kidding around, playing a joke, looking to poke fun at me. But when I look at him, I see he means what he says. He's looking around like he's admiring the view for the first time.

Ben releases his arm from around my shoulder and leans forward, intertwining his fingers together. He looks back at me, a small knowing smile forming on his lips.

"This isn't one of our places," he says.

I look around the park again. The playground off in the distance, the path following the lake, rows of wooden benches spaced out on either side of us, the magnolia trees back in full bloom, just as they were a few weeks ago.

That's when it hits me. The magnolia trees. I realize now what I've done. I've brought Ben to a place that reminds me of Jax.

The man in black.

My stomach starts to twist into an unbelievably tight ball, and it feels like someone is squeezing my chest to where I struggle to breathe. Ben notices immediately and quickly jumps to his feet, kneeling down in front of me. His hands rub up and down my thighs.

"Just breathe. Everything's going to be okay."

I shake my head, disagreeing. I let this happen again. God, how horrible this must be for Ben, to again have Jax thrown in his face, to have my life without him surround us like this.

"Babe. Look at me," Ben says softly. I lift my eyes to meet his. How different mine must look from his right now. His are full of understanding, love, and support. All he must see is panic, insecurity, guilt.

"I'm not mad," he tries to reassure me. "This is a good thing."

I shake my head. "You should be mad," I voice. He should be, but he isn't. "Why aren't you?" I ask, my voice dropping.

His lips press together, and he squeezes my thighs before he stands and sits back down beside me. Out of the corner of my eye, I see his chest rise as he inhales deeply.

"You know why," he answers.

I look up at the sky, my eyes burning. I hope that if I keep my head held up high long enough, the tears will disappear. But my vision only becomes more blurry. I drop my head back down and feel my tears fall down my cheeks.

"But I love you," I whisper.

He looks sad, but more so for me than him.

"I know. And I love you. More than anything. More than I ever thought possible. More than I ever believed I'd be capable of. The minute I saw you..." he says, turning towards me. "I saw everything I never knew I wanted. But there it was, right in front of me. All wrapped up in defiant eyes, an angry look. You pulled me in with every push you gave. And it made me crazier for you." He stops for a second, a small smile appearing at his own

words. "I wanted that future for us more than anything."

I sniffle, wiping my tears into my sleeve. "And now?"

His eyes roam over my face, committing it to memory, for what I suspect is the last time.

"Do you know my greatest fear?"

"I didn't think you were afraid of anything," I say.

His lips quirk up a little before becoming serious again. "My greatest fear is that someone else was meant to be the love of your life."

His confession throws me, silences me. Never did I ever think he'd be worried about such a thing. How could he think that? Why would he think that? I open my mouth, ready to assure him no one could ever take his place, but he's too quick.

"It's also my greatest hope," he says quietly.

I blink, unsure I heard properly.

"Ben..."

"There is nothing more important to me than your happiness, Rachel. If I thought this could make you happy..." he stops, unsure how to continue.

"Seeing you does *make me happy," I protest.*

"Do these dreams make you as happy as a painting? Or a hat?"

His words are jarring. They sound like an accusation, but I know they aren't. They hurt because they are reminders of Jax.

"I need you to hear this, Rachel. Really hear this." He shifts his body so that he's facing me fully. "No part of me wants you to spend the rest of your life alone, too wrapped up in missing me."

I lift my hand and rest it against his cheek. "But I'll always miss you."

Ben turns his face and kisses the open palm of my hand. "And I'll miss you, every day. But there's more for you than just this. More waiting outside of this bubble. More life to live. And I need you to live it. For both of us."

It's hard hearing him say all this. Mostly because it sounds like he's trying to let me *go.*

"We never got to say goodbye," his voice takes a sad tone. "Maybe that's what all this is about. We were so busy planning the beginning of our life together that we weren't prepared for the ending of it."

If I thought hearing anything he said earlier was difficult, it doesn't come close to this. Is that what this has been all about? Needing to say goodbye? Were these dreams a way to pull us apart instead of bringing us back together? I move into him, lifting my legs up onto the bench and cuddling into his side. The need to be as close to him as possible is overwhelming. He wraps his arms around me and holds me tight. We stay silent for a few minutes, wrapped in each other.

"Nothing can break us," I mutter into his chest, repeating words he once told me.

"Nothing," he answers. "But that doesn't mean you didn't need putting back together."

I shake at the truth of his words.

"He did that. You were happy. I want that for you," he whispers into my ear.

It's so hard for me to understand that.

"How can you want that? If the roles were reversed, I'd want you longing for me the rest of your life," I say into his shoulder.

I feel the rise of his chest, a light laughter shaking my resting head.

"We both know that's not true," he says, lifting my hand and kissing it.

He's right, but I still can't bear the thought.

"Do you love him?" he asks.

I press my face into his chest, unable to look at him when I nod. It feels wrong, admitting it to Ben, but I've never been able to keep anything from him. Even if I didn't answer, he'd know.

He can see right through me like no one else.

"I'm sorry," I whisper.

"Don't be."

"I'm not ready to say goodbye." I burrow my face further into his chest, my tears staining his shirt.

His lips kiss the top of my head. "So, let's not. How about, 'See ya in sixty years?'"

I shake my head. "That's too long."

"Nah. It will fly by. You know how I know?"

I lift my face to meet his. His eyes are so full of certainty in what he's about to say that I have no choice but to believe whatever it is.

"Because you are going to have the best life. It's going to be full of fun and new experiences. A family. Your life will be so full, you'll wish time would slow right down."

His words fill my heart with such love for him. I reach up, wrapping my arms around his neck, pulling him down for a kiss. I pour every emotion I have into what I know will be our last one. And he kisses me back with the same intensity, same passion.

When he pulls back, his lips find their way lower, to my neck, then the curve of my shoulder. I feel his lips move against my skin as he speaks.

"You made my life worth it."

I let out the cry I've been holding in and grip him harder, holding him closer. I try and hold on to this moment as long as possible, but I can already feel Ben starting to fade away. I'm waking up, and I only have a little time left before I have to say goodbye to him forever.

I pull back and look at him, hoping I can figure out the words before it's too late. But then right as I'm about to say something, he smiles and winks. Just like he used to.

He already knows everything I wanted to say.

chapter 25

WAKING UP THIS morning, I feel a mix of emotions. Relief. Sadness. Hope.

And finally, closure.

Every bit of last night's dream felt so real—every touch felt, every look given, every confession made. Telling someone you love that you've fallen in love with another, there's no describing that feeling.

I am so incredibly lucky to have been able to love Ben. Even luckier that he loved me back. Now I can be thankful for our time together instead of angry for it being cut short. The things I've learned about myself, life and love because of Ben have made me into the woman I am today.

And because of that, I do owe it to Ben to start living my life. For today and tomorrow and the day after that. Today is the first day I will leave yesterday behind.

Even though my run last night made my legs angry at me today, I get up, get dressed, pour some coffee into a thermos and head out the door.

I walk this time. I walk along my usual path, through my familiar neighborhood, passing houses I usually am only able to take a quick glance at. At this speed, I am able to take in more detail than I ever did before. I notice how the house on the corner has slightly different color shutters on the lower level windows than the uppers ones, how the house across the street has the most beautiful hydrangea bushes growing along its side—things I've passed every day for years but seem to only notice for the first time today.

I'm so lost in my thoughts about last night that it's not until my body stops and sits down on a familiar wooden bench that I realize I've walked to where things began—in the park, under the magnolia trees. The day Jackson Perry sat down beside me on this very bench and smiled at me.

I wasn't ready for him then.

I've been lucky enough to have two men come into my life and change me. One made me who I am, the other saved me from who I was becoming. One will have a piece of my heart forever, the other has filled it completely.

Three weeks have gone by since the night I left Jax, and I have missed him every second of it. I have been nothing but miserable. I can't regret leaving that night because without that, I probably never would have gotten my chance to say goodbye to Ben. And I needed to if I was ever going to be able to fully open myself up to love again.

Today is the first day I will be that person.

My thoughts are disrupted by the vibration in my pocket.

"Hey."

"What did I say?" Tess scolds.

My back straightens against the bench, immediately put on edge.

"What do you mean?"

"Didn't I specifically tell you *not* to go and talk to Paul? Because I feel like I did. I feel this way because I remember specifically saying, '*do not* to talk to him.'" Her voice is hushed but angry.

Shit.

"Umm..." I squint up towards the sky, trying to come up with an excuse Tess might accept.

"Umm? That's the best you can do?" she questions.

"Well..."

Silence comes over the phone for a minute. I try to think of what I can say to defend myself, to make her see that I only wanted to help. Then I hear a small laugh escape from Tess.

"Did I scare you? God, I hope I did. You deserve a scare for going behind my back."

"Huh?" Clearly I'm confused over what is happening here. "You're going to have to back up. Am I in trouble or not?"

I hear her laugh before she continues to speak in a hushed tone. "No, you're not in trouble, even though you should be. You went behind my back! Fucking unbelievable. Me! Your best friend!"

"Well from the sounds of your laughing, it seems like it's a good thing I did. So are you going to explain or are you just going to keep ridiculing me? And why are you whispering?"

"Paul's in the shower. I don't want him to hear."

Paul is in Tess's shower? This early in the morning? I smile.

"Let's start with how Paul got to be in your shower this early morning," I suggest.

"Fine, but just know, I'll remember this betrayal!"

"Yes, fine. Whatever," I agree. "So, shower?"

"I guess after you went behind my back and had a little chat with him, he had some asshole epiphany. He showed up at my work last night while I was in the middle of a fitting for a male swimsuit segment. Could not have been at a better time. The look on his face when he saw all those guys in speedos, fuck, I wish I had a camera. I'd make postcards and send them to everyone he knows," she says. "He came storming up out of nowhere, thrust some cheap grocery store flowers against my chest, telling them to back off a little. Can you believe that shit?"

I try to hold in my own laughter, picturing the scene in my head.

"I can hear you," Paul's voice sounds in the background.

"I'm having a private conversation!" Tess yells back at him.

After a few seconds, she comes back. "Okay, he's gone."

"So? Then what? Did your heart go pitter-patter?" I ask giggling.

I hear her snort. "Who the fuck do you think I am? Of course not. I got right up in his face and told him to leave. Unacceptable behavior. He can't just walk into my place of work and act all Tarzan and expect me to be Jane. I'm the fucking Tarzan in this relationship!"

"I'm not seeing how all this ended with him in your shower."

"He refused to leave until we talked so I told him to wait in my office. I left him there for forty-five minutes."

"He waited that long?" I say, surprised.

"He's lucky I only had him wait that long. After the weeks of bullshit he put me through, he got off easy!"

I laugh.

"Long story short, as soon as I walked in, he apologized. Groveled, really. For how he's been acting for the last few weeks," she says. "He said he realized he let some of his insecurities get the better of him. About us, my job. Where we may end up."

"So you kissed and made up?"

"No. First I told him he had to get over his male chauvinist attitude and welcomed him into the twenty-first century. I also told him that if he ever put me through something like this again, he'd be lucky to have kids one day." Then her voice softens. "Then I looked down at the pitiful bouquet of flowers he had in his hands—the price tag was still on the wrapper for fuck's sake. I realized it was the first time he'd gotten me flowers. Gotten me anything. He was there, he was sorry, and he was asking me to take him back. And that's all I wanted."

My heart fills. "I'm so happy for you. That's amazing, Tess."

"If you ever tell him I said that, I'll kill you," she threatens.

"Secret is safe," I swear.

"I thought I'd need some grand gesture or that I'd want to make him squirm longer. I guess I didn't. I knew the minute he walked into the studio, we would leave together."

I see now that Tess's hard exterior has finally found a crack, someone who is able to soften her.

"Then I made him get on his knees and give me an orgasm for every week he was a dick. And he did." *And she's back.* "So I guess I should say thanks." I can hear resolution in her voice. "Who knows how long it would have taken him on his own. Men are so fucking stupid."

I smile. "He would have figured it out sooner or later."

"Well, I'm just happy it was sooner. The vibrator was getting a little boring."

"Ew!" I scrunch my face. "Too much!"

I hear Paul yell something in the background. "Got to go. He still has a lot of making up to do."

"Okay, that's enough!"

Tess laughs. After a few seconds, she sneaks in one last comment. "Just goes to show you what a sad bouquet of sunflowers and an apology can get you."

Her voice practically screams her double meaning. But it's going to take more than an apology to fix things between me and Jax. For starters, I need to be ready to fix things. I don't have more time to think about it because Tess just can't help herself.

"Happy endings…all night long!"

"Okay, I'm hanging up now."

I MISS JAX. Terribly.

Everything around me reminds me of him. The brownies in C'est Bon, a bride's honeymoon plans in London, the roar of a motorcycle. The most obvious is the branches of magnolia flowers I ordered for no other reason than to just have in them in the shop. Tess thinks I'm filling the void he left with things that remind me of him. She may be right.

It's late in the evening and I'm finishing up inputting invoices into my computer at work when Tess calls. Before I even say hello, she's already talking.

"He's at home. You need to go and finally fix this."

The music is loud in the background. I remember her mentioning going out for drinks with Paul and some friends.

"Dylan's here. Sophie brought him. Did you know she's still been seeing him? What a secretive little bitch," she deviates. "Anyway, I asked about Jax. He said he's at home."

My heart speeds up at the mention of Jax's name as it always does, but it's quickly followed by fear and insecurity. It's been weeks since we've seen each other. For all I know, he may not be at home alone. The thought turns my stomach to acid.

"I don't even know if he'd answer the door," I say.

"He will." She sounds so sure. "Rachel, you're in love with him aren't you?"

The answer to that is a resounding yes, but it doesn't do anything to help ease my fear of seeing him.

"Then go there. He deserves to know and you deserve to be able to finally tell him!" she says before hanging up.

I pace my office back and forth, simultaneously talking myself into and out of going over there. I know it's cowardly, but the risk of rejection is a hard one to face. I know how awful that sounds considering how I rejected him only a few weeks ago.

But I needed that time.

I needed to let go, to stand on my own without the fear of losing parts of me that make me who I am. I needed time to realize I want a future, I want the life Ben would have wanted for me.

More than anything, I needed to realize how deeply I am able to fall in love again. At the risk of being rejected, I know Jax deserves to hear it too.

He deserves to know it all.

WALKING INTO THE lobby of Jax's condo building, I'm surprised I don't stumble over my own feet. My nerves so heightened, my body is moving almost robotically. I have to concentrate on placing one foot in front of the other the entire time.

It's nearing ten in the evening and walking past me is a small group of women heading out for a night on the town. They all look gorgeous. Each with their hair and makeup done, wearing short skirts and killer heels. I immediately wished I had gone home first and changed out of my jeans and off the shoulder t-shirt. I try to remember if I put makeup on this morning. Even if I did, I'm sure it's all but rubbed off by now.

I walk over towards the security desk and am caught off guard when the older gentleman remembers me.

"Ms. Miller, it's lovely to see you again."

I smile nervously. "Thank you," I look down to his name tag, "James."

"Jimmy, please. Here to see Mr. Perry?" His eyes wander down to what I'm holding in my arms. How does he remember all this?

My nerves keep me silent. *What if Jax refuses me entry? What if Jimmy calls up and then has to tell me Jax doesn't want to see me? What if he already has a guest?*

Jimmy looks at me expectantly, waiting for me to answer. I feel my cheeks flush.

What the hell was I thinking coming here? Too much time has passed. Jax is probably relieved he doesn't need to deal with me anymore. I'm about to apologize to Jimmy, turn and make a dash for the lobby doors, when I hear his voice.

"Rachel?"

Jimmy looks past me, his head leaning slightly to the side. His eyes dart from behind me then back, like he's watching a tennis match.

I take a deep breath and turn slowly, gripping tightly to the glass vase in my hands. I do my best to act casual. I try and smile but the minute my eyes find his, I falter, my nerves too strong. But it's his expression that guts me. Aside from the mild look of surprise, his face is void of any other emotion. Stoic.

"Hi," is all I manage.

His eyes quickly scan over me, and once again, I berate myself for not going home to change. I could have at least freshened up a little before I came to declare my love.

"What are you doing here?" he asks.

I hear the shuffling of papers behind me and am reminded that we are not alone. I quickly glance behind me to where Jimmy is, not doing a very good job at hiding his eavesdropping. I take a few tentative steps towards Jax, hoping for a little more privacy.

But with every step closer, my mind gets a little foggier. I smell a bit of his aftershave mixed with soap and shampoo. His hair looks damp like it's only just been towel dried. He's wearing a pair of light jeans with holes at the knees. He's in a t-shirt and flip-flops, holding keys and mail in his hands. He's the most beautiful thing I've ever seen.

"Can we talk? Maybe go upstairs?" I'm so nervous, my heart is beating so fast I fear the possibility I'll pass out.

Jax looks beyond me towards Jimmy and then back in my direction. His eyes fall to my arms and what's in them. He gives a small nod. "Sure."

We start to walk towards the elevators and Jax raises his hand, waving towards the older, snoopy gentleman.

"Mr. Perry. Ms. Miller," Jimmy bows his head in reply.

As soon as we are in the elevator, I let go of the breath I've been holding. I try to regain some composure, feeling better that Jax has at least agreed to speak with me. I can't stop looking at him through our mirrored reflection in the elevator doors. He notices it too. His eyes give nothing away, only fleeting glances. It takes everything in me to hold back and not beg for forgiveness right here and now. But his hard exterior and expressionless face tells me I should go slowly if I have any chance at making this work. Neither of us says anything during the entire ride up, only the hum of the elevator filling the small car.

As soon as the elevator reaches Jax's floor, the doors open and he waits for me to exit first. I'm a few steps ahead of him as we walk towards his door. I feel his eyes boring into the back of my head, and I quicken the pace a bit. I wait for him at his door, his eyes stay glued to mine until he's standing mere inches from me, then looks away to unlock the door. Being this close to him after all these weeks has my body in overdrive. I feel my skin radiating heat, small goose bumps rising on my arms and legs. I stare at his side profile, his freshly shaven face, his Adam's apple moving slightly as he swallows. It's only when I hear the click of the lock that I look away.

He opens the door, swinging it inwards and gestures with his hand to step inside. Memories of the last time I walked through this door flood my mind. Him in the kitchen, strapping on my black British cap, our kiss, our…everything in the bedroom. His apartment hasn't changed much since then. A small sigh of relief escapes me when I see the painting still hanging above the mantle.

I feel Jax walk past me, our arms brushing against each other as he moves. He drops his mail on the counter and turns back around, leaning against it, crossing his arms over his chest.

He's waiting for me to say something. I guess I'm the one who should start since I came here looking for him. I just don't know where to start. His mannerisms are hard to read. His body is stiff, but his face is curious, softening it slightly. My mind is pressed with thoughts. I try to decipher them and come up with a clear and hopefully meaningful beginning. Instead, I say the first thing to pop into my mind.

"I made a mistake."

Stepping away from the counter, he releases his arms, dropping them to his side and raises his brows slightly in surprise.

My mind continues to swirls with everything I want and need to say. *Do I apologize first? Do I tell him how much I've missed him? Do I ask for another chance? How do I begin to explain these last few weeks?* The weight of all these questions is as heavy on my shoulders as the large glass container that I hold in my arms. Realizing I'm still holding the large vase, I extend the offering to him.

"These are for you," I say, taking a few steps closer to him, lowering the vase to the counter top. The branches of magnolia flowers stand out against the otherwise empty space. I look over at Jax who's watching me put the flowers down.

"Thank you." His voice is quiet, uncertainty laced through it. "Like the ones from the park." He extends his arm and delicately touches a few of the petals with the tips of his fingers. He looks over at me and shows a hint of a smile. It's the first bit of emotion I've seen from him since I've come here.

"Yeah, that was sort of the point," I say.

He doesn't say any more, waiting for me to continue. I take a deep breath, walking further into his condo. I feel him watch me slowly walk around the room. Maybe I should start off easy, ask him about his day and work my way from there. A slow and steady pace into the hard stuff. But Jax eliminates that possibility pretty quick.

"Rachel, what are you doing here?"

His voice is close so I know he's followed me into the room. I can feel the tiny hairs on the back of my neck stand at his close proximity. I sum up my courage, ready to tell him why I'm here. I clench my fists, close my eyes and count to five before I turn.

But as soon as I face him, all bravery leaves me, and I become a scared, vulnerable girl, afraid the man she loves doesn't love her back anymore.

"That night, I'm sorry I left like that. You didn't deserve that. *We* didn't deserve that."

I see him take a deep breath, bringing his hands to rest on his hips.

"No, we didn't."

I take a few tentative steps towards him and am thankful he doesn't take any steps back. I know I have a lot of explaining to do, and I hope he's open to hearing it.

"You took me by surprise," I start. He raises his eyebrows just slightly, but his eyes remain focused on my face. "I wasn't expecting you or even looking for you. I didn't think falling in love again was a possibility for me. I didn't even want it." I pause, looking down and swallowing the lump in my throat. "But it happened. And I felt…terrible."

I hear Jax take a step closer, the sound of his flip-flops smacking quietly across the floor. When I look back up, I can see it was hard for him to hear me say that.

"I felt like I was betraying Ben. His memory. Our life together. Every moment I spent with you was a moment I wasn't thinking about him. And I don't mean you were simply a distraction. You were more than that. More than I was ready for at the time."

I watch Jax look down and scratch the back of his neck, contemplating everything I've just said. When he finally looks up, his eyes are kind but closed off. I know it then, he's not going to forgive me. He's not going to move past this.

"Rachel…" he starts.

"Please don't give up on me," I plead. "I still have so much to tell you." I feel my window of opportunity getting smaller and smaller with every second that passes. I need to be able to tell him everything I came here to say. He needs to hear it at least before he turns me down.

He looks up at me, his face resigned. "These few weeks were…tough. Tougher than I thought they'd be. But it gave me time to think."

My hope starts to dissipate and my fear of being rejected resurfaces.

He continues, "I know this might sound harsh, I don't mean it to, but I know no other way to say it."

My heart starts to crumble. I want to stop him before he says anything that could end us before we truly begin. I round up all the determination I have left and take those final steps towards him, taking his hands in mine.

"Jax…" I plead.

"I can't compete with a ghost, Rachel. I'll never be able to win."

He slowly removes his hands out of mine and takes a step back. The pain is unbearable. I need to do something. Say something to make him understand. Let him know there is no competition. I know my eyes are pleading for him to stop. To forgive. To give me another chance.

"Earphones," I blurt out.

He looks at me, obviously confused.

"That first day in the park. You reached over and pulled my earphones out. That's the first time I felt it," I say.

His eyes fall into small slits. He shakes his head, still not understanding.

"That was the first time I felt my heart beat for you. It was small, like a tremor. But it was there, and I felt it. I've felt it every day after that too. Getting stronger and stronger. When I got on your bike for the first time, my heart wasn't beating fast out of fear. It was because of how close we were. When we stood right here and hung that painting up, a pull started. I know you felt it too. I could go on and on. Tell you exactly how it felt when you finally kissed me on my doorstep. How nothing else existed to me in that moment but you. And what we shared here? I know you believed me when I told you how much I wanted it. I know you saw it. And I did!" I take a breath. "You knew what you were doing to my heart. And you were so gentle with it. You understood what was happening before I did, and you were so patient. You waited for me to catch up."

I take another step closer and let him know I'm not finished fighting for us yet. "Now I know what my heart has been telling me for weeks. I've finally caught up. And I'm terrified it's too late, that your feelings have changed. Please tell me it's not too late."

He shrugs his shoulders, shaking his head. "Falling in love is easy, falling out of it…"

I take another step closer, leaving us only mere inches apart. I can feel the apprehension radiating off his body. As nervous as I was to come here and tell him my feelings, I see now that he's just as nervous to keep feeling his.

"I told him about you," I say. His eyes meet mine and I see a glimmer of…something. Something is better than the resignation I saw earlier. "I know that may not sound like a lot, but for me it was everything. To tell him about you. My feelings for you." I pray he sees how sincere and truthful I am with what I'm about to say.

"There is no competition. I'm so sorry I made you feel like there was. I'm so sorry I wasn't more truthful with you, that I didn't tell you how scared I was. How scared my feelings for you made me. My feelings for you grew so quickly I didn't know what to do. How to behave."

His face softens, and it urges me to continue.

"My heart wanted you. This. *Us*." I gesture my hands between us. "Faster than my head was ready for. Please believe me now when I say that they are now both in the same place."

"And where's that?" He asks quietly.

"They're both screaming how much I love you and praying you believe me enough to try again."

As soon as those words leave my mouth, I feel a weight lifted. No matter what he does or how he reacts, knowing I told him the truth feels right.

His body stiffens and he moves closer—so close that our bodies are touching. "Say that again," he demands.

Relief in knowing I have no reservations admitting it, I repeat myself.

"Jackson Perry, I love you. I'm in love with you. And I hope you still love me enough to give me a chance to show you."

His nostrils flare just the tiniest amount before he answers with the words I've been waiting, hoping to hear.

"I'm going to kiss you now."

My heart explodes.

"Good, because I've been wait—" before I can even finish, his lips crash down on mine.

I feel him clutch my head in his hands as he pushes his tongue into my mouth. He's forceful, but I match his tone eagerly. This kiss is different than any other kiss we've shared. It isn't experimental or tender or emotional. This kiss is primal, possessive. Jax is branding me as his as I'm branding him as mine.

I feel him bite my lip with enough force to have me flinch but moan the next second when he runs his tongue over the sensitive area. His hands come down, one gripping my hip, the other touching the skin of my lower back. I run my hands through his still damp hair. It's smooth as silk, and I tug on it when he nips at my neck. This time he's the one to moan. I feel his hands grip my sides and he lifts me, urging me to wrap my legs around his waist. My arms come around his neck, holding on as he carries me down the hall towards his bedroom.

Once there, my back rests against the wall, my legs squeezing his hips, keeping him close. Our lips separate for only a moment as I feel my shirt being lifted above my head. He throws it over his shoulder before his eyes roam downwards to my chest. A simple white lace bra seems to have him in a trance. When he looks back up, one side of his mouth tilts up.

"Last time I took it slow. I don't think I'll be able to this time."

His words have me squirming against him, rubbing myself against the hardness I feel through his jeans. I feel a small rumble of laughter come from him, his shoulders shaking. He moves his hips away, out of reach.

"Keep doing that, see what happens," he threatens with a grin.

"Kind of the point, isn't it?" I say. He's amused by my answer.

Last time he wasn't the only one who went slowly. I was timid and nervous, afraid even. This time, my want and need for him are the only feelings I have.

My hands reach for the hem of his shirt and I pull it over his head, breathing a sigh of relief once our skin touches. Jax pins me to the wall with his hips so he can use his hands to undo the clasp of my bra. Once that's gone, his hands are all over me.

"I've thought about this so many times over the last few weeks," he says between kisses and licks on my chest. His hands hold my breasts, lifting them up so he can kiss each one, his tongue circling each nipple. "Tell me. Tell me you've thought about this too."

I pull his head up to mine and look him in the eye. My hands grip the sides of his face, making sure he sees me when I say this.

"I have," I promise.

That seems to be good enough for him because his lips come crashing down on mine once again as he starts to walk us towards the bed. He doesn't lay me down on the mattress gently but drops me in the middle of it. I use my feet and hands to climb up higher and watch as he climbs on his knees onto the bed. He starts to undo his belt, followed by the button and zipper of his jeans. He looks over at me and nods towards my pants.

"Those. Off."

I giggle, my hands undoing my pants, but I'm distracted with him pulling off his own and his boxers along with it. My fingers start to fumble with him naked, on his knees between my jean-clad legs. He sees me watching and grins. His hands come up and finish undoing my pants and he starts to pull them down my legs, taking my panties with them. With no more clothing between us, we both can't keep our eyes and fingers from roaming, exploring—mine to every hard inch of him, his to every soft inch of mine.

My hands are ripped from his body when I feel him grab my ass and lift me in the air, my legs thrown over his shoulders has he lays down flat on the bed. Last time, I stiffened with nerves when he wanted to taste me. This time, my hands run through his hair pushing his face closer. With every lick, kiss, even bite, I moan. A few times, embarrassingly loud, but it only seems to turn Jax on even more.

"I love that sound," he murmurs between my legs.

His arms come up, filling his hands with my breasts. I can't help but grind against him as I feel my nerves start to tighten. My back arches off the bed when I come, my breathing fast and short. I can feel Jax grin as he removes my legs from his shoulder, kissing the inside of each thigh.

His eyes meet mine as he kisses his way up my body. "I love the way you look right now. Flushed and panting."

"I love the way I feel," I say, hoping my grin conveys just how good I feel right now. Just as Jax is about to rest on top of me, I push his chest away, moving out from under him, reversing our roles.

"My turn," I say.

He raises his upper body slightly, resting against his forearms and watches me as I kiss down his chest, stomach, below his navel. My fingers trace the lines of his pelvis and when I grip him, I see his stomach suck in. I lick my lips making sure they are wet and slippery before I take him in my mouth. I hear him let out a loud exhale as I take him further down. As equally as he is hard, his skin is incredibly soft. I love hearing the sounds he makes every time I move up and down, sucking him harder. My eyes look up from what I'm doing and see him watching me. He sweeps some of my hair away from my face, giving him a clearer view. The look on his face lets me know that he very much likes what I'm doing. It's not long before he sits up a little more and his fingers lift my chin, moving my mouth away from him.

"No more or this is going to end before I can fuck you."

I softly kiss the tip and slowly crawl up his body, our lips meeting, our tongues dueling. Sitting up fully, he spins us so that I'm on my hands and knees. He kisses up the length of my spine, moving up to my shoulders, to my cheek and takes one of my hands, resting it on top of the headboard. He does the same with my other hand. I feel his fingers graze the length of my arms and the sides of my ribs. He pulls a condom from his nightstand and finds his place back behind me again. I hear the sound of the wrapper being torn and I shiver with anticipation.

"I'm going to need you to hold on," he growls.

My hands clench against the headboard, ready for whatever he wants to give me.

With little warning, he slams into me, filling me. I hear myself let go small sounds of surprise at just how unyielding he is, but they quickly turn into pants once he starts to move. Over and over he pulls almost all the way out before pushing all the way back in. His hands hold on to my waist, giving him the leverage he needs to move in and out as fast and as hard as he wants.

Although I'm enjoying it, and he is too, I know there is more going on than simple lust. He's working out his frustration on me for what I put us through. And it's okay. He needs this. I need this. We need this to be able to move forward.

"Say it again," he says between thrusts.

I look behind me, unsure of what he means. His eyes meet mine. They are filled with something I've never seen from him. Greed.

"Say it again," he repeats, gentler this time. Then I understand.

"I'm yours," I tell him. His lips don't smile, but his eyes do. "And you're mine," I add.

With that, I see his lips quirk. "Yes, I am."

EXHAUSTED AND SATIATED seems to best way to describe my state right now. Jax was right when he said he wouldn't go slowly, but the second time, he was softer, gentler. And now we are taking the time to talk to each other.

Lying on our sides, facing each other with only a bed sheet covering our naked bodies, we say the things we didn't get a chance to earlier on. He let me know hard it was watching me leave. I let him know how hard it was for me to keep moving. I promise to tell him more about Ben someday, about my past and my hopes for our future. He promises to listen and wait until I'm ready. I again try and explain why it was so hard for me to admit my feelings for him.

Most importantly, we say *I love you* enough times to make up for the weeks of being apart.

"I'll never get sick of hearing or saying it," he said laughing after I told him how love sick we must sound.

Jax falls on his back, pulling me to him, curling me into his side. My head rests perfectly on top of his chest and his arm switches from playing with my hair to skimming my bare back with his fingers.

"I really missed you," I say quietly.

His fingers still on my back. I feel his lips press against the top of my head.

"Me too."

"I saw you. A few weeks ago," I reveal.

I feel his head and chest lift from the pillow, turning to his side, facing me. "You did? Where?"

"At a restaurant. I was walking back from a meeting and there you were." I watch as his memory plays back the last few weeks. "You were with Jessica," I add softly.

His eyes open a little wider, remembering. "We had a business lunch."

"She definitely looked like she was making you *her* business."

I cringe at how that sounded. After everything I've put him through, I have no right to pass judgment. Even still, I can't help it. I press my face into the pillow, embarrassed. His fingers push my hair back, and when I try to bury my face even further, he takes my pillow out from under me, giving me nowhere to hide.

He's grinning, amused. Even through the dimness of the bedroom light, I can see his eyes shining.

"Were you…jealous?"

"NO!" *Yes. Terribly so.*

"Are you sure? Because…" his fingers trace my eyebrow, giving me away.

I blow out a large breath. "Fine, yes. I saw the two of you and didn't like it. Happy?"

His smile couldn't be bigger. "Extremely."

I roll my eyes and turn my body, facing away from him.

"Oh, come on," he says laughing, trying to turn me back in his direction, but I refuse to move.

I feel him roll on top of me carefully, his bare chest resting against my back. I feel him kiss my shoulders, making his way up to my neck to the spot just behind my ear that causes me to react each time.

"You have no reason to be jealous," he murmurs in my ear before his teeth and lips lightly suck on my earlobe. "There is no one but you. There has been no one but you since that first night at the bar." His voice changes at the memory. "You looked so scared that night. Frightened. I knew it then."

I turn my head and look at him.

"I knew it then. That I wanted to be the one to calm you," he places a soft kiss on my lips. "It's been only you."

With that, he answers the question I've been too afraid to ask. I couldn't blame him if he dated, but the sense of relief that washes over me that he hasn't is enough for me to turn onto my back and face him fully. My fingers play with some of the longer pieces of hair that's fallen over his forehead.

"Just you," I promise him back.

He kisses me long and soft. Part of me can't believe the hardness I'm feeling poking my stomach but when my own body starts to react, I completely understand. Before we start to move things along again, I feel him roll off me and reach for his phone that's sitting on the bedside table.

"What are you doing?" I watch him slide his fingers against the screen and start typing out a message.

"Emailing my assistant. Telling him to cancel my meetings for tomorrow," he glances over at his alarm clock. "Today actually."

"Oh?" I try to act disinterested, but the goofy grin plastered on my face is a sure giveaway that I'm very interested in what may have trumped these meetings. I lift the bed sheet up, covering the lower half of my face. "Something come up?"

"You're a terrible liar," Jax grins. "And you and I both know something's been coming up all night."

I giggle into the sheet.

Jax puts his phone back on the bedside table before lifting the sheet and rolling back on top of me.

"I thought that after I kiss you all over and feel every inch of you again," he says between kisses to my chest and neck, "we'd maybe get a few hours of sleep, and then I could take my girlfriend out for breakfast."

If my heart wasn't already beating fast, it accelerated at the word "girlfriend."

"How does that sound?" Jax lifts his head slightly, his eyes scanning my face, looking for a reaction.

I know he isn't questioning about how breakfast sounds. I take his face between my hands and kiss his slightly swollen lips.

"Sounds perfect."

epilogue

Jackson

Ten Months Later

IT TOOK ME a little while to find the right spot but after asking the groundskeeper, I was finally led in the right direction. The snow has all melted and the grass is just starting to turn green again. It's a mess to walk through, but I've been holding this off long enough. I'm not sure if it's manly pride or honorable gentleman that's brought me here today. Maybe it doesn't even matter, but it's something I know I have to do.

There isn't anyone around, at least not that I can see. It helps knowing I don't have an audience considering how strange I already feel being here. A small gust of wind breezes by, blowing some of the dead leaves from the previous year away. Once I reach my destination, I smile a little, recognizing the uniqueness of the bouquet already laying there. After a while, I've come to recognize Rachel's work.

I don't feel the pang of jealousy so much anymore, knowing that she ensures a new bouquet is laid here every week. I know it's not her bringing them here every time. Lately, she's had her delivery driver do it. She only comes on certain days now. Two of which are engraved on the marble stone I've come face to face with.

I lay my own bouquet of white roses that I bought from a corner store on my way. I thought it best not to tell Rachel where I was going. I don't like to keep things from her, especially with how open we've become with each other, but this is something private I needed to do. Man to man.

"Hello, Ben," I say, brushing away any stray branches, flower petals and leaves that cover the stone.

I know the fact that this will be a one-sided conversation doesn't make it fair, but fairness is not something I'm really going for. I look down at the bouquet next to mine, a beautiful mixture of creams and yellows.

"The bouquet Rachel made is really beautiful. I'm sure she spent a good amount of time on it."

At first when she told me she would bring a bouquet here every week, I was a little jealous. And truthfully, worried. Worried that maybe she hadn't let Ben go as she told me. She assured me that it had nothing to do with us, but it was more a sense of responsibility. She also added that he deserved them, that he should never feel like she's forgotten him. I guess it was a little hard to understand at first, knowing that she still felt that kind of responsibility towards him, but I knew I had to get past my own insecurity about it. She told me once that I wasn't competing with a ghost. I had to make the choice to believe her.

Even now, months later, she still feels the sense of responsibility to make sure he's taken care of, that his final resting place is always taken care of. But she's reached a place where she's okay with that responsibility not falling solely on her shoulders. For that, I'm selfishly grateful.

Looking at the well-kept stone, I am strangely at a loss for words.

"I thought I knew what I was going to say, but I guess I don't." I take a deep breath and look around the cemetery. I know they are supposed to be depressing and sad, but I find them to be some of the most beautiful places in the city. Quiet and peaceful. I look down at the stone in front of me, the engraving on it catching my eye.

Benjamin Tyler McAvoy

Loved by all who knew him.

I smile at the words, knowing how true they are. Knowing the feeling of being loved like that, by someone who does it so fiercely. It's amazing what you can have in common with a complete stranger.

"I came to let you know about my plans."

I pull the ring box that I picked up earlier today out of my jacket pocket and start spinning my hands.

"I'm not looking for your approval or blessing—her dad already gave me that. Her mom cried when I stopped by to show her. I guess I'm just here to make you a promise."

In the months that have passed, I have managed to fall in love with Rachel more and more every day. I know that sounds cliché, but it's true. And just when I think I've reached my limit, she does something or says something that will make me laugh or smile, and I know I just fell more in love with her. My eyes move from the ring box back to Ben's name.

"I'm sure you can relate."

A lot has changed since the night she came to my condo. Our relationship has changed. It's become more than I expected. It's become everything to me. I believe she feels the same, at least I hope she does. She pretty much lives at my place which doesn't bother me one bit. Except that I've come to see that she's a bit of a slob. Constantly leaving dishes in the sink, shoes anywhere but in the closet. Last night's clothes are always piled on the floor. I've cleared out space for her in my closet so she never needs to rush home for clean clothes. Most are on the floor by her side of the bed.

"Was she always a slob?" I ask. "I mean, don't get me wrong, I love having her around, but Christ. I've had to hire a housekeeper to come once a week. She doesn't know about that, by the way."

Another breeze hits, the smell of spring wafts through in the air.

"Look, I know this is weird, me being here talking to you in a way I'd never want another man talking about her, but I guess our situation is...unique." I lift the ring box up in front of my face. "No one but her parents and you know about this. I haven't even told my parents yet. Probably because I'm mildly terrified. I know she still thinks about you. Especially on certain days." My eyes shift again to the date of birth and death engraved on the stone.

"But I know she loves me, and I know she's happy. Sometimes when she doesn't think I'm looking, I catch her watching me. It's hard to describe the look, but the way it makes me feel? It's like I could rip open my chest and serve her my heart on a platter. Those are the times I'm not so nervous about asking. Those are the times I see how much she loves me."

"I guess I'm here to tell you that she's happy. And to promise you that I'm going to do everything in my power to make sure she stays that way for the rest of her life. And I hope you're good with that."

I stand, feeling better. Feeling relief at knowing I've said all I came to say. Proof that I'm okay with Ben being a part of Rachel's past because I am her future. And hopefully, Ben can be okay with that too.

I WALK IN the door with my arms full with grocery bags. On my way to the kitchen, I trip on one of Rachel's running shoes.

"Fucking hell," I mumble.

I put the bags on the kitchen counter and see Rachel come out of the bathroom. I'm about to tell her I could have broken my neck when I see her wrapped only in a towel. She looks at me and smiles. And with that, I forget all about her stupid shoe. She walks towards the kitchen, leaving a trail of water drops behind her.

"What's for dinner?" she says peeking over the counter.

"Your favorite," I tell her. I look in the bag until I find what I'm looking for. I pull out two boxes of macaroni and cheese.

She laughs. "Perfect. I'm starved. Just going to go put on some sweats."

I watch her walk down the hall to the bedroom. She drops her towel at the door, not even thinking about it. This girl. She's not trying to seduce me, but she does anyway.

I take a breath, telling my now growing hard-on to sit back down.

I quickly make dinner, setting the food out on the table, grabbing plates and utensils when Rachel reappears. She's dressed in pj shorts and one of my t-shirts. There are many looks of Rachel I love, but this is my favorite. Her legs are shiny from the lotion I know she just applied. Her breasts are beautiful mounds hidden under my worn t-shirt, nipples softly poking against the thin cotton, an indicator that she's not wearing a bra. As much as that's a turn on, it's more of a turn on knowing I'm the only one who gets to see her this way.

We sit, ready to eat, when she asks me about my day.

"Just had some overdue errands I had to run," I tell her.

She tells me about her day and new expansion plans for the shop. Her excitement over it is evident on her face as she goes over the details. After we finish eating, she gets up and comes around the table, standing behind me. She wraps her arms around my neck, her damp long hair falling over my shoulder.

"That was delicious. Thanks," she says kissing my neck.

"No problem," I smile.

"I have a few calls I need to make for work. Mind if I use the office…after I help you with the dishes?"

I bark out a laugh for a few reasons. One, because she's asking permission to use the office as though it's not already half hers. Two, because I know she won't do the dishes.

"I've got the dishes. Go make your calls."

I feel her smile against my skin before kissing it once more and leaving to make her calls. I start to gather the dishes and any leftovers. I put the food in the fridge, empty the clean dishes from the dishwasher and reload it. I'm hand washing our wine glasses when I feel her standing behind me.

I continue to clean wondering if she's going to say anything, but she doesn't. I know she thinks I don't know she's there, but she has no clue that every hair on my body stands on end when she's near.

I turn my head, catching her off guard and before she's able to wipe that look off her face.

That look that has my heart exploding in my chest. That look that tells me I'm the only one.

That look that tells me she's going to say yes.

acknowledgements

I DON'T EVEN know where to begin in thanking everyone who supported and encouraged me over this past year while writing *This Is Love*. From the simple questions to how the book was coming along to friends begging to read it early, it's all been very overwhelming.

This novel is my first and with it came a large learning experience. Not only in what I was capable of doing, but in what others are willing to do to help me achieve.

Indie Solutions for answering my questions, some of them silly, some not. For guiding me in the right direction when I had no idea where to go. But mostly for putting me in touch with my editor.

Megan, words can't describe what you did for both *This Is Love* and my confidence. Your ideas, comments, and words helped make this book what is it…a better version of what it was. Thank you for letting me know what made you smile, laugh, angry, cry and smile again. Thank you for telling me when I had to change something, when I was using a word too much or when something I wrote was too distracting and needed to be cut. More than that, thanks for continuing to be my friend long after your work was done.

To all my beta readers who took the time out of their busy schedules to read *This Is Love*. Everyone's time is valuable and to know that you took that time and used it to read this story really warms my heart. Keely, Beth, Tara, Jamie, Christine, Laurie and Nikki…thank you!!!

To Okay Creations for the beautiful cover… You listened to my vision and made it come true.

JT Formatting for answering all my questions and even researching a few things for me…Thank you for all your help and your work on making these pages that I agonized over for months so pretty.

My friends and family who always asked, inquired, wondered when this book would be ready. For talking about it to their friends, sharing it on their social media sites and who were anxiously awaiting to read.

My mom who read the first draft and in true mom fashion told me I didn't need to change a thing. A huge lie but so supportive! My dad who would call me with ideas, my mother in law who had a list of people she couldn't wait to share the book with.

My husband, who when I told him I was going to write a book told me to go for it. He said the success of this book wasn't in how many people read it, but in me simply finishing it. Thank you for letting me do my part.

At the beginning of this journey, I emailed someone and told them my plan. She emailed me back, (a complete stranger) telling me how great she thought it was and to go after my dream. She promised that one day, she would read *This Is Love*. That promise was one of the things that kept me going in this journey, so thank you Colleen.

And finally to anyone who took a chance on this book, a

chance on me, thank you so much. I hope you enjoyed this story and will come back for more!

~Caroline xo

about the author

CAROLINE NOLAN WRITES stories about love and all the beauty and ugliness that comes along with it. She lives in Toronto with her husband and their fur baby. She is currently working on her second novel.

Caroline can be found online at
www.facebook.com/authorcarolinenolan